The soldier's mind was so clouded with anger that he didn't see the shadowy form until it was far too late.

As if by some dark magic, it materialized right in front of him. Its arms moved so fast the soldier wasn't entirely sure they had.

He tried to scream, to alert the others of this sudden threat, but he couldn't open his mouth.

His jaw felt like pudding, wobbly and wet. Confused and horrified, the soldier reached up to feel what had happened to his face.

The shadowy form snapped his neck before he realized his lower jaw was completely gone.

Other Titles by E. R. Torre

Shadows at Dawn (Short Stories)
Haze

Corrosive Knights Novels

Mechanic
The Last Flight of the Argus
Chameleon
Nox
Ghost of the Argus
Foundry of the Gods
Legacy of the Argus

The Dark Fringe Novels

The Dark Fringe (with John Kissee)
Cold Hemispheres

Chameleon

By

E. R. Torre

Book Cover Design by ebooklaunch.com

All Other Interior Artwork by E. R. Torre

Please visit my website:

www.ertorre.com

Comments or questions? Email me at:

atrocket@aol.com

ISBN: 0-9729115-6-1

ISBN 13: 978-0-9729115-6-6

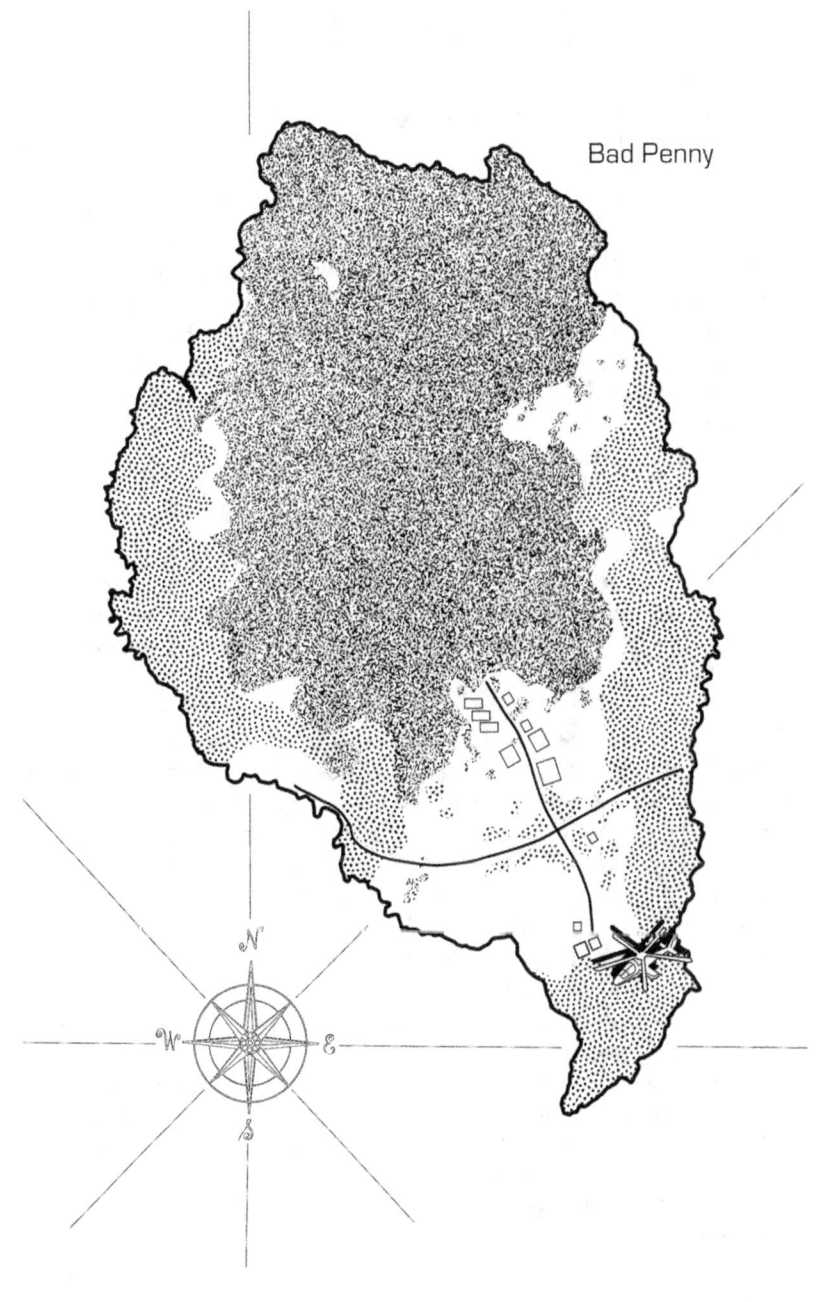

PROLOGUE

THE BLUE MOUNTAINS, ARIZONA.
OCTOBER, 1925.

He awoke to the bitter taste of blood in his mouth and a searing pain coming from somewhere –he wasn't quite sure where– below his chest. He tried to move his hands but couldn't. He tried to move his feet and they wouldn't. For a second, despair mixed with confusion filled his mind. Had he fallen? If so, was his neck broken? His spine? Was he paralyzed? He tried to remember what he was doing just before…just before the darkness.

He tried to remember where he was.

It was a little before ten in the morning. Even at that early hour, the desert sun was beating down hard and he was on his horse following a faint trail leading away from town and into the desert. He was thirsty and scared. Someone else, someone he cared for deeply, was also subjected to these unbearable conditions.

The fear took a lifetime to lift. The pain below his chest eased, until he knew it was nothing more than a heavy bruise. His breathing grew more relaxed. He opened his eyes and, unwittingly, let out a moan. As he did, he detected movement from a few feet away. Beyond that moving shape laid the night sky and the stars. A vivid full moon looked down upon him and his companion. It was nearly midnight. There was the smell of rot in the area, of flesh baking in the sun…

"You're up, Sheriff?"

The words came from the moving shape. The voice was ancient, timeless.

The figure crouched before a small camp fire. In its flames, he saw the skeletally thin man. The smell of rot came from him. The skeletal man eyed the Sheriff for a few seconds, as if checking on livestock, before his attention returned to the fire.

The Sheriff leaned back, exhausted. A cool breeze washed over the makeshift camp. It sent a prickly cloud of sand over him. The Sheriff closed his eyes, but just a little too late. Sand leaked into his watery eyes. He pulled forward, instinctively trying to bring his hands to his face. He couldn't. The Sheriff tried again, harder. Still nothing. His hands were pinned, somehow stuck behind his back. No, not stuck. He was tied up.

For a moment, the Sheriff felt an odd sense of relief. He was not paralyzed after all. Instead, he was a prisoner. He blinked several times, until his eyes were clear and he could see again. He stared down the length of his body and saw a thick rope tied around his legs, as well. The last of the fog lifted from his head. The painful memories returned in full.

"Where is she?" he yelled.

The winds shifted once again, sending smoke from the fire in his direction. He smelled cooking meat. The old man didn't turn. His focus was on the meal. He was confident of how well he roped his captive.

The Sheriff rolled to his left, pulling his body into a sitting position. He took a long, close look at his surroundings. He was lying at a corner of a cul de sac made up of enormous boulders. The Sheriff was somewhere in the Blue Mountains, of this he was sure. At some point, the old man ambushed him. The Sheriff was taken here, to the old man's hiding place.

The Sheriff moved his head, trying desperately to see more of the area. He spotted the old man's camping gear laid out beside the fire. A sad, gnarled piece of wood lay to one side. A canteen, the Sheriff's, sat on it. Off to either side of the campfire were deep crevasses in the rock, the way into and out of the cul de sac. Pitch black shadows marked each opening. The rest of the area consisted of walls of black rock.

She was nowhere to be seen.

His panic grew. The Sheriff stared hard at the old man, noting the crudely sown patchwork of fur covering his body. In the old days, when he was a little boy, he saw a few prospectors wear these crude, handmade clothes. None were quite this grotesque. Stitched into the left shoulder of the old man's clothing was a raccoon's head. Its eyes were hollow; its mouth open, as if delivering one final, horrible scream.

"Where is she?" the Sheriff repeated. Though his voice was weak, there was plenty of venom left in his tone. He wanted the old man to turn, to acknowledge him. To say something. Anything. But the old man remained where he was by the campfire cooking his meal.

The Sheriff shook his head. He could do little. He thrust his body up as high as he could while fighting the pull of the ropes.

He caught more glimpses of area around the campfire. He saw shadows behind boulders and cracks in the stone walls. His daughter *had* to be near. She was tied up just like he was. She was hidden away. Somewhere close by.

The smell of cooking meat grew stronger. Very dark thoughts came to the Sheriff's mind.

"Where is she?" he repeated a third time. His voice no longer carried any fury. There was more than a hint of fear.

The old man stood up. In his withered hand was a long, thin twig. Speared through it was a strip of meat, freshly cooked. He faced the Sheriff.

The old man's face was smeared with mud and greasy filth. His stringy gray hair was pasted down. It looked like he hadn't seen a bath in years. The old man's eyes, however, were bright blue and almost glowed in the darkness, as if they possessed an inner light. The old man rubbed his free hand in the fur covering his chest. There, stitched into his clothing, was another animal's head.

A possum? The Sheriff wondered. *Or perhaps a rat?*

This creature's head was stretched beyond recognition. Its expression was also one of despair.

"Your daughter's not here," the old man said. His voice was so bland it lacked any emotion at all. He pulled a small strip of meat off the twig and placed it into his mouth. As he did, the Sheriff realized the old man's teeth were, unlike everything else about him, almost perfect. They were remarkably straight and spotless. Given his age and hygiene, it didn't seem possible the teeth were natural. But where would a desert rat like him get such a set of well-made false teeth?

"Why did you take her?" the Sheriff demanded.

The old man smiled. He spit out the strip of meat he had placed in his mouth moments before and pulled another strip off the stick. He leaned in closer to the Sheriff.

"You hungry?"

The Sheriff didn't reply. Despite his despair, despite his fury, and despite the dark thoughts swirling in his mind, he *was* hungry. He was also very thirsty. He last ate early in the morning. Right before...

It was unusually *cool and windy that morning.*

The Sheriff finished his breakfast and put his plate away. Normally, he'd walk little Jessie to school, but today she awoke late and was taking her time getting ready. She looked unusually tired.

"Catching something?" the Sheriff asked.

Charlotte ran her hand over Jessie's forehead.

"She's running a little warm," she said. "But nothing terrible. Let's give her a little time."

The Sheriff eyed his daughter with great suspicion.

"You can make it to school?"

"I don't know, Pa," she replied.

"It's bad to miss class. Any class."

Little Jessie frowned.

"I really was sick last time," she insisted.

The Sheriff couldn't help but smile. It was an old argument, the circumstances of the "big fever" she supposedly suffered a little over a month before. Her illness happened to coincide with a math test Ms. Fitzpatrick was giving.

"You have any tests today?" the Sheriff asked.

"None, Dad."

"Next big test is in a couple of days," Charlotte said. "Ms. Fitzpatrick told me so."

"See Dad?" Jessie said. "I'm not making up anything."

The Sheriff thought about that while Charlotte folded her hands.

"If she goes to school and she feels worse, she can always tell Ms. Fitzpatrick to take her back home," Charlotte said.

The words momentarily brightened the girl's face. So much so that she had to force herself not to look *too* happy. Her efforts made the Sheriff laugh.

"There you go, giving her ideas," the Sheriff said.

The happiness on Jessie's face turned into a pout.

"Daddy, I'm not well," she insisted.

"Ok, Ok," the Sheriff said. He took a look at his watch before eyeing Jessie's cereal bowl. She wasn't even halfway done with her breakfast. "You gonna finish that anytime soon, Jessie? I got to get to work."

"Yes."

Charlotte patted the girl on her head.

"Tell you what, dear, I'll take her to school," she said. "You best get to the office before you're late."

"I'm the boss you know."

"Not 'round here," Jessie said while looking up at her mother.

"Our daughter's wise beyond her years," Charlotte said.

The Sheriff chuckled. He walked to his wife's side and gave her a hug.

"Yes ma'am," he said. "I'm just the lowly servant of this humble abode."

"My mama always told me it was good to know your place in this world," Charlotte said.

The Sheriff gave his wife a passionate kiss.

"Even better when you're at ease in it," he said.

The Sheriff released his wife and leaned down to kiss his daughter on the cheek. He paused before doing so.

"This won't make me sick, will it?" he said.

"You're never sick, Daddy," Jessie said.

"That's not true," he said and kissed his daughter on the cheek. "We all get sick now and again. Next time we tell you it's time to go to sleep, it's time to go to sleep."

The Sheriff ruffled Jessie's amber hair and winked at his wife before stepping out into the street.

The Sheriff drove a dusty 1920 Chevrolet Model T truck around town. It was his usual routine, checking up on the small town's hot spots for any sign of early morning disruptions. He paid particular attention to the area in and around Johnson's Bar. The place could be lively, even at this hour. He was relieved to find that the very few people milling about the streets were doing so quietly and minded their own business. He recognized and knew each and every one of them for it was difficult not to in a town this size.

A little over a half hour later, when he was done with his rounds, the Sheriff parked his truck before his office on Main Street. The truck's engine was still rattling while he exited.

"Take it easy," he told the noisy vehicle. "You're gonna wake everyone up."

The engine let out one final gasp before shutting down. The Sheriff shook his head.

Technology.

He removed his hat before stepping up to the door to his office.

It was ajar.

The Sheriff stiffened. Very few people had keys to his office. There was his Deputy and the Mayor, but neither was known to come by this early in the morning. There was also Gertrude Smith, but she came in during the night to clean the place. She never left the door open and she never stayed much beyond ten P.M.

The Sheriff couldn't help but think he was dealing with an intruder.

But who would break into his office? There was nothing of value inside and no prisoners in any of the four cells.

Doesn't matter. The door is open and it shouldn't be.

The Sheriff cautiously pushed the door fully open and entered the front office area. He kept his hand close to his gun belt, alert for any danger. Inside, he found all was where it should be and nothing out of place.

Nothing obvious, as it turned out.

For when the Sheriff finished his quick search for any mysterious strangers or stolen items and sat behind his desk, he spotted the folded piece of paper. Unlike his Deputy, the Sheriff was a neat man. When he left the office late last night, his desk was clear. The Sheriff picked up the paper. Had the Deputy come in early and left him this note? Was there trouble outside of town?

As the Sheriff unfolded the paper, he noticed how dirty it was. Smudges of mud made the writing on it nearly illegible. Before reading the note, the Sheriff grinned. The Deputy was a young man with a wicked sense of humor. Perhaps this note was a prank he was playing to get back at him for that disastrous blind date he arranged a fortnight ago with Mrs. Allen's daughter.

The Sheriff shook his head and laughed at that memory. The laugher died the moment he read the letter's contents.

I have your daughter. I'm taking her to the Blue Mountains. If you want to see her again, meet me there. Come alone. I will see you coming. If you don't come alone, your daughter dies. I will wait only until 9:00.

The Sheriff frowned. If this was a prank, it was in poor taste. He folded the paper and glanced at his wrist watch. 8:15 A.M. There was no way he'd reach the Blue Mountains' eastern edge by 9:00 A.M. Maybe by 9:30, but not by 9:00. Whoever had his daughter wanted him out of town. Quick.

He felt a thin, ice cold trickle of sweat roll down his cheek. When he reached to wipe it away, his Deputy arrived.

"Good morning," the young man said and walked to his desk. After sitting, he pulled a folder from a drawer and skimmed over its contents.

"I said good morning."

"Good morning," the Sheriff replied.

"You're awfully quiet today."

The Sheriff said nothing.

"Case in point," the Deputy muttered after a few seconds. "Hey, did you see him?"

"Who?"

"That old prospector," the Deputy replied. "What's his name? You know, the one that comes around town once a month or so to pick up supplies and sell whatever gold or junk he finds out in the boonies. Foul smelling dude. He practically threw himself on me at the Cantina. And I was enjoying such a nice breakfast—"

"What did he want?"

"Not all that much, really. Just to see you is all. I got the feeling it was important, whatever it was. I told him if he hurried he might catch you at school, with your daughter."

The Sheriff nodded. It took every last bit of inner strength to keep from jumping out of his seat and running from the office.

Come alone. I will see you coming. If you don't come alone, your daughter dies.

"I...I have an errand to run," the Sheriff said. He pocketed the muddy paper. "I'll be back later."

The Deputy nodded.

"I'll hold the fort," the Deputy said. "Not that there's ever all that much to worry about around these parts. I'd say we're in for another easy day."

On the street, the Sheriff jumped into his truck and drove directly to his daughter's school.

Jean Fitzgerald, the school's superintendent, was outside waiting for the last of the children to show up before closing the school's front door. She waved as the Sheriff approached and exited his truck.

"Good morning, Sheriff," she said. "How's Jessie?"

"She...she isn't here?"

"No sir," Mrs. Fitzgerald replied. "Your wife brought her a half hour or so ago, and she and the other kids were playing out back. Then one of them comes to me and says Jessie wasn't feeling well and was heading back home."

The Sheriff digested that information.

"She was feeling a little sick this morning," he said, his voice barely calm. "I...I came by to see if she would make it through the day. I guess she didn't."

Mrs. Fitzgerald gave the Sheriff a warm smile.

"Well, you tell Jessie we miss her. I hope she's back tomorrow."

"She will be."

The Sheriff returned to his car and raced away. He drove to his house, but stopped a little way down the street for he spotted his wife tending the garden in the front of the house. Charlotte's mind was clearly on her work and there was no sign of Jessie. Charlotte wiped sweat from her forehead. She had obviously been working outside for a little while.

You wouldn't be tending to the garden if Jessie was inside the house, sick, the Sheriff thought. His eyes turned down, back to his wrist watch.

I will wait only until 9:00.

His watch read 8:25.

This was insane. Too insane to be a prank. Though he desperately wanted to believe otherwise, his child was kidnapped. He again looked at his wristwatch.

8:26.

The Sheriff pressed down hard on the accelerator and spun his truck around. The Blue Mountains were due west of the Devil's Ravine. There was a trail leading in that direction, but there was no way his truck would make it through that wasteland of sand and brush.

The Sheriff drove to Robertson's Stables. Old man Robertson was a blacksmith, but with the arrival of the automobile, blacksmiths and horse stables were fast becoming a thing of the past, even in a small town like this one. The Sheriff recalled the many times he chided old man Robertson for living in the past.

At this moment, however, he couldn't be happier with this backward thinking resident. The Sheriff parked his car at the stable's side and checked his revolver. It was loaded and ready. He reached into the back seat of his truck and grabbed his rifle from its case before running to the stable's front entrance.

Old man Robertson was there, sweeping the floor. The pungent smell of horse manure assaulted the Sheriff's nose. This was another reason the horse trade was going extinct, the Sheriff thought. Cars would never be as hazardous to the environment as those foul smelling animals.

"I need one of your horses," the Sheriff said.

"You do?" Robertson said, a smile wide on his face. "What's a matter, that contraption you ride in ain't reliable enough?"

"What do you have?"

Old man Robertson's smile disappeared when he realized just how tense the Sheriff was.

"I got a few to choose from. What are you looking for?"

"You wouldn't happen to have an Arabian?"

"'Fraid not," Robertson said. "But if you want distance, I got a strong mare."

"I need the strongest you've got," the Sheriff said. "And a canteen."

Old man Robertson dropped his broom and led the Sherriff to his stable's first stall. A magnificent white and brown mare stood within, her saddle already on.

"After sweepin' up, I was gonna take her for a trot," Robertson said. "She's the strongest I got, Sherriff, and she's ready to go."

The Sheriff opened the stall door and grabbed the horse's rein. He tugged at it, harder than he should, and the horse protested.

"Easy, Sheriff," Robertson said.

The Sheriff eased off. He rubbed the horse's side until the animal calmed down.

"About that canteen?" the Sheriff asked.

Robertson grabbed one hanging on the stable wall. He used a hand pump beside the stable's door to fill it. When done, the Sheriff took the canteen and walked the horse outside.

"I gotta go," he said.

"Where to?"

"The Blue Mountains. If anyone asks, tell them I'll be back soon."

"They'll ask?"

The Sheriff nodded. His watch read 8:36.

"I really have to go."

The Sheriff mounted the mare and galloped at full speed down the street. In less than a minute he was out of town. A couple of minutes later, he was on the trail leading to the Blue Mountains. His only hope was that the prospector would see him coming alone, and not do anything to his daughter even though he wouldn't make it to the mountains in time.

"You hungry?" the Prospector repeated.

"Thirsty."

The Prospector walked back to the campfire and returned with a canteen. It was the same one Robertson gave the Sheriff back at the stable. He unscrewed the canteen's top and placed the opening over the Sheriff's mouth. The Sheriff took a very deep pull of the liquid. It was warm and tasted stale, but considering his thirst, it was the best damn drink he'd ever had.

"Now," the Prospector said. "Food?"

"Yes."

The old man pulled one of the largest pieces of meat off the twig. He held it in his hands, waiting for the Sheriff to open his mouth. But the Sheriff didn't do so. Instead, he said:

"What is it?"

The Prospector's eyes lit up.

"What is it?" he repeated, his voice a whisper. Images of Jessie filled the Sheriff's mind. He could barely look at the meat. Had he failed his daughter so completely?

"Tell me what it is."

The Prospector let out a laugh.

"It isn't easy finding fresh meat in the desert," he said. "Rest easy. I'm many things, but I'm no cannibal."

The Sheriff let out a heavy sigh. There was little reason to believe the Prospector's word, yet his answer sounded sincere. Or perhaps, the Sheriff thought, he was *that* hungry. The Sheriff reluctantly allowed the Prospector to put the meat into his mouth. It was a tough chew, but like the water, it tasted nothing short of heavenly.

"What is it?" the Sheriff asked.

The Prospector scratched his head.

"My apologies, Sheriff. We're eating your horse."

The Sheriff let out a groan. He wanted to spit the chewed meat into the crazy old bastard's face. But he needed the nourishment if he was to regain his strength and didn't want to anger the crazy bastard. Not until he had his daughter.

The Sheriff heaved with every swallow yet forced the food down until it was gone.

"More?" the Prospector asked.

The Sheriff nodded. He was given another bite. This one went down easier. He already felt strength returning to his body. It was only then he realized how weak he was. After finishing a third portion, he looked the old man in his eyes and asked:

"Where is my daughter?"

"She'll live," the Prospector said. He retreated to the fire.

"Why did you take her?" the Sheriff asked. "She's only a little girl. You need...you need to let her go back home, to her mother."

The Prospector let out another chuckle.

"Did you really think this was about her?"

The Sheriff frowned.

"You wanted to get *me* out here? Why in God's name...?"

The Prospector returned to the Sheriff's side. He had another piece of freshly cooked meat in his hands.

"I brought you out here because you need to see something," he said and offered the Sheriff more meat.

"That's it? You wanted to show me something?!"

"Yep."

The Sheriff found it hard to contain his fury.

"Why didn't you just ask?"

"I could have," the Prospector admitted. "There are many things I could have done differently. But time's short and the opportunity sorta presented itself."

The Prospector pointed to one of the dark passages leading out.

"We're going that way."

The Sheriff stared down that dark passage. He felt his flesh crawl. The situation was even more dangerous than he thought. During the Great War, while he was in the trenches, he'd seen many fellow soldiers lose their minds because of the stress of battle. It was the reason that, upon returning to the United States, he had forsaken a promising new life in Boston and moved to the desolate state of Arizona. He found a peace here that eluded him in the big city. In the years since, he made his life in this quiet, and very small, world. He found his calling in law and envisioned growing old and, eventually, dying here, as far removed from the problems of the rest of the world as he could be.

But the Sheriff now realized there was danger in this solitude as well. This old man, who likely lived his entire life among the plains and deserts, had also succumbed to madness. What unspeakable things had his precious little daughter experienced during the course of this day?

"What do you want to show me?" the Sheriff said, gently.

"If describing it was enough, I would have done so back in town," the Prospector said. "You'll see, soon enough."

The Prospector approached the Sheriff. As he did, he produced a blood stained Bowie knife. He held it before the Sheriff's face.

"Easy," he said. "No funny business."

The Prospector cut the rope from the Sheriff's legs.

"Get up."

The Sheriff got on his knees. His legs felt like slices of dead meat. The Prospector grabbed one of the Sheriff's arms and helped him stand.

"This way," he said.

They walked out of the cul de sac and followed a long crevasse. It was very dark and the Sheriff had opportunities to make a move on the Prospector. He didn't. He felt the point of the Bowie knife against his back and knew that anything he tried in these dark, unfamiliar surroundings could result in injury…or worse. Besides, he needed to know where the Prospector hid his daughter. Otherwise, he could spend days searching in vain for her. There was absolutely no way he would let her die here, alone and thirsty.

"They're coming for me," the Sheriff said. "I told old man Robertson where I was going."

"That explains it," the Prospector replied.

"What?"

"Maybe five hours ago a posse left town. Big group. They were headed this way. You're a popular guy."

"Can't say the same about you," the Sheriff said. "When they find you…"

"That young Deputy of yours was leading the posse."

"He's a good tracker," the Sheriff said. Despite his attempts to sound convincing, doubt crept into his voice.

"He could use more experience," the Prospector said. "Before they left town, I laid down some tracks heading to the southern passage of the mountains. Your Deputy found 'em. He followed them and kept going in that direction. I figure it'll take his group until early tomorrow morning before they get back. By then our business will be over."

They worked their way through a twisting maze of rocks and parched wood, often ducking or climbing mounds of crumbly debris. Though it was a difficult trek, the passage they were in grew wider and the light from the moon made their walk less treacherous.

After nearly a half hour of moving through the rock corridors, the Prospector laid a hand on the Sheriff's shoulder.

"Over there," he said. He pointed to another cul de sac.

The Sheriff gazed in that direction. He was surprised to see a shadowy figure standing before a boulder. It looked like a man, but he was completely immobile. He stared up at the Moon. Littered around him were a backpack, a small shovel, a pick, and a pan. Prospecting gear.

"Who's that?" the Sheriff asked.

"You'll find out soon enough," the Prospector said.

He pushed the Sheriff into the cul de sac. As they approached the figured, the Sheriff realized he wasn't looking at a man. Rather, the figure was a sleek sculpture of a man. It appeared to be in the process of emerging from the rock itself. The figure was covered in a fine orange grain, the same that made up most of the weathered rock formations in this part of the mountains. However, there were parts of the sculpture that reflected the light of the moon.

"What is it?" the Sheriff asked.

"Why don't you take a closer look?"

Despite everything, curiosity got the better of the Sheriff and he moved in. His mind filled with questions. Was the figure made of stone or metal or was it a combination of both? But how was this polished metal coming out of stone? The Sheriff was no longer sure of what he was looking at. The figure was clearly not flesh and bone, but neither was it a rock sculpture.

"Go ahead," the Prospector urged.

The Sheriff's concern for his missing daughter was momentarily set aside as he drew even closer to the figure. Soon, he stood directly before it. The figure was at least six feet high. Its lower body was fused to the rock below.

Fused.

That seemed the only explanation, for several chips of hardened rock cracked away at its base, revealing the polished metal skeleton. In the Moon's light, the metal was incredibly beautiful.

"I don't understand," the Sheriff said.

"It's been here a very long time," the Prospector said. "It took me many, many years to find it. Many more years to dig it out. Now she's fixed."

"Fixed?"

The Prospector walked to the Sheriff's side and produced his Bowie knife.

"I'm going to release you now," he said. He stared deep into the Sheriff's eyes. "You're a strong young man and I'm sure your first inclination is to attack me. Maybe you're even thinking about how you're going to kill me. Let that anger go, Sheriff. You've got a reputation for being a decent man and we shouldn't fight. Even if you think there's reason to."

The Prospector drew the knife closer to the Sheriff.

"Let me clear up a couple of things before I set you free," the Prospector continued. "First off, it wasn't my intention to bring you here the way I did. I'm sorry you lost that mare. You were riding her real hard and she tripped over a rock a mile or so back and broke her neck in the fall. You just about did the same."

The Sheriff glared at the old man.

"I know," The Prospector continued. "The mare's death is my fault. Anyway, I gave you plenty of care afterwards. For a while, you were done for. Luckily, I know a few things about medicine. I healed you up and took some meat off your horse for nourishment. When you see the horse's remains, after all this is done, you'll know I was telling you the truth."

"What about my daughter?"

"She never left town."

The Sheriff frowned. *What the hell?*

"Now, I'll admit, I seriously thought about taking her to draw you out here."

"In the name of God, why?"

"Come on, Sheriff. If I had come to your office and asked you to ride out all this way alone with me to look at some sculpture, would you have done so?"

"No," he admitted.

"Besides, this meeting here needed to be just between the two of us."

The Sherriff shook his head in frustration.

"What about my daughter? What do you mean she never left town? Where is she?"

"Right now? I'm guessing she's in her bed, sleeping."

"Explain yourself."

"In the morning, I saw you leave your house and, a little later, your wife and child walked to school. I got close enough to hear your wife tell the teacher your child might be catching a cold. She gave the teacher permission to let your child return home if she wasn't feeling good. They talked a couple of more minutes before your wife left."

The Prospector smiled.

"I may be old, but my hearing ain't too bad. Your daughter's hearing ain't too bad either, because she also heard everything her mother said and, kids being kids, decided after playing around a bit with her friends that she'd had enough of school for the day. So she pretended to be a whole lot sicker and that got her teacher's attention. She let your child head back home on her own."

The Sheriff gritted his teeth. The idea of his daughter walking alone with this old man following her...

"That was when I made my move. I stopped your daughter a short distance from the school and gave her some change. I told her the drug store had a fresh supply of peppermint sticks. Last I saw, she was on her way there, to see if that was the case."

The Prospector chuckled.

"Kids. Anyway, I found your Deputy eatin' breakfast in the saloon and told him I was looking for you. I ran to your office, broke in, and left you that note. I made it as menacing as I could, hoping that would make you move instead of think. Otherwise, you might have searched a little harder in town for your daughter. Of course, there was a risk you'd run into her anyway, but it was worth taking."

"How did you know I wouldn't round up the posse myself?"

"As I said, the note was designed to...encourage you...to rush. With that note and the Deputy telling you I was looking for you, I figured you'd put two and two together and guess I was the one that took your daughter. You being a young and strong man and me being old and feeble, I also figured you'd think you didn't need no posse to take care of me. All alone."

"I'll see you jailed for this."

"No," the Prospector said. "I don't think you will."

The Prospector gazed at the statue.

"It's time you were free," he muttered.

True to his words, the Prospector cut the rope from the Sheriff's arms. The Sheriff drew his hands forward. They felt like pieces of wood. He rubbed them until they were no longer stiff.

The knots were effective, though not so tight that he would suffer lasting pain. From the corner of the Sheriff's eye, he noted the Prospector putting away his knife.

Now or never.

The Sheriff let out a yell and spun around. He grabbed the Prospector's ragged jacket and slammed the old man against the rock wall.

"You will pay for this you bastard."

The Sheriff swung at the old man's face, intent on removing every one of those unnaturally white teeth from his mouth.

His fist was stopped in mid-flight. To the Sheriff's shock, the Prospector held it firm, unmoving.

"We'll deal with your anger later," the old man said.

The Sheriff tried his best to free his hand, but couldn't. The Prospector's grip on his fist was like a vice.

"You need to see him," the Prospector said.

"Him?" the Sheriff yelled back. "You mean that statue? Are you truly insane?"

"You won't think so in a couple of minutes," the Prospector said. The smile disappeared. "There was a reason I needed you here, Sheriff. You and no one else. You know what the nations of this world are capable of doing to each other."

"What the hell are you talking about?"

"You were in the Great War," the Prospector said. Sensing the Sheriff's anger ebb, he released the man's hand. "There isn't anyone else within five hundred miles who knows what you know."

The Sheriff's anger had given way to pity. The Prospector was indeed crazy. He didn't need physical punishment. He needed someone to care for him. The Sheriff took a step back.

"What is it that I know?" the Sheriff asked.

"Your military might," the Prospector said.

"What does that have to do with—"

"Touch him," the Prospector insisted. "Just touch him."

The Sheriff took another step back. He shook his head before facing the rock and metal sculpture. Behind him, the Prospector remained perfectly still. He said nothing more, for he had said all he needed to say.

The Sheriff let out a deep breath. During the Great War, he faced so many horrors, from mustard gas to tanks to bullets and bombs hurled down from the skies. The Prospector was right:

There wasn't anyone within hundreds of miles who knew the military might of the world powers like he did.

But why did that matter? Why bring him to this statue?

Despite his anger, despite the certainty the old man was crazy, the Sheriff could not deny a growing sense of curiosity. The Prospector showed incredible ingenuity getting him here. Why go to such trouble? What could possibly be so damn urgent about seeing –about *touching*– this thing before him? As much as he hated to admit it, the Sheriff *was* interested in it. Whatever the hell it was.

You're here, a voice deep in his mind told him. *What harm is there in doing what the old bastard wants? Why not just touch the damn thing and get it over with?*

The Sheriff fought the urge and tried to think of a reason to not do what the old man asked. Yet as eager as he was to get back to town and his family, he knew he'd do so only after doing what the old man asked of him.

You're here.

As if he were in a dream, the Sheriff finally relented. He approached the statue until he stood directly before it. He gazed at it for a few seconds, appraising it. The light of the Moon revealed the statue's featureless face. Blank eyes stared up and away at the stars. The figure's mouth was open, as if in mid-scream. The statue's face reminded the Sheriff of the old and weathered Roman and Greek statues he saw in museums. On the figure's lower left arm was exposed a very large patch of metal. It seemed like the rock sediment of the statue was hardened skin, the metal bone. Below, rock formations surrounded and encased the figures' legs. Though the Sheriff didn't know much about geology, he knew enough about the formation of this rock to estimate this particular object had been here for many, *many* thousands of years.

His eyes came up and again settled on that very large patch of metal. The Sheriff was transfixed by this sight. The metal glowed in the Moon's light.

So shiny. So very shiny.

The Sheriff swallowed and shook his head. Whatever logic he possessed managed one last, pointless protest. This whole thing *was* crazy. Why wasn't he on his way home, to see his family? To see his daughter? To make sure she was indeed safe?

What was he still doing here?

That protest was duly noted and allowed to drift away.

The Sheriff reached out and, with only a slight hesitancy, touched the exposed metal.

At first, he felt nothing. He let out a breath he didn't realize he was holding. Still nothing. The Sheriff felt foolish. After a couple of seconds passed, he felt like he was going to laugh. What exactly did he expect? He was dealing with a person that should be locked up and—

The Sheriff felt heat at the tips of his fingers. He looked down at the statue's exposed metal and, in his eyes, it appeared to...*glow*. But it couldn't. It was just metal. How could it...?

Fear gripped the Sheriff.

What have I done?

His eyes moved from the metal to the statue's eyes. They were still wide open, looking up at the night sky. And then, very, very slightly...they *moved*. They moved until the statue was looking directly at him.

The fear turned to panic. The Sheriff wanted to pull back, to run with all his might. The heat at his fingertips became red hot. He wanted to run, but he couldn't. He felt a jolt of pain. It emanated from his fingertips and radiated through his hand, then his arm, then his body. His entire body felt like it was on fire and he tried to scream, to move, but he couldn't. He stared at the statue and the statue's eyes looked deep into his...

...and, as the Prospector promised, all was revealed.

1

EIGHTY YEARS LATER

If one happened to be out in that damp forest carrying a flashlight on this particular night and shined it in the right place and at the right time, the small, soiled animal making its way through the low lying brush could easily be identified –further assuming you also happened to be a zoologist– as a rattus norvegicus. To the more ordinary observer, the animal before you was the all too common brown rat. Even with that information, it would take a near supernatural awareness and perception for anyone to realize this particular rat's final moments of life would, in turn, lead to the deaths of so many others.

She moved along slowly as her body was far heavier than usual. She was pregnant, fifteen days into a typical twenty one to twenty three day gestation. She was also very, very hungry. The rat darted forward. At times, she stopped to sniff the air and turned her head from side to side. This allowed her highly sensitive ears to listen to everything going on around her. Course corrections were made and the rat picked her path. She continued working her way through the thick forest brush.

Hunger was a near constant the past few days and her erratic movements reflected a growing irritability. At one point, she let out a low level hiss. Perhaps it was a warning directed to other creatures she sensed lying unseen around her. Then again, it might well have been an almost human curse directed at her current fate.

She hurried along and looked and listened and sniffed, until she came to a full stop. Her ears and nose twitched almost in unison, and her head turned slowly to her right. She remained in place a full ten seconds, a lifetime given her current pace, and absorbed the sensory data while ignoring the now extreme hunger gripping her body. She blinked, as if making a decision and, after a few more seconds of deliberation, moved on to the right, until she came to a stop before the smooth metal wall.

She sniffed at the wall and clawed at it with her paws. She found a hold for her nails and pulled herself up and into a standing position. With a very ungraceful leap, she was over the wall and on a flat plain. She sniffed some more, moving forward until a draft of cool air brushed past her whiskers. It came from somewhere below, and with it came the delightful smell of food. The rat leaned down, attempting to press her body closer to the source of that smell, but she was stopped by a thin and unmovable barricade.

Though she couldn't know it, between her and the distant food was a wire mesh. She sniffed some more, taking in the odor coming from below. She released an excited, and frustrated, squeak. Her goal was so very close, yet this thing before her impeded all progress.

The rat pushed her nose into the edge of the mesh. She pushed and pushed until, finally, a piece of it gave way, though not enough to allow her entire body entry. The rat pulled back. She sniffed the edge of the mesh and moved along, poking and prodding until, finally, she found a loose corner. With a little more prodding, she worked her way in.

The joy of entry to the place that promised food was followed immediately with horror. She fell far faster than her mind could process. And then, just as abruptly, she landed with a jarring thud.

The rat squealed in pain as thick drops of blood rolled out of her mouth. There was serious damage to her body, she knew, yet she fought through it and, after a few seconds, staggered to her feet. The triumph was temporary. She could not remain standing and lay back down. She panted hard and her eyes closed.

Her body became very still.

When she awoke, the pain was even worse and dry blood coated her mouth. She cautiously rose and found her legs were not broken. Much of the pain she felt came from her stomach. She could no longer feel the movement of her offspring within.

The rat took a couple of steps and realized the world around her was radically changed from her forest walk. There were no leaves swaying and the ground was no longer sandy and damp. She was in an immense, cool, and very slippery metal tube. It angled downward, and she had to fight both the slippery floor and the pull of gravity. She did not want to fall again.

Though the searing pain urged her to remain in place, the hunger –and the lingering smell of food– motivated her to keep going. The smell rushed past her on the breeze and up and back to the forest where she came from. Cautiously she moved on, driven even more desperate by the promise of a meal. She moved on until she ran into another wire mesh.

This one, she found, was even more solid than the last and far too strong to push through. She circled around, hoping to find some weak point, driven nearly mad by the smell and the pain.

Perhaps it was at that point that she knew she was going to die.

The realization made her even more desperate. If she was to die, she would do so with a full belly. She retraced her steps, re-examining the edge of this new barricade. She discovered a small cavity and pressed her head into it. Within, she felt a series of long, flexible rods.

Wires.

They were not edible but, perhaps, she could chew through them and somehow squeeze by. She set about doing just that, her work fevered and aggressive. Sharp teeth made progress against the wires, and soon enough one of them was chewed all the way through. The rat pushed past it, ignoring the fact that the cut wire brushed up against her small body.

She chewed on a second wire. This one proved even easier to work through. As she chewed, her excitement grew. She would find the food that had brought her here, to this place of pain. She would fill her belly. Her last moments would be happy ones.

She made it only halfway through that second wire before being hit with two hundred and twenty volts of electricity. The rat's body convulsed only once. Her death was instantaneous.

Around her, all was quiet. All was dark. For the moment.

Then, from somewhere far, far below, came a low, throbbing alarm.

From deep down below appeared a flood of lights. The sounds of footsteps –many footsteps– were heard. Some walked, most ran. Their actions were frantic, as frantic as the rat's. Had the rat lived, she would have surely heard the shouts.

After five minutes and twenty seconds, all was silent once again.

But the damage was done.

2

Agnes Livingstone was a week shy of her sixtieth birthday and, as was her annual mid-October custom, put in for her two week vacation. She eagerly looked forward to it, especially this year. She worked as a systems analyst for the better part of thirty years and was a widow of a little more than a year and a half. After her husband unexpectedly passed, she fell into a depression so deep that her friends and co-workers worried whether her melancholia would affect her life and work.

Nearly a year to the day of her husband's death, Agnes met a fellow widower while out in the food market. His name was Charlie and he had a twinkle in his eyes and a roguish charm Agnes found impossible to resist. Soon, they were inseparable and Agnes' melancholia lifted. Much as she still missed her late husband, Agnes made the surprising realization that she had successfully moved on, and her life was once again full of promise.

She eagerly eyed the clock mounted at the end of the oversized office, where all her fellow systems analysts worked in their individual cubicles. There was one hour left in her shift and one hour before she was on vacation. Charlie and she would be off to Rotterdam. At this time tomorrow, the glowing widow thought, she'd be with her new sweetie on a cruise ship taking a round trip along the beautiful Scandinavian coast.

So eager was she for her shift to end that she hurried through the latest satellite images, skipping past them as if they were a bothersome friend's bad family pictures.

In part her rush was also because the images were virtually identical to those she processed the day before and the day before that. They covered the same general terrain and it was her job to notice any irregularities from previous days.

As she worked, her mind wandered back to thoughts of Charlie and her vacation. She clicked the computer's mouse and the next satellite image appeared, but her eyes had drifted from the all too familiar image and to the windows on the north side of the room. There, she saw the buildings along Whitechapel High Street and, without meaning to, she let out an audible sigh. Her sigh was immediately followed by a sharp grunt, this one coming from somewhere behind her. Surprised, Agnes spun in her chair and found Corporal Thomas Hedley, her boss, standing beside the entrance to her cubicle. His arms were folded across his chest.

"You scared me," she said.

Corporal Hedley shook his head. He surveyed the room and noted several of his staff looking his way.

"Get back to work," Hedley told them.

Like scared gophers, the curious staffs' heads disappeared into their respective cubicles. When the Corporal was satisfied the others were minding their own business, he entered Agnes' space and leaned in close to the widow. He too eyed the Whitechapel High street.

"I know the hour is late," Hedley whispered. "But could we trouble you to finish your work *before* your vacation starts?"

Agnes gave her boss a warm smile. Despite his gruff demeanor, Hedley, more than any of the others in this office, showed the most concern for Agnes during her tough times. He, more than any of the others, lent her a hand and offered her a shoulder to cry upon.

He can be a bear, Agnes thought, *but there's no denying underneath it all is a very caring man.*

"Yes sir," Agnes said.

"He won't leave without you," Headley added before retreating from the cubicle.

"I know," Agnes whispered.

She shook her head and again focused on the computer monitor. She clicked through the next series of images, finishing the daytime satellite photos and shifting to the nighttime thermals. One followed the other and nothing appeared out of place.

Agnes let out a yawn.

She tried hard not to look at the clock or out the window.

Be professional, she admonished herself. *Even if you only have a short time before—*

The thought died quickly.

The thermal image before her looked much like all the images she just examined but something stood out. The thermal was almost entirely dark. The darkness was punctuated by a very small rectangular group of lights. The lights were square blobs, man-made but amorphous in shape. None of those six lights captured Agnes' attention. No, it was the seventh light south of the others that intrigued her. That light was very faint.

Had it not been for Agnes' familiarity with previous nights' thermals taken at the time, this oddity might well have escaped even her attention.

She clicked her mouse button a few times and another display appeared on the monitor. It was another thermal image, this one taken two nights before. She moved that image to the left of the screen until it was side by side with the previous night's image. She compared the two, checking to see if this ghostly seventh light was an artifact.

"Are you for real?" she muttered after a while.

She clicked the mouse button a few more times, getting a close up of a small section of the faint light in the otherwise absolute black. She sharpened the image and boosted the contrast. She tired other enhancements to make out a shape. She turned the image around, spinning it clockwise and counterclockwise.

She was so engrossed with the thermal image that she didn't notice her fellow workers pack their gear and begin leaving. The day shift was over, but Agnes continued, her mind focused entirely on this small, mysterious blob of light. After a while, all the cubicles were empty and Agnes was the only one left in the large office.

"Agnes?"

Agnes spun in her chair. Corporal Hedley again stood beside her cubicle. He pointed at his watch.

"I thought you were eager to start your vacation?" he said and smiled. "You aren't planning to apply for overtime, are you?"

Agnes let out a laugh.

"I didn't think we had the budget."

"We don't," Hedley replied. "So what say you get out of here and go enjoy yourself?"

"I will sir," Agnes said. But she didn't move from her desk. Instead, she faced her monitor.

Hedley frowned. He approached Agnes and looked over her shoulder.

"What has you so entranced, my dear?"

"I'm not sure," Agnes replied. "It's something...At first I thought it might be a glitch, some kind of camera glare. I'm still not sure..."

Hedley looked at the image.

"Rectangular electronic light source."

"Yes. But faint. Too faint."

Agnes pulled back on the image and compared the faint lights with the other six regular lights she saw in each of the nocturnal pictures.

"Maybe they had a party and put up some low watt lights?"

"No," Agnes said. "It's too faint, even for that. It's almost like..." She let out a chuckle. "It's almost like these lights are coming from underground."

Thought she didn't notice it, Hedley stiffened. His eyes were suddenly razor sharp and took in every single detail of the image on Agnes' screen.

"I must be losing my mind," Agnes said after a while.

Hedley's stare didn't deviate.

"I think you were right the first time."

"About?"

"I think it's a glitch," Hedley said. "Probably a software problem."

"You think?" Agnes said.

"Nothing to worry about," Hedley said. He reached over Agnes' shoulder and switched her monitor off. "When the tech boys come in, I'll have them run some diagnostics. By the time you're back, everything will be fine."

"Are you sure? You don't want me to double check?"

Hedley shook his head.

"Agnes, my dear, what I want you to do is enjoy your vacation."

"But sir—"

"That's an order."

Agnes nodded.

"Wouldn't want to keep Charlie waiting," she said and giggled.

"Indeed."

Agnes grabbed her purse and locked her desk drawers. Hedley accompanied her to the doors leading out of the office. She used her security pass to open the door and stepped out. Beyond the doors was a long white corridor. At the end of the corridor and standing beside a fortified metal double door, the facility's exit, stood two armed military guards.

"Have a good time," Hedley said.

"I will," Agnes replied. She walked to the end of the corridor and officially signed out. She looked back once more and waved to her boss before exiting.

The warm smile on Hedley's face disappeared the moment she was gone. He pulled his cell phone from his pocket and hit a button. After a few seconds, he was in contact with his superior.

"Mister Vulcan, this is Corporal Hedley," he said. His voice was low, his words to the point. "We found something."

Hedley was silent for a few seconds.

"Yes sir," he continued. "You most definitely should take a look."

He was again silent and nodded before hanging up and pocketing his cell phone.

"This room is on lockdown," Hedley said to the guards at the end of the corridor.

He then retreated into the office and approached Agnes' monitor. He turned it on. After a few seconds, the thermal image reappeared. Hedley stared at it.

As he did, a shiver ran down his back.

3

**THE MARISE TRENCH, ATLANTIC OCEAN.
THREE WEEKS LATER**

The HMS *Avenger* crawled along the Marise Trench at a steady five knots.   Though the powerful British nuclear submarine was equipped with state of the art Rolls-Royce pressurized water reactors and capable of speeds exceeding 29 knots, it maintained the very reduced pace over the last twelve hours. During that time, the submarine literally hugged the sea's bottom, rarely rising more than twenty feet from the muddy silt some two to three hundred feet below the surface of the Atlantic Ocean.

While normally capable of holding over one hundred officers and servicemen, the submarine was staffed by a skeleton crew of forty three.   They went about their business quietly, most amazed at the amount of space there was within the normally tight confines of a vessel such as this.

The ship's Captain, Jonathan Elliot, watched his staff go about their business from the confines of his chair on the bridge. His weary face reflected what on the surface appeared to be only a detached interest. His crew, however, knew better. While on the bridge, the Captain's thoughts were sharp and focused.   Any screw up, however small, would be pointed out and, depending on its level of severity, quickly –maybe even harshly– dealt with. The person responsible for said screw up would either efficiently correct their error or be forced aside. If the latter occurred, there was a good chance the service man's –or woman's– days in the Royal Navy were over.   When traveling in a submarine whose cost spiraled a billion pounds *over* its already sky-high budget, only the very competent need apply.

At that thought, Captain Elliot frowned. It seemed almost everything in the military nowadays was judged, first and foremost, by its cost. He entered the Navy just after the Cold War ended. Then, nations were focused on self-preservation far more than the funds needed to pay for this survival. Things changed as the Cold War receded in time. The fear of global annihilation was, for the most part, gone. Few worried about all out nuclear conflict.   Dangers still existed, of course, but attitudes had changed...

Captain Elliot sighed.

He wished those attitudes by the people in power remained more consistent.   Today, bean counters carefully eyed every expenditure.   New programs and innovations took longer to approve and initiate.   During the Cold War, departments were aggressive, inventive.   Today, the military felt like it was in neutral.

Until, that is, they call you out to carry on a mission like this one.

Captain Elliot cradled a cup of lukewarm, sugarless black coffee and considered taking another swig.   He was awake and on duty for over thirty hours and needed every bit of help he could to stay focused on the task at hand.   The mission, to put it mildly, was intriguing as hell.

On paper, the *Avenger* was still under construction at one of the massive docks in Barrow, on the east coast of Great Britain.   In actuality, the newest member of the *Astute* class of submarines was secretly launched a full two weeks before.   Though he was now the Captain of this vessel, Elliot was not involved in her launch.   It was only afterwards that he was briefed on her departure.   The story had him in awe as it was a thing of clever beauty and worthy of the Cold War era stories he read or the programs he watched on the BBC when he was much younger.

For just before her launch, the *Avenger* was replaced with a massive hallow frame mounted on a platform within the secure construction site.   Large opaque curtains disguised elements of the supposed construction, while several hundred "workers" filtered in and out of the work site, giving the impression the naval vessel was still in the process of creation.   The deception was made for any ground level spies, as the construction site was inside an enormous closed hanger and all but invisible to satellite imagery.   This intrigue was authorized by officials in the highest levels of government, and all because of this current mission.

While heavy boat traffic filled the area around Barrow, the *Avenger* was silently released.   She used a noisy trawler as surface cover and mirrored that ship's movements from below, eventually slipping out of port and hitting the high seas.   For a week a skeleton crew comprised of technicians and scientists ran the *Avenger* through her paces to ensure the submarine was seaworthy.   She was.   The only equipment on board that remained unfinished were her torpedo and missile systems. For this mission, such offensive and defensive systems were unnecessary.

From there, the crew headed south and east across the Atlantic and, in a circuitous route, made their way farther and farther west. Four days before the submarine met with another trawler. On board were Captain Elliot, his handpicked staff, and two very special passengers.

In the dead of night the group boarded the *Avenger* and Captain Elliot officially took over. Off they went, traveling farther west and south, until they were within hours of their destination. When this mission was over, the *Avenger* would retrace her path and a few days later return to her birth at Barrow and conclude her construction. In a matter of weeks and with the usual official fanfare, the *Avenger* would be formally launched, with no one knowing she already had one mission under her belt.

Until then, Captain Elliot and his crew were like phantoms crawling along the ocean floor, existing where they should not, performing a mission no other nation, and very few within Britain herself, knew about.

Captain Elliot sipped some of the cold coffee.

This whole situation, when looked at from a distance, seemed just like the type of adventure he longed for. Yet after that initial adrenalin rush was gone, the prevailing emotion within the vessel was one of constant, oppressive tension. For out here, the submarine and her crew were most certainly on their own. Should the *Avenger* be damaged or disabled, it would be up to Captain Elliot and his personnel to resolve the problem. Radioing for help, unless and *only* if the situation was deemed life threatening, was strictly forbidden, for any outgoing signal, even in coded form, would be heard by the many ears out there whose job it was to listen. Locating the source of that signal, while not without its difficulties, could be achieved to within a general area by any foreign power. And even if those powers couldn't locate the submarine's exact position, the fact that there was a phantom signal sent from a phantom vessel was enough for a clever intelligence agency to guess the *Avenger* –or some other "nearly" complete submarine– was already in operation.

More investigation might expose the vessel's mission and this was *not* an option.

Captain Elliot finished his coffee and stifled a yawn. It was because of the delicate nature of the mission he remained on deck after so many continuous hours. Everything had to proceed smoothly. Everything. Even if he knew almost nothing about the mission's ultimate goal.

"We're exiting the trench," the Navigational officer said. "No traffic detected."

Captain Elliot nodded.

"Bring her up slow, to one hundred feet," he said. He took a deep breath and added: "Follow the plan. Absolutely no deviations."

There was nothing more to say. Captain Elliot glanced at his watch. Local time was 2:14 P.M. It would take at least two more hours before the *Avenger* reached her destination. From there, he would have to consult one of his two onboard "special guests" about the mission's next stages. If all went well, he was told, this guest would finish whatever he needed to do precisely twelve hours later, at which time the submarine would have its man back on board and would begin the journey back home.

That time can't come soon enough, Captain Elliot thought.

Just under two hours later, Captain Elliot wandered through the main corridor of his vessel. Like his staff, he was not immune to marveling at the lack of personnel he normally dodged while making his way through these tight corridors.

In the Captain's hand was a fresh cup of coffee. Though the deep drag of exhaustion was almost crippling, the fact that the *Avenger* had reached her destination without incident provided some small measure of relief...and renewed energy.

He chuckled.

It's either that or I'm suffering from a severe caffeine overdose, he thought.

Regardless, the level of tension within his vessel was noticeably diminished, and several crewmembers sported actual, honest-to-God smiles. With this phase of the mission over, all that was left for the Captain and his exhausted crew to do was enjoy a few minutes of well-deserved rest. Their next orders would come soon enough.

Captain Elliot walked up to one of the many metal doors lining the personnel corridor. For a second he paused. For several seconds, actually. The exhaustion, he realized, was getting to him. For a moment, his mind felt like it was stuck in quicksand.

Easy now, you'll be able to rest soon enough.

Captain Elliot rubbed his face with his free hand and, gently, knocked on the door in front of him.

"Come in," a voice called out.

Captain Elliot slid the door open and stepped inside. He stood in the first of the submarine's twelve private quarters. On the left side of the room was a bed. On it was a fresh set of clothing. On the other side of the room was a small metal desk. Directly in the middle and on the opposite wall was an open door leading into a cramped bathroom. Stepping out of that bathroom was a handsome young man in his early thirties. He wore form fitting bicycle shorts and was drying his dark, damp hair.

"You're early," the young man said. His voice was pleasant and energetic. In the very little time Captain Elliot had talked with him, he found it hard to dislike the lad. Hard, but not impossible.

Captain Elliot handed him the cup of fresh coffee.

"Yes, we're ahead of schedule," Captain Elliot said. ""We thought you'd—"

"—like to know," the young man concluded. He took the offered drink. "Thanks."

"You're welcome."

Captain Elliot folded his arms and looked the room over. It wasn't the Grosvenor House, certainly, but it was positively luxurious compared to private quarters on either the *Swiftsure* or *Vanguard*-class submarines.

The Captain's gaze and attention eventually returned to the young man. He drank from the cup and placed it on the metal desk. He then turned to the clothing on the bed and dressed. Every item he wore was jet black and made of a dull, non-reflective material. It was a perfect covert ops outfit: form fitting and difficult, if not impossible, to spot in darkness.

The young man grabbed the black shirt. As he put it on, Captain Elliot noticed a series of scars along the lower left side of the man's back. Had he not been paying attention, the Captain might have mistaken the scars for an elaborate, if abstract tattoo.

The wounds were deep, yet not deep enough to hinder the young man's movement. Given their pattern, they appeared the result of some kind of shrapnel tag. The Captain wondered how close the young man was to the source of the explosion that caused these wounds. A little closer and he might well have been cut in half.

Where did you get them? The Captain wondered. *Afghanistan? Iraq? Or perhaps somewhere a little more exotic. Somewhere we, at least officially, aren't supposed to be. Like we are now.*

The Captain scolded himself for wasting time on such thoughts, yet his eyes lingered on the young man's wounds. He noticed another, darker scar higher up on the right side of the man's back. With a start, he realized it was an old bullet wound. The Captain forced his eyes away. The wounds were another fascinating element which added to the overall mystique of this quiet passenger.

Quiet passenger.

It was as good a description of both the special passengers on board his vessel. However, while Captain Elliot had access to the young man, the other older passenger might as well be quiet *and* invisible. Captain Elliot was first introduced to them on a deserted, windswept coastline near Ilfracombe. They, along with Captain Elliot's skeleton staff and another senior official, were waiting for the transport which eventually delivered them all to the *Avenger*. At the time, Captain Elliot approached the young man and the other, older passenger and offered his hand. Their handshakes were firm and impersonal. When he introduced himself to them, only the young man reciprocated.

"You can call me Michael," he said, while the older man stood to the side.

It wasn't his real name, of course. Given the parameters of the mission and the way information was delivered, that much was obvious. Captain Elliot took the hint and decided to keep the conversation very short. He ultimately left his special passengers alone and focused on his staff. He made damn sure everyone was ready for what was to come. When the transport finally arrived, the entire group boarded in silence. A few hours later, they were transferred to the *Avenger*. The young and older man retired to their individual rooms and remained there for the length of the trip. Only once, late in the first day of travel, did Captain Elliot see Michael walking the ship's corridors. He appeared lost in thought and paid little attention to the scant personnel passing him by.

Captain Elliot shook his head.

When he was Michael's age, he was approached by the SIS and offered a position most likely in line with that of this young man. In Captain Elliot's case, the SIS proved the wrong path. His true love and devotion was to the sea. In the years since his entry into Her Majesty's Royal Navy, Captain Elliot's rank and reputation grew, until he had a reputation for being one of the more capable senior officers in the fleet. Standing before this young man, Captain Elliot couldn't help but wonder about the path not taken.

Captain Elliot looked up, and was surprised to see Michael looking at him. How long, the Captain wondered, had he been staring at the young man's wounds? He cleared his throat and said:

"We are currently at a depth of one hundred feet and at the proper coordinates."

"Exactly?"

"Yes, exactly," Captain Elliot said a little more irritably than he wanted. "We can bring the *Avenger* up for insertion within fifteen minutes of your say so. Assuming, of course, you desire such action."

The last words came out even more strained. If Michael noticed, he didn't say anything. Instead, he looked at his watch.

"Excellent," he said. He was fully dressed in his inky black outfit. It made him look compact, smaller. "You're certain we haven't been detected?"

"Absolutely."

Michael reached under the bed and produced a backpack. It was compact and made of a dull green plastic and had a heavy duty seal which, no doubt, kept the contents within dry. The young man unzipped the top of the backpack and reached inside. Though he couldn't help himself, Captain Elliot noticed a change of clothing within. The clothing had a familiar green camouflage color.

The young man pushed past the clothing, revealing several pieces of dull metal equipment. As with his current clothing, they were all black. He grasped something at the bottom of the backpack and retracted his arm. In it was a Heckler & Koch USP handgun in a black leather holster. The young man pulled the gun free and conducted a quick check. As he did, Captain Elliot stiffened.

"Guns make you nervous?" the young man said.

"We're in a nuclear submarine under a hundred feet of water and a stranger on my craft is holding a handgun."

"We're on the same side."

"So I've been told. Despite this, you're not a member of my crew. Seeing someone I know so little about carrying a handgun makes me very nervous. Usually."

"Usually? Are you implying you're not quite so nervous right now? Am I that trustworthy?"

"No."

"Then why the lack of concern?"

"Because you're carrying blanks."

The young man leaned back. A knowing smile worked its way onto his face.

"Am I?" he said.

"Of course. I've taken the mission seriously from the very beginning, but clearly what we're engaged in is a training operation."

"And you know this because?"

"Because of our current location."

"You assume we are near our destination."

"Aren't we?"

"Yes."

"Then you're carrying blanks. There's no doubt about it."

The young man removed the clip from his gun and drew a single cartridge. He handed it to the Captain. The Captain looked at it for a few seconds before handing it back.

"If you wish, you may look through all my ammunition," the young man said.

"I...I don't understand," the Captain muttered.

The young man replaced the very real cartridge back into the clip and slid the clip back into the gun. He then thrust the gun into its holster and tightened the holster's strap around his shoulder. He once again reached into his backpack and produced a small flash drive. He handed it to Captain Elliot. Despite its small size, it felt heavy.

"These are your instructions," the young man said.

Captain Elliot approached a panel on the wall. He inserted the flash drive into a slot and the panel's screen came alive.

"Use your RMS access code."

Captain Elliot typed in his access code and information appeared on the monitor.

"Verify the code," the Captain told Michael.

"Project Onyx. 90112."

The verification codes were proper. Captain Elliot read his new instructions. His eyes grew wide.

"What is this?"

"It's your next destination as well as where you are to surface," Michael said. "You were quite correct, Captain. We are only a few miles from our destination. I want to get to shore no later than 1730 hours. You will pick me up exactly twelve hours afterwards, unless, of course, I send word for an earlier pick up."

Captain Elliot shook his head.

"This is madness," he said. "The only thing out here is—"

"I'm well aware of what's out here, Captain," Michael said.

Captain Elliot drew a sharp breath.

"All right," the Captain said. As painful as it was, he and his crew's role in this mission was little more than being chauffeurs for Michael and his mission.

And whatever the other "special" passenger's mission –if any– was.

"We'll...we'll be there at the appointed time," Captain Elliot finally said. "Might I ask a question?"

"Of course."

"The sun sets in this part of the world at approximately 1820 hours. Is it wise to pursue...to pursue whatever it is you're after while there is still light outside?"

The young man smiled but said nothing. A dull anger grew within Captain Elliot. Michael was playing a child's game: You can ask any question you want but there was no guarantee you would receive answers.

"Very well," the Captain said. He took a step back, toward the door. "I'll be getting back—"

"Wait," the young man said.

Captain Elliot stopped. From within the backpack and stuffed underneath some of his compact equipment, the young man produced a small envelope. He walked to the Captain's side.

"The Royal Navy demands subservience," Michael said. "And this is...this is a most unusual mission. Believe me, I am sympathetic."

Michael held the small envelope out.

"Perhaps we could help each other."

Captain Elliot stared at the envelope. It was addressed and stamped. With a start, Captain Elliot realized what the young man wanted him to do.

"This is against regulations."

"The hell with regulations," Michael said. For the first time since meeting him, the young man's voice held emotion. He opened the envelope and removed the letter.

"Read it," he said. "No codes, no reveals. No microdots or invisible ink or any other SIS bullshit."

"I can't do this."

"Of course you can," Michael said.

The young man remained before Captain Elliot with letter in hand. He said nothing more but pleaded his case with his eyes. After a few moments, Captain Elliot relented. He took the letter and read it. When he was done, he folded it and stuffed it back into the envelope.

"Addressed to your mother," Captain Elliot said.

"We haven't been on the greatest of terms," the young man said. "Our duty as officers is to Queen and Country. Personal issues are often lost in the wash. This particular mission snuck up on me. I could not refuse the call, but I don't want to leave things as they are back home. Especially if I were to not make it."

"I sympathize," Captain Elliot said. "I truly do. But even if you didn't return, I couldn't send this. It is against protocol."

"So is telling you the details of my mission," Michael replied.

The implication hung heavy in the air.

Send my letter and I'll satisfy your curiosity.

"This is nonsense," the Captain said after a few seconds. "In all these years of service, I have yet to lose a member of my crew. What makes you think that's a possibility?"

"We do not choose our missions, Captain. There are missions that take months of careful planning. The ones that consider and reconsider even the tiniest of details. Those missions have the highest likelihood of success and the lowest likelihood of...tragedy. Then there are the other missions, those executed in haste, usually because the window of opportunity is open only for so long. Unfortunately, by their very nature those missions have a higher likelihood of failure."

"What you're asking me to do could get me court-martialed."

Michael said nothing. The anger within Captain Elliot grew. How dare this young man try to play with his emotions and sense of duty in this way. He wanted to be done with this, to head back to the bridge. *Fuck* Michael and *fuck* whatever it was he and his superiors at SIS were up to.

But Michael's letter remained in the Captain's hand. Despite his anger, despite his desire to follow protocol, he still held it.

"I offer you clarity, Captain," Michael said. "You won't have to stumble in the dark. All I need is for you to put that letter in a mailbox, should I not make it."

"And if you do make it?"

"You rip the letter up and we forget we ever had this conversation," Michael said. "From where I sit, you get the better part of the trade."

The Captain's eyes danced between the letter and Michael. The SIS agent was right. If Michael's mission was a success, this entire incident would be irrelevant. No harm, no foul. And even if something bad did happen to the young man and Captain Elliot did send the letter, he had to admit its contents were innocuous. If he should drop it into a mailbox when he got back to London, who would know?

Very slowly, the Captain folded the envelope and pocketed it.

"Thank you," Michael said. The young man's eyes turned away. In that moment, he looked much older than his age.

"You will make it through the mission," Captain Elliot insisted. "Afterwards, we'll share a bottle of Slivovitz, Mister Jennings."

The young man smiled.

"Jennings is my mother's maiden name, not mine," he said. "As for the Slivovitz, I'd be delighted to share a small cup. I don't think my system can handle more than one."

Michael held out his hand and Captain Elliot shook it. The handshake was firm and impersonal, just like the first time. The young man's smile was gone. Perhaps, Captain Elliot thought, it had never really been there to begin with.

"We will be surfacing at 1700 hours," the young man said. "Sharp."

"Yes sir," Captain Elliot replied.

Michael sat back on the bed. He said:

"You wanted information, Captain," Michael said. "Go ahead. Ask your question."

Captain Elliot made sure the door leading out of the room was locked. This was about as private as they would get. The Captain leaned close to the S.I.S. agent. His voice was a whisper.

"I have only one question," Captain Elliot said.

"I figured as much," Michael replied.

Captain Elliot frowned and said:

"Why is British intelligence infiltrating a U.S. military base?"

4

BAD PENNY MILITARY BASE, 1735 HOURS

Steve Cibos carried a rifle that, in the early evening gloom, was indistinguishable from the many models readily available to soldiers in the various branches of the U.S. armed forces. His pace was unhurried, his manner casual. He walked this path hundreds of times before and had yet to tire of it. Though it was part of his job to patrol the shoreline, he found the walk allowed him to clear his mind before beginning the second part of his shift.

Steve wore standard black patrol fatigues accented with white embellishment and labels. Smoke rose lazily from a cigarette he cradled between the fingers of his right hand. He took another deep pull before pausing a moment to stare out at the sea.

The waves gently lapped against the shore some twenty feet away. It was a big difference from the month before, when a tropical wave, not quite a tropical storm, skirted to the south of Bad Penny. The night was filled with howling wind and heavy rain while the coast was battered by dangerous surf. For a while, it felt like the end of the world. All the result of a tropical wave.

Steve grinned. If that's what a strong tropical wave was capable of, he'd hate to face a hurricane. Like everyone else, he was just as shocked about the pandemonium left behind in New Orleans after Katrina. It was hard to believe one very strong storm could knock civilization on its collective ass.

The MP tossed his now spent cigarette into the water. He stood there, watching the waves for a few moments and enjoying the calm. Though he didn't really want to, he reached into his shirt pocket and pulled out another cigarette.

Bastard things, he thought as he lit it up and took a long pull. *One of these days I'll give you up. For good.*

Nonetheless, he lost himself in the pleasant buzz of nicotine and enjoyed the moment. There wasn't a single cloud in the sky and the water looked so damn inviting. This was the life, even if he was stuck in the fucking military.

Steve finished his second cigarette of the afternoon and dropped it to the ground. In a single, lazy motion, he stepped on it and crushed it underfoot. His eyes drifted back up to the blue sky and his solitary thoughts as he continued his walk, out and away.

This was just as well for the young man hiding in the bush a few feet away. Had he wanted to, he could have reached out and grabbed the crushed cigarette. As it was, he was glad his mission hadn't derailed in its first few minutes.

Michael wiped water from his wet hair and stole a glance at his watch. As was usually the case, his schedule and reality had already clashed, though as of yet he wasn't running behind all that much.

Still, the delay was a problem. He only had so much daylight left to find what he was looking for and leave, preferably without having to use any of the very real ammunition in his handgun.

When he was sure the M.P. was sufficiently far away, Michael got to his knees and silently wandered off into the jungle, in the same general direction the M.P. had originally come from.

In the early evening hours, as the sun was just beginning to set, if you looked across the street you could see a few buildings evenly spaced and spread out over a distance of a half-mile, five on one side and six on the other. The buildings were separated by a narrow paved road. If you weren't looking closely enough, the town would appear to be like any other very small town in the United States.

But only if you weren't looking closely enough.

Three of the buildings, a cluster in the town's center, were shaped like drab concrete blocks and rose up two floors each. They were free of any flourishes or signs and all were painted a dull gray. There were no signs indicating specific stores or sales or any of the usual attempts to draw clients in. To the south was a black and silver warehouse and next to it was a lean two story building that had a pair of beat up gas pumps sitting before it. This small gas station, like the other buildings around it, bore no corporate logo.

Further down the south side of the town and past a dense tropical forest was a small two story control tower, on the top of which protruded a series of antennae and satellite dishes. Next to the tower was another smaller building and another, more modern, gas pump. Immediately south of this was a large, square, concrete landing pad. Had this been Any Small Town, U.S.A., you might expect a single propeller crop duster parked in the grass and an old man sitting in a wicker chair, sucking on his pipe or cradling a glass of lemonade while enjoying the early evening breeze. Instead, in the middle of the landing pad and taking up that space like a burly tank was a gray MH-60R Sea Hawk multi-mission helicopter.

The presence of this helicopter, perhaps more than anything else, would dispel any remaining notions one might have that this was an ordinary small town. Now alerted to this inconsistency, a more thorough inspection by the viewer would reveal that *all* the vehicles in this town were far from ordinary. There were at least five Humvees and an equal number of M939 transportation trucks, all painted in a familiar camouflage green, parked under trees and difficult for the casual observer to spot.

Not that casual observers existed in any quantity around here.

Fishermen from the nearest islands some seventy five miles away knew to avoid Bad Penny, even though there were no explicit warnings posted along her beaches. From time to time a single Cyclon Class Patrol Boat skirted along her waters, discouraging the locals from coming too close to the chain of islands, of which Bad Penny was but one. The military presence was low key and rarely overwhelming, which was in line with the fact that the islands were primarily used for military training.

At least that was the description offered by the U.S. Armed Forces.

The young man delivered to this island via the British submarine *Avenger*, however, knew this wasn't quite the case. He had made his way to the island's southern outer edge and, now dressed in camouflage gear, lay nearly invisible within a wild bush. In his hands was a pair of compact binoculars. Through them, he surveyed the Bad Penny's air base as the day slowly wound down. Though his breathing was even and his outward appearance calm, his mind raced. The British agent known as Michael hoped to make it to the center of the base and find his target well before sunset. He had already failed in this endeavor, and the weight of the missed deadline was a concern.

Time was running out.

Samantha Aron's eyes fluttered open as the dying rays of the sun broke through the window. She winced and turned to get away. Anything to continue sleeping. Even in her present hazy state of mind, she knew this was the wrong thing to do, yet she felt so damned comfortable in bed.

"I know what you're thinking and you can't stay there forever," a formless voiced called out to her. "You'd better get up."

Samantha dismissively waved her hand and the bothersome voice offered a genial laugh.

"Seriously, you better get up," the voice insisted. "They're waiting for you."

"Let them," she said.

"They have you on such a quick turnaround..." the voice persisted.

Samantha moaned at that thought.

"...and you have people and supplies to fly out—"

Samantha jerked into a sitting position. Her eyes shot down to her wristwatch.

"It's nearly six thirty!" she said. "Why didn't you wake me up?"

Warren Bligh emerged from the bathroom. He was completely nude and incredibly striking to Samantha's eyes. She could look at him for hours, but unfortunately –very, *very* unfortunately– she didn't have the time. Warren caught her stare and smiled. He removed the toothbrush from his mouth.

"I've been trying to get you up for the past half hour," he said. "If I knew all it took was to show myself off—"

Samantha jumped out of bed, equally nude.

"I needed the sleep," she explained as she rushed past him and into the bathroom.

Before closing the door, however, she took a few seconds to admire her lover's back side. Her gaze lingered.

"Did I really say I needed sleep?" she said and shook her head before closing the door on her lover.

He was left with nowhere to spit out the foamy toothpaste.

Dressed in her slick black flight outfit, Samantha burst through the door leading out of her cabin. Though most of the staff and officers in Bad Penny were stationed in the barracks, certain officers with specialized skills, including pilots, were allowed to reside in one of the ten small private cabins in the military town. These cabins were the last remnants of a failed golf course and surrounding community that was never completed.   Facing foreclosure and bankruptcy, the U.S. Government instead swooped in and took over the island while the cabins were still in relatively good shape.

Today, they were crawling with bugs and were small by the standards of your average home owner, but they afforded privacy, something which was in very limited supply within the armed forces.

A cigarette dangled out of Samantha's mouth and a small duffel bag swung against her side as she stepped into the early evening dusk. She was in the process of slipping on her flight jacket, something which proved considerably harder to do with the duffel bag in the way, when a voice called her back to the cabin door.

"You're leaving without as much as a goodbye?" Warren said.

Samantha stopped in her tracks and spun around. A warm smile appeared on her face and she couldn't help but giggle. Warren was standing at the door, toothbrush still in hand. He hadn't dressed yet, which Samantha really appreciated. Then again, he still had the foamy toothpaste on the side of his mouth. It was the high cost of being exiled from your own bathroom.

"When I get back, the first thing I'll do is teach you how to properly clean up after brushing your teeth," she said. She walked back up the stairs leading to the cabin door.

"Before or after you teach me how to dress?" he replied.

"For you, that knowledge is completely useless," Samantha said. "I'd go so far as to say it should be forbidden."

She wiped the toothpaste from the side of Warren's mouth and embraced her lover. They kissed, gently, twice.

"I'll miss you," Samantha said.

"So will I," Warren replied.

They kissed once more. A series of catcalls interrupted their embrace. A pair of Marines walking down the street and toward the Mess Hall further south paused in their tracks to watch the show. Warren extended his right hand and flipped them the bird.

The Marines laughed and continued their walk. Samantha, too, managed a laugh.

"How very rude of you."

"What, this finger?" Warren said. He tried, but utterly failed, to look innocent. "Why it's quickly becoming Bad Penny's unofficial greeting."

"You don't say?"

Warren offered Samantha another smile. He noted her arms were tight around his naked waist.

"Something tells me you have a real hard time letting go of things."

"Just certain things," Samantha said.

"Your passengers are waiting."

"Let 'em."

"That's all well and good. But if you take any longer, I might just get a call from brass."

"Oh? You're going to arrest me?"

"We M.P.'s take our duty seriously."

"Spoil sport."

"Go on. I'll be waiting when you come back. Just don't take too long, OK?"

"I'll be back before you know it."

Samantha gave Warren a final kiss and ran down the stairs and to her Humvee, which was parked a few feet from the cabin's driveway. The vehicle's tires squealed against the pavement.

In her rearview mirror, she saw Warren, still standing by the door in all his nude glory, waving as she drove away.

"I must be crazy," she muttered. "Who in their right mind voluntarily leaves something like *that* behind?"

The buildings of Bad Penny passed quickly as she drove south though the small town. Several more officers exited the weight room building at the center of town, every one of them also heading south toward the Mess Hall. Samantha felt a pang of hunger and wished she had awoken early enough to join them for supper. Unfortunately, there was no time.

After passing the Mess Hall, she entered the dense tropical forest separating the town from the airbase. Halfway through that forest she stopped at the base's only four way intersection. Roads leading east and west to the beaches on either side of the island and were rarely used. They were covered in nature's debris: dead leaves, mud, and palm fronds. Samantha nonetheless looked to her right and left and held for a second. In the distance, beyond the bushes and undergrowth to the southeast, she spotted a small building almost completely hidden among the trees. It was an old, rusted one story tool shed. Or at least that's what the higher ups claimed it was.

Few believed it.

Despite the fact that the building was small and showed the ravages of age and weather, there were always at least two guards sitting in equally weathered beach chairs before its entrance. Every time she passed the intersection, they looked like they were engaged in a particularly intense game of cards, yet never once did they fail to notice her. Their very mean looking M16A2 assault rifles were always close beside them, ready for use. Such weapons seemed like overkill considering the rusted shack they were guarding.

Few visited it, but those who did, Samantha noticed, carried a curious yellow ID badge. She spotted similar badges in other bases a few times before. The people who carried them were often high ranking officers who were not known to fraternize with grunts or pilots. Whatever the people with the yellow badges were doing in this particular shack and on this particular island, Samantha was pretty certain it involved things requiring considerably more than a Phillips Head screwdriver.

Samantha shook her head. She was far from a seasoned military veteran, yet knew almost all the bases had their very own "special" or off-limits areas. In her sometimes fertile mind, she imagined the people who frequented these places were engaged in equally special operations. Or, as her friend Eleanor told her a very long time before, they were spooks.

Spooks. The words conjured dark images. Images that—

With a start, Samantha realized she was still parked at the intersection staring at the shack. Had she been in a real city, she would have had a pile of vehicles with very angry drivers stuck behind her.

"You picked some time to daydream," she muttered while stepping on the accelerator. Her Humvee drove past the intersection.

It was pure luck. Pure *bad* luck.

Or so Michael thought when the Humvee came to a stop at the intersection. He had only a second to fall flat on his stomach and lie among the weeds. Because of his haste, he couldn't be sure how well covered he was, and feared just enough of him was exposed for the driver to locate him.

Take it easy, he thought as he tried to check his anxiety. *See how it plays out.*

So far, it played out very badly. Very badly indeed.

The Hummer came to a full stop and didn't move. A second passed, then another. And another. The vehicle remained still.

What is he waiting for?

Michael moved his head just a little, until he had a view of the Humvee. To his horror, he realized the driver was looking in his general direction. Through the weeds, he spotted the driver's – *her*– stare. She was gorgeous, and in any other place and at any other time he would have been flattered to see such a knockout look his way. But not here. Not now.

With great care Michael released his handgun from its holster. With even greater care, he slowly aimed it at the vehicle's sole occupant. If she spotted him, there was little he could do. His mission dictated he could not be found. It dictated he absolutely could not be captured. That left him with few alternatives. If the driver of the Humvee did indeed see him, he would have to take her out, simple as that.

He aimed his gun higher, until the silenced barrel was lined up directly at the driver's head. She still hadn't moved. She was still looked in his general direction.

Fuck.

Michael took a deep breath. She spotted him. She *had* to. There was no other reason for her delay.

Michael gritted his teeth. The gun was aimed directly at her. All he needed to do was pull the trigger. That was the easy part. Afterwards, he'd have to dispose of the vehicle and the body, all of which would take precious time. Time he simply didn't have.

This mission is good and fucked.

Michael released the air in his lungs and took another breath.

Now or never, he thought.

He was about to press the trigger but, at the very last second, paused.

She's looking in my direction, he thought. *But not at* me. *She's looking past me.*

Michael eased his finger from the trigger and slowly lowered the handgun. Very, very carefully he turned his head to follow the lady driver's stare. He spotted the weathered shed in the near distance, some twenty five meters off his right shoulder, and immediately recalled seeing it on the daytime satellite imagery Intelligence brought him.

He never thought much of the structure. It was just a small nothing surrounded by larger, no doubt juicier targets. But as the seconds passed and the lady driver continued to stare at the shed, Michael realized there was good reason for doing so.

He spotted the two guards sitting before the shed's entrance pretending to play cards. Pretending. The movements of their eyes gave them away. They were focused on everything around them *but* the card game, and increasingly curious about the Humvee stopped at the intersection.

Michael drew another breath.

What are you guys guarding?

Behind him, he heard the Humvee's engine roar to life. The vehicle moved on.

Thank you for your guidance, he silently told the departing female driver. *Maybe my luck isn't so bad after all.*

The guards by the shack relaxed once the vehicle was gone. Their "card game" was momentarily forgotten as they took several minutes to check their surroundings. Michael, for his part, followed suite, examining the shack and the forest beyond. It took him seconds to spot another pair of guards. They were on either side of the shed's entrance and some fifty feet deep in the woods. Like Michael, they were dressed in camouflage fatigues and almost completely invisible. They carried rifles with scopes –standard sniper gear– and had a laser-like focus on everything going on around the shack. There was little reason to pretend otherwise.

You're a very lucky fellow after all, Michael thought.

Not only had the Humvee and its driver pointed out his target, but because he was forced to fall to the ground and hide, he had also escaped imminent discovery by the snipers. Had he continued walking only a few more feet, he would have passed the cover of the trees and been spotted by the snipers.

Michael scowled. It was very possible there were more snipers out there, and a near certainty that the shed had even more levels of security.

Michael assessed his options. There was no way he could approach the shed from the front. Despite the forest, that area was too well guarded. Going in from the rear was possible, but that meant dealing with the snipers. Once he made it past them, he had to find a way into the shack. He couldn't use the front door, obviously, so his hopes rested on finding an alternative entry. Given the shack's size, it seemed unlikely the structure had a back door. Yet he had to get information on whatever was going on in there without alerting anyone to his presence.

This was the key to the mission and it was the reason the *Avenger* was launched in such secrecy. Michael's superiors had to know what the Americans were up to in Bad Penny. They were equally adamant that no American know of his arrival *or* departure.

Michael frowned.

This last fact was the only truthful thing he told Captain Elliot after showing him the very real ammunition in his weapon. Michael's superiors knew it was impossible to keep Captain Elliot completely in the dark about the mission, especially when their inside man was released just off the coast of Bad Penny, a well-known, if small, American military base. Michael's superiors authorized him to tell the Captain a cover story, should his curiosity prove difficult to contain. The story was simple: The mission was designed to test the British Navy's stealth capacity. It was a dry run for future operations involving penetration and insertion directed at hostile governments. Only a select few in the U.S. Army and the British Navy were aware of this test. This meant the *Avenger* and all aboard had to take this challenge as if it were the real thing.

In *all* respects.

Captain Elliot was furious, of course, both regarding the secrecy of the mission and the potential danger he put his men in. He swore he would file a grievance with the Admiralty when the mission was over. Taking real weapons with real ammunition into a training exercise was beyond the pale. Before leaving Michael's quarters, Captain Elliot pulled out the envelope Michael wanted sent to his mother.

"If this mission is bullshit, why the hell would you fear for your life and ask me to send this letter?" he spat.

"Isn't it obvious?" Michael replied. "Only a few people know this is a practice mission. To everyone else at Bad Penny, I'm an intruder."

"Why carry live ammo? Why risk hurting someone?"

"Believe me, I'd rather not," Michael replied. "If I'm spotted by any of the U.S. forces on the island, I give up and let them take me prisoner. I have no such option with the island's wildlife, some of which are quite dangerous."

Despite his anger, the Captain kept Michael's letter to his mother. He exited the agent's room, only to call him a few minutes later. He was very happy to report the submarine was in place and ready to lose the SIS agent, at least for 12 hours.

A little later Michael was on the beach, examining the top secret thermal images released through the Intelligence Collection Group. It showed the heat signatures released by Bad

Penny's secret underground base during that night a couple of months ago, but it was impossible to discern the entry point for said base.

The Americans were very clever for a very long time. To everyone else, Bad Penny was a small military facility used solely for training and, given the recent world-wide conflicts, a place for much needed rest and relaxation. It seemed everyone on the island was living between far more grueling assignments.

British Intelligence gave Bad Penny no thought until they happened upon these particular thermal scans. The Americans kept their base relatively "dark" each night. All electronic or thermal activity was minor, up until the "event" happened.

The "event" might well have been the result of a fire, a blown fuse, or some other unexpected glitch. Maybe, some thought, foreign powers had penetrated the base.

British Intelligence might never know. But whatever happened that night, the underground base lit up and sent faint electronic and heat signals that showed a broad and, until that moment, completely unknown underground structure. The signals lasted exactly five minutes and twenty seconds. A very, very short time. Yet long enough, especially if you're lucky to have someone intimately familiar with the previous satellite imagery around to see the difference.

British Intelligence, it turned out, was very lucky.

The United States is our greatest ally, it is true, but even best friends hide secrets from each other. The SIS was curious what the Americans were hiding at Bad Penny. A flurry of information sifting followed, and it was found that the leading minds in several U.S. Intelligence Agencies, from the DIA, ONI, MCIA, and SIGINT had at one point or another visited Bad Penny. Their trips were top secret of course, even though the method of transportation proved shockingly casual. These personnel entered the base via standard helicopter flights in the company of groups of very green cadets.

It was the very definition of hiding in plain sight.

Still more investigation revealed Intel officers from the Navy to the Air Force to the Department of Defense to the CIA had also made discrete visits to the lonely island. Their stays were often lengthy, at least a week or more, and whatever they accomplished remained completely unknown. It was truly unusual to see so many different intelligence departments converge upon this one, relatively small base.

As if this wasn't enough to pique the British Intelligence's curiosity, an official logged on to Google Earth and made a quick check on the satellite imagery of the area. When he found that most of the buildings in Bad Penny were Photoshopped out and those that remained had their positions significantly altered, there was no longer any doubt that the Americans were hiding something worth investigating.

Michael took another look at the camouflaged snipers on the perimeter of the tool shed. They remained in place, ever vigilant. He bit his lower lip.

It was time to move.

5

Samantha passed the intersection and drove deeper into the thick woods. A chilling shade covered her vehicle. The road was a straightaway so Samantha hit her lights and floored the accelerator. Base higher-ups and the MPs were never happy with speeders, but since they weren't around to see her...

"...it never happened," she finished the thought out loud.

The Humvee was doing fifty when she spotted the radar dish and antennae jutting over the forest. She was only moments away from the landing pad and slowed. The forest was gone when she reached her destination.

The outer perimeter of the landing pad was encircled with a tall wire fence. At the entrance was a guard gate. Samantha brought her vehicle to a full stop before the gate and produced her papers. Steve Cibos, the M.P. on duty at the guard gate, eyed her.

"Going a little fast back there, weren't you?" he asked as he wrote in his log book. It was standard procedure to catalogue all the comings and goings within the island, and Steve's face reflected what a mundane chore that was.

"I don't know what you're talking about," Samantha replied. She pulled a fresh pack of cigarettes from her chest pocket and offered it to Steve. The M.P. made sure no one was watching before snagging the pack.

"You're a bad girl," he said. "You know how hard I've been trying to give up on this shit?"

"I've just about kicked the habit myself."

"How in the world did you manage that?"

"By giving away my smokes to people like you."

Steve let out a laugh.

"You've got other distractions, from what I hear."

"What could you possibly be talking about? We pilots are always level and clear."

"That's not what Warren says."

A smile worked its way onto Samantha's face.

"Maybe the vision gets a little foggy when it comes to him," Samantha said and offered Cibos a wink. "You take care of him while I'm gone."

"If I take care of him anyway like you do, I'll be marched out of the service," Cibos said. He waved Samantha on. "Now get going before they blame me for your being late. Again."

Samantha offered a mock salute and drove into the landing pad area. In front of the one story control tower was a small parking lot. Samantha parked her Humvee in one of the handful of spaces and hurriedly exited the vehicle. She couldn't see through the tower's reflective glass but nonetheless waved at whoever was inside. She'd be talking to them soon enough.

In the distance, on the pad itself, sat the *Little Charlie*, an SH-60 Seahawk helicopter. It was her current assignment. Standing to the side of it were five officers, two men and three women.

Small group today, Samantha thought. Some days she carried more gear than passengers. Today looked like that was the case.

Samantha recognized only one of them, a tall, muscular, light brown haired woman named Becky Waters. Samantha knew her only because so much gossip surrounded the soldier. Becky Waters was considered an excellent recruit and drew high marks from her superiors in almost all aspects of her training. But she was a quiet loner who didn't care much to keep company with any fellow soldiers. Perhaps it was inevitable, given the relatively small size of the base and the chatter among the personnel, that wild rumors and innuendo developed around her. Fellow soldiers questioned almost every aspect about her, from leering sexual gossip to concerns about her sanity. The last person to openly question her on either of these topics, a burly private from Southern Command, lost his two front teeth.

Becky Waters and the soldier were reprimanded, but so too was the entire company. The higher ups, obviously, were aware of the gossip and would no longer tolerate it. For the time being, the rumors stopped and Becky Waters was left alone.

Samantha grabbed her gear from the passenger seat of her vehicle and jogged to the *Little Charlie*. She saluted the group as she walked by them. They had already been processed by the M.P.s and were ready to go.

"Sorry for the delay," she said. She opened the door leading into the chopper and waved the group in.

The standing officers collected their duffel bags in silence and walked to the vehicle's entrance. Their faces were stone cold.

"Come on guys, time's a wasting," Samantha kidded them.

None of her passengers cracked a smile.

"Tough crowd," Samantha muttered.

Samantha was the last to enter. She stepped into the cockpit and found her co-pilot, Frank Masters, sitting in his chair and running a check of the chopper's instruments. Frank was in his forties and, despite graying hair and a band of wrinkles around his eyes, looked youthfully fit. At least from the neck down. To Samantha, he was a no-nonsense old timer who delighted in sharing (or, as others put it, *boring*) you with stories of the "good old days". In time Samantha realized the so-called "good old days" encompassed his whole career up to, give or take, the previous month.

"Glad to see you decided to join us," Frank said. "Mind you, the passengers had plenty of fun standing around in the heat waiting for you to arrive. Almost as much fun as I had baking in this fucking cockpit."

"You could use a few more minutes," Samantha said. "You're still a little pink."

Frank shook his head.

"I'm going to have to talk to Warren. That boy's a really bad influence."

"Are you kidding? *I'm* the bad influence. Besides, you could have turned the A/C on."

"Now now, for the betterment of the environment, this man's army is going green. Such wasteful uses of energy are verboten."

"Damn, must have missed that memo," Samantha said. "And here I was, using the high A/C in the hummer all the way here. You know, I just about froze."

"That's it, rub it in."

Samantha chuckled. She stared at the computer displays before her and worked a separate keyboard, checking the helicopter's systems.

"What's the weather look like?"

"Winter's coming in early this year. Weather net says the temperatures in Alexandra are expected to drop into the teens with a possibility of up to two feet of snow. There's a strong front passing through even as we speak."

"And there you were complaining about the heat. If I had my choice, I'd take this over temps in the teens any time."

"You're obviously not a skier," Frank replied. "You don't know heaven until you've hit the slopes."

"I'll take your word for it," Samantha replied. "Now, are we going to get the fuck out of here or what?"

A sarcastic applause erupted from the cabin. Samantha laughed.

"The natives grow restless."

"Indeed," Frank said. "Let's get everything in order and be off as soon as possible. I'd hate to be the first military helicopter pilot in history to face a mutiny."

6

Michael eased into a depression in the forest floor. His movements were slow and calculated to minimize noise. He pushed aside the leaves from the bush before him and spotted the sniper lying a little over twenty feet away. For several long minutes, the sniper was frozen in place. Michael knew he could stay that way for a very, very long time. Much longer than the British agent could afford to wait.

Michael ran through some options. There was little chance to make it around the sniper, nor any conceivable way to render him incapacitated without alerting his companions. With his silencer, Michael could take him out but, as with the Humvee driver, killing any officer on this island was obviously meant as a last resort only.

As Michael pondered his options, the sniper suddenly moved. For a second Michael's muscles flexed. He was ready to attack.

Did they spot me? Were they closing in?

Michael didn't dare breathe. He watched with horror and fascination as the sniper slowly crawled from his position. His hands were on his weapon, but his weapon hung low to the ground. He rose to a crouch before moving away. *Away* from Michael and toward the shed.

Michael felt a wave of relief. The sniper hurried his pace and reached the rear of the shed. Once there, he stood up and waved to another of the snipers that lay to Michael's far left before producing an entry card and pushing it into what appeared to be a rusty slot. A small metal panel slid open, revealing a sophisticated hand scanner. The sniper laid his bare right hand over the scanner and it was flooded with a green light. The door built into the shed's rear wall silently slid open and allowed the sniper inside. Once in, it slid shut.

Probably need to take a piss, Michael thought. One sniper out of the way, but the other guardians remained in their places.

On the plus side, there's a rear entry into the shed. On the minus side, I need to avoid guards and snipers while somehow producing an entry card and a proper hand scan to get inside. Once in, who knows what other security measures the Americans have waiting.

Michael frowned. Going in through the shed's front –or rear–entry was impossible. For a few seconds he considered his options. The frown on his face grew deeper.

Are there any other options?

Michael slid back into the bushes. All missions presented unique difficulties as well as possibilities. He reviewed his goal and it was simple: He had to get into that tool shed and find out what the Americans were up to.

The frown faded.

Correction: He had to get into the base *below* the tool shed.

If getting into the base via the shed was impossible, then he had to find an alternate way in. One that didn't require hand scans, identification cards, or the scrutiny of security guards. His mission was still borderline impossible, but at least there was a glimmer of hope.

Michael scanned his surroundings. He eyed several trees and bushes and vegetation. Whatever little optimism he had of fulfilling his mission slowly, inevitably, faded. He could spend hours moving through this bush without finding anything. His eyes settled back on the tool shed.

Now what?

He would have to look around, hope to find—

A sound came from his right. Something had pressed down against the dry brush.

Shit, Michael thought. He had missed one, or more, of the snipers? Had his shaky luck finally run out?

Michael reached for his combat knife. He eyed his surroundings, figuring out where the noise came from, trying to find the intruder who had made it so close to his position.

He saw no one. He saw nothing.

Michael remained still.

Let them come to you.

He flattened his body against the ground. A single bead of sweat rolled down the side of his face. A mosquito buzzed by. In the far distance, a bird called out to its mate.

The source of that initial noise, whatever it was, remained a mystery. Was his stalker unsure of Michael's position? For that matter, *was* he being stalked? Could the noise have been produced by someone –*something*– else?

After several quiet minutes passed, Michael backed up into the bush. He took his time and turned his head to the right, to try to get a clear view past the foliage. He couldn't. Carefully, so very, very carefully, Michael reached out and pushed them aside. As he did, and he saw what lay beyond, the tension in him broke to the point he was forced to keep from laughing out loud.

Walking parallel to him was a small brown rat. The rat walked erratically, moving from side to side as if searching for something. It stepped through a patch of withered leaves, producing almost the exact same sound Michael heard moments before.

Michael turned to his left and looked at the remaining Sniper. The guard was still in place, blissfully unaware of Michael's presence. Michael let out a very relieved breath.

That was interesting. If it gets any more interesting...

Michael shook his head and put the knife away. His gaze returned to the rat. To his surprise, it was no longer there.

Out of curiosity, Michael tried to find it. He was unable to do so. Michael shrugged. There were better things to do than worry about a rat.

Then again...

Michael looked at the last place he saw the creature. Though he couldn't explain why, he was suddenly curious as to where it had gone. He looked around for a few seconds while doubts grew.

This is ridiculous, he scolded himself while crawling to the last place he saw the creature. He spotted the remains of a faint trail in the sand.

What are you going to do now? Follow her home?

Another movement, to his right, drew Michael's attention. The rat was there, walking past more bushes and eventually stopping before what appeared to be a tree trunk. The tree trunk's ragged top was covered in dense bush. The rat's nose was twitching as it stood up on its rear legs. It smelled something within that tree trunk and bush.

Michael watched the bush move gently in the breeze. Something about the movement seemed...odd. There was no breeze at the moment, yet the bush kept moving. Almost as if...

Michael frowned before hurriedly crawling to the tree trunk. As he did, the rat scurried away.

Later, Michael thought.

The British agent examined the thick green bush, fascinated by its impossible dance. Michael reached up and grabbed at a leaf. When he did, his eyes opened very wide. The leaf was plastic! He released it and felt along the length of the bush.

The entire thing was fake!

Michael let go of the phony bush and examined the area around it, searching carefully for any security devices or motion sensors. Satisfied there were none, he gently pushed the bush aside. The top of the tree trunk, he found, was covered in a thick wire mesh. It was from within that mesh, down below the ground, that the stream of air that moved the bush originated. It was an air duct.

Michael felt the tree trunk. It too was phony, sculpted in cement and painted in the colors of rotted bark. The entire illusion was damn good.

Michael again removed his knife from its sheath and reached for the top of the tree trunk. A series of screws kept the wire mesh in place. Michael unscrewed three of them, enough to pull a section of the mesh up. He bent and folded it in half. By doing so, he created a hole big enough to fit into.

Michael put the knife away and, after making sure the remaining sniper hadn't moved, reached into his backpack and produced a small flashlight. He turned it on and aimed the beam into the dark hole. The light revealed a shiny aluminum tunnel. It dropped five feet down before branching off to the south and north. Because it was releasing air into the outside environment, Michael reasoned it was some kind of purging system, used to rid the underground base of airborne contaminants.

Michael swore. He left his miniature air tanks on the beach. Should something poisonous be released through this duct while he was inside...

That's a risk you'll have to take. Look at the bright side: You didn't have to kill anyone. Not yet anyway.

Michael turned the flashlight off and gave his surroundings one final look. The second sniper was emerging from the shed's back door and returning to his post. The first sniper waved at him as he did.

You didn't earn your keep today, Michael thought. *It's time for me to earn mine.*

He eased his body into the air duct.

7

The passengers aboard the *Little Charlie* waited for liftoff. Becky Waters sat farthest from the cockpit and, true to form, stared out the window while ignoring her fellow passengers. She didn't purposely do this to be rude: Her mind was on other things. She was nearing the end of her tour of duty and in two months she was a free woman. She thought about falling back into society. She'd do so like a newborn for she had no family, no job to return to, and, at the moment, no serious prospects. She didn't fear facing this nebulous future. Neither did she have any regrets that her tour of duty was coming to an end.

"Gum?" came a voice to her left. Its source was a short, dark haired and very muscular man seated beside Becky. He held out a pack of green Juicy Fruit and offered a far too-warm smile along with a puppy dog stare.

"No thanks," Becky replied. Her monotone spoke volumes about her interest in either the gum or continuing the conversation.

The man shrugged. He was experienced in being shot down by members of the opposite sex.

As they say, the soldier thought. *When one door slams in your face, there's always another nearby.*

The man shifted to his left. Sitting to his other side was a much younger female soldier. Her face was filled with anxiety. She looked like she dreaded the upcoming flight. She had the look of a very green recruit.

"Gum?" the young man repeated. His smile and eyes were back in their place, along with whatever charm he could muster.

"Thank you," the newbie replied.

"My name is Howard Bartlett," the young man continued. The puppy dog eyes were replaced with a friendly twinkle. *Now we're getting somewhere!* He held out his hand.

"Alicia Cunningham," the newbie replied. She hesitated but shook the man's hand. "This is some helicopter, huh?"

"She's a Sikorsky SH-60 Seahawk," Bartlett replied matter-of-factly. The smile on his lips was syrupy.

"You're a pilot?" Alicia asked.

"No. I prefer keeping my feet on the ground."

"You didn't try out at least?"

"Well, you see..."

"You weren't good enough?"

The smile on Bartlett's lips noticeably dripped.

"No," he said. Though he tried to contain it, there was considerable defensiveness in his reply. "I didn't want them. But enough about me—"

"How fast can she go?"

"You're real curious, aren't you?" Bartlett said.

"Knowledge is power."

"I...guess so," Bartlett said. "Her top speed is a buck fifty. Her service ceiling is nearly twenty thousand feet."

Worry filled the rest of Alicia's face.

"Twenty thousand feet?" she repeated. "I was wrong. Ignorance *is* bliss."

"She's a classic, very safe," Bartlett continued. "If the pilots fly her right, you'll hardly know we're in the air at all."

"I never did care for flying," Alicia continued. "I get air sickness real easy."

She eyed the narrow space between herself and the talkative soldier.

"And when I get it, I get it *real* bad," she warned him. "If I were you, I wouldn't want to be anywhere near me when we lift off."

Whatever twinkle was left in Howard Bartlett's eyes faded. He nodded and leaned in closer to Becky's seat. While Becky glared at him, she had to fight hard not to laugh. Alicia might be a newbie to the armed forces, but the way she brushed off Bartlett proved she was a veteran at getting rid of unwanted pests.

The man sitting in directly in front of Alicia's seat, Dan Thompson, was also forcing himself not to laugh. He witnessed the entire conversation and the wolfish eagerness in Bartlett's approach to the ladies bordered on desperate.

Thompson leaned back in his chair and looked to his right. Sitting next to him was the last of the helicopter's five passengers, a blonde knockout that couldn't be more than twenty four years old. Even in her bulky fatigues, Thompson admired the hell out of her curves. But what intrigued him the most were her crystal clear green eyes.

Like Becky Waters, the blonde kept mostly to herself during the wait on the landing pad. She offered absolutely no insight into who she was or where she came from, which intrigued

Thompson all the more. He noted the tags on her duffel bag and, thus, knew her name: Jennie Light.

Too bad the flight isn't all that long, Thompson thought. Jennie Light was most certainly someone worth getting to know well. Unlike Bartlett, Thompson was shy and not the best of talkers. Meeting and greeting women usually proved difficult. He considered a few introductions, subtle ice-breakers that would, hopefully, lead to more (any!) meaningful dialogue with Jenny. But after mentally running through a series of progressively worse introductions, he hit a wall.

They're all *terrible*, he thought glumly. He eyed Howard Bartlett and shook his head. *I wish I was carrying some gum.*

In the chopper's cockpit, Samantha finished her pre-flight check. She got out of her seat and stepped into the passenger compartment. The passengers eyed her with a mix of anger and impatience as she walked to the helicopter's side door and stepped out.

"Now what?" Thompson asked, his mood shifting from sour to downright hostile.

"Relax, grumpy," Samantha replied. "Gotta give this bucket a quick visual check."

"No one did that yet?"

Samantha pointed back to Frank, her co-pilot.

"He insisted it was my turn," Samantha said. "Don't worry, in a couple of minutes we'll be out of this paradise."

8

Michael found the skeletal remains of the rat a few feet from the duct's juncture. It died nibbling through the exposed wires near a mesh fence. It was curious that no one had removed the body or, even more importantly, fixed the wires the rat cut.

Carelessness?

Maybe. And, equally possibly, a case of hubris. When you have a secret base on a remote island operating for who knows how many years without anyone suspecting its existence, there's always the danger the powers that be get just a *little* lazy.

Michael examined the wires the rat chewed through. It was impossible to guess where they led to or what they fed, but he had a suspicion, based on the rat's level of decomposition, this might have been the source of the base's nighttime illumination three weeks before. If that was the case, the wires most likely fed some kind of electronic dampening equipment. The fact that the cut wires weren't fixed suggested the base's electrical engineers figured out some alternate path to feed this particular charge.

Michael released the wires and focused on the mesh. He removed the screws that held it in place and set the obstacle aside. He then crawled along the length of the duct until it turned ninety degrees and continued straight down. The duct dropped for at least thirty, if not more, feet. Michael held his hand over the drop and felt cold air rising from below.

"No place to go but down," he muttered.

Michael removed his small backpack and fumbled inside it before producing a black rope and a sturdy but thin j-shaped grappling hook. He thrust the hook onto the edge of the duct until it pierced through the metal and held fast. When he was satisfied the hook wouldn't slip, Michael tied his rope to it before gently dropping it into the hole.

Michael then removed a pair of gloves from his backpack and put them on. He slipped head first down the hole.

As he descended, the air grew colder. This proved very uncomfortable, but not nearly as uncomfortable as his head-first descent. Michael knew there was no other way to go, as the passage was too tight for him to spin around before going in.

Michael tried his best to ignore the blood pounding in his head. He passed a branch, then another branch in the duct and, rather than explore each one, he decided to go all the way down first. If he didn't find anything at the bottom, he would work his way up to these other levels.

Presently, he reached his destination. He estimated it lay three to four floors down. At that point, the air duct made a sharp horizontal turn. Michael slid forward, bending with the tube and becoming horizontal as well. He allowed time for his stomach to settle before crawling forward.

At the end of the duct he found a vent outlet. Between the outlet and Michael was a high speed fan. It sucked the air from the room beyond into the duct. Michael peered through the rotating blades and found the room beyond was a very sophisticated laboratory. Several tables filled the floor. Upon them were computers, books, and folders. To the left of the room was a huge metallic object which, although Michael couldn't be entirely sure, nonetheless looked like an electron microscope.

Michael pushed forward and to his left to see what he could of the other side of the room. When he did, his mouth dropped.

Towering over everything else were three large metal and glass tubes. They stood upright against the west wall and looked like oversized caskets. Cold steam rose from what appeared to be several hundred small tubes snaking into and out of the bottom and top of each of the caskets. A blue tinted glass allowed anyone standing before them to see their contents. Unfortunately, from where Michael lay all he could see was a hazy frost.

What the hell are these Yanks up to?

Each of the caskets was large enough to hold an adult body. Indeed, that's what they seemed designed for. The fact that there was an icy buildup on the inner glass further suggested the caskets were cryogenic units of some kind, designed to freeze whatever –whomever– was inside.

Michael rubbed his chin.

If this was the case, who were they storing?

Adolph Hitler.

Despite the seriousness of his mission and the magnitude of his discovery, he smiled at his own joke.

I think I saw that film before, Michael thought. *Leave it to the Americans to secretly freeze Adolph Hitler after the war. Then again, maybe they're storing Walt Disney. Maybe both.*

Michael let those frivolous thoughts drift and considered more realistic possibilities. Could the people in the caskets be victims of some highly contagious disease? That didn't seem likely. The United States was an incredibly large country, and quarantining people anywhere deep within the fifty states was easy enough. There was no need to bring them out here to the middle of the Atlantic. Besides, there were signs posted around the room warning of high voltage and freeze/fire hazards, but none regarding biohazards. Though it wasn't much to go on, it was Michael's experience that Americans were obsessed with safety warnings, even in their most secret places. Therefore, no biohazard warning meant no biohazards present. The people in the caskets were likely clean.

So what were they up to here?

Michael suppressed an excited smile. Though he had no clear idea –yet– of what the American's were doing, it appeared his superior's very high stake gamble in sending him on this mission would pay off.

He removed a small black digital camera from his backpack and took several pictures of the laboratory. He made sure each picture captured a clear image of the room beyond the duct. So engrossed was he in this that he was surprised when a man in his sixties with white, thinning hair and a white goatee appeared in his view.

The man stopped directly before one of the caskets and was likely in the room all along, though obviously outside of Michael's limited view. The man took a pair of thick glasses out of his lab coat's pocket and placed them over his eyes. He examined the readings on a computer monitor beside one of the caskets and jotted some information on his clipboard.

You look exactly like the type of person I'd find in a place like this, Michael thought.

The elderly man went about his business, jotting a few more notes on his clipboard after reading the remaining computer monitor displays beside each of the caskets. He did this quickly, finishing his job in a matter of minutes before turning away from the caskets.

When he did, Michael frowned.

On the man's left side and tied to his waist was a thick black belt and a large black sheath. Inside the sheath was an equally large Bowie knife. Michael had to look twice to make sure he wasn't seeing things.

What the hell are you doing with such a blade? Michael though. He shook his head. *Perhaps the old man fancies himself Rambo, or maybe Tarzan.*

The man finished taking his notes. He let out a yawn and gazed at his watch. Though his job in this secret room within this secret base was most certainly unique, his just performed gesture was universal: The old man was tired and looking forward to finishing his shift.

The man picked up a cup from one of the tables. His footsteps receded as he left the room.

Michael listened for any other sounds. All he heard beyond the whirl of the fan was a low level humming coming from the computers and the machines that fed cold air into the caskets. He carefully looked over the room one more time for security devices. He spotted two cameras screwed to the wall. Both aimed at the caskets. It was hard to tell from where he was if there were any others aimed at the center of the room.

Michael wondered if he could lower himself into the laboratory and get a closer look at the caskets. His curiosity over who -or what- was inside them became unbearable. But did he dare enter the lab? He was certain that if he left right now and delivered the photographs he had taken to his superiors, they would consider his mission a success. With these photographs, they could figure out what the caskets were and make an educated guess as to what cargo they might contain.

But they, like he, would wonder exactly what was inside those caskets. They, like he, wouldn't be happy to go all this way into the American's base without getting that particular bit of information. But to get it, Michael needed to exit the safety of the air duct. He needed to get inside the room.

He needed to stand right where the old man stood.

Michael stewed on that for a few seconds.

What are you hiding? He thought. It was both a question and a temptation. *No risk no reward.*

Michael took a deep breath and decided on a course of action. He disconnected the electrical wires running to the fan before him. The blades slowed and stopped. He then pulled a screwdriver from his backpack and unscrewed the bolts that held the fan in place. He laid the device against the air duct wall and slid to the outlet vent that separated him from the laboratory. It took him only a few seconds to remove it.

When he was done, he grabbed a black ski mask from his backpack and put it on.

Michael stuck his head out of the vent's hole for a quick peek before darting back into his hiding place. In the second or two his head was exposed, he confirmed there was no one else within the laboratory. He also spotted another pair of cameras along with the two focused on the caskets. One was aimed at the side of the caskets while the other was aimed at the door leading into the room.

The news couldn't be any better: Michael could exit the air duct and enter the laboratory unseen, provided he kept his body tight against the side wall.

Michael took several deep breaths.

Let's do this.

He left his hiding place, pressed his body as tightly against the laboratory wall as he could, and slid down to the floor. Once there, he crouched behind one of the laboratory tables.

He crawled under that table and approached the caskets, all the time making sure he wasn't in any of the cameras' points of view. It was hard to keep his excitement in check. He had a very limited, at best, time to do his work and worried how long the room would remain empty. Still, Michael couldn't hurry. He needed to move slowly and carefully, lest he expose himself. After what seemed like a lifetime of crawling, he was under the table nearest to the caskets.

He spotted shadowy forms inside them. The forms appeared human.

Incredible.

Michael took more pictures. As amazing as the sight of those forms was, the frost on the glass was too thick to make out any facial features or even the sex of those within.

Michael finished taking his pictures. He was satisfied with his work. If the pictures taken from the air duct were a success, then those taken from within the laboratory would certainly be considered a *rousing* success. The Americans were cryogenically storing people in those three caskets. This much was verified. Nonetheless, Michael was not satisfied. His eyes hadn't strayed from the shadowy forms.

Who the hell are you?

Michael bit his upper lip. He was only a few feet away from the answer. Only feet away from solving that mystery. But to do so, he had to get even closer. And to do *that*, he would expose himself to the security cameras.

All of them.

Michael eyed the door leading into the laboratory, then the vent. Thoughts whirled in his mind.

If he were to risk it all and get the identity of the people in the caskets, would he have enough time to get out? Could he escape the island before it was locked down?

The Americans didn't know he was here and they certainly had no idea of how he entered the laboratory. Hell, they didn't even remove the rat's corpse. Perhaps after all these years of working here, they had entirely forgotten about the air duct.

Michael weighed his options.

He could take the safe route and leave right now and turn in some very valuable information to his bosses. Or, he could expose himself but be rewarded with *all* the secrets of this base.

There really wasn't a choice.

They don't pay you the big money to take the easy road, he thought. *No risk, no reward.*

It was time to move.

Michael crept along the far wall until he was directly below the camera monitoring the laboratory's sole entrance. The British agent needed only a few seconds. If the Americans were complacent enough about their security down here, he would fully use this to his advantage.

He removed the Heckler and Koch handgun and checked to make sure it was loaded and ready before returning it to the holster.

Just in case.

He then carefully placed a chair from behind one of the tables to the spot under and just out of sight of that camera. He climbed on the chair and stood inches from the camera's lens. From within his backpack he pulled out a small rectangular case and opened it. Arranged in tight order within were several small tools. Michael removed a pair of pliers. He worked on the back of the camera, freeing the metal plate that hid the device's inner workings. Exposed were several small circuit boards and wires. Michael examined them. Once he found the cable he was looking for, he clamped down on it with his pliers. If he did this right, security would see electronic snow on their monitors.

Michael released the wire and quickly lowered himself to the floor. Once he released the cable the security monitors would be clear of all static. Michael hid under the table and waited. The seconds ticked by. A minute. Then another.

No one showed up to check on the camera.

Good.

The Americans *were* too comfortable.

Michael returned to the chair and climbed onto it. He used his pliers as he did before, but this time tore the wire from its place. Whoever was watching the camera feed once again saw static. But this time the static resulted in the camera going completely dead. Michael hoped the earlier static before the camera's complete blackout would mistakenly interpreted as a technical problem rather than an emergency. Security would certainly come, but he hoped the previous static would have them walking here instead of running.

Doesn't matter, he thought. *You're on the clock.*

Michael jumped down from the chair and ran to the table closest to the door leading into the laboratory. Now that he wasn't visible to security there, he pushed a heavy table against the door. By barricading the door, he bought himself another few precious seconds. Hopefully, it was all he'd need.

Michael removed the Heckler and Koch from its holster and aimed the gun at the remaining cameras. He fired once, twice, three times. Each bullet found its target, shattering the other cameras in the room. Security would most certainly know something was wrong, but they now had to contend with his barricade.

Michael ran to the three caskets and looked in.

He swore.

The frost that covered the glass front of each of the caskets was very thick. Even from a few inches away, it was still impossible to see who lay within.

Michael hurriedly examined each casket's computer controls, looking desperately for any button or lever that would allow him to open any one of them. He found the proper controls, but they were activated by two separate keys and, based on the computer monitor that lay beside the second keyhole, a password as well.

"Shit," Michael swore. There was no way he could get past those security measures in the time he had.

Did I stick my neck out all this way only to fail?

Frustration overwhelmed the British agent. His target lay so very close. So very, *very* close.

Michael let out a deep breath and made a decision. He was in this way too deep to stop now. He faced the first of the three caskets.

"The hell with you," he said.

He aimed his handgun at the thick glass and fired.

9

Samantha entered the helicopter after conducting her visual inspection. She was subjected to a rain of thunderous applause from some very impatient passengers.

"You're a bunch of smart asses," she told them as the sarcastic applause died down.

"We are leaving today, aren't we?" her co-pilot called out from the cockpit. "At least before midnight?"

"And you're the biggest one of them all," Samantha called out. The smile on her face faded and she addressed her passengers. "All right folks, some basics for those who don't know. First off, make sure you're strapped in. Wearing seatbelts is mandatory. Secondly, these choppers make a hell of a lot of noise. Grab the headsets on the walls behind you and put them on. They will muffle the engine and allow you to hear any instructions coming from yours truly. That is, if I should bother informing you about anything. The headphones have switches which allow you to talk to each other in something less than a scream, although for the life of me I don't know what any of you could possibly want to talk about."

The passengers grabbed and put on their headsets. Samantha made sure everyone was strapped in before entering the cockpit. As she sat down, Frank shook his head.

"We aim to please?"

"Must have missed that particular class," Samantha said with a wink.

She put on her seatbelt and headset. Frank did the same while working the controls. The Seahawk's motor coughed to life. Outside, the helicopter's rotors began a lazy spin which quickly built up to a high speed. The roar of the engine grew loud enough to seep through the headphones. Samantha looked back at her passengers and switched her microphone to the intercom setting.

"We're off in just a couple of minutes, ladies and gentlemen," she said. "Once we clear the base, your stewardesses will serve our in-flight meal. On the menu is the new chicken and pasta MRE's. Rumor is they taste a little like chicken, though that is only a rumor and should be treated as such. Afterwards, sit back and enjoy our in-flight movie. It's a beautiful and tasteful, although some have argued thematically obscure, French film called *Clouds Passing by Your Window*."

Frank sighed and clicked on his microphone for cockpit-only chatter.

"I know you never stop, but I have to know: Do you ever slow down?"

Samantha chuckled. She switched from the intercom to cockpit and communication mode and said:

"This is MT-1034. Standing by for clearance, Clarence."

Within Bad Penny's flight control tower were tables and file cabinets loaded with charts and forms. In a corner was the electronic equipment. The building's walls were thick glass windows. From within, the flight control crew had an outside view in all directions.

Two technicians currently occupied the room. One of them faced away from Samantha and her helicopter. He was wearing headphones and humming softly to himself. The other was seated before the main computer displays. His attention was on the Seahawk.

"Holy shit, Samantha," he said. "Are you guys really ready to go? Over."

There was a crackle of static.

"You awake, Lombardo?" Samantha replied. "I'll have you know, I'm absolutely surrounded by smart asses today. Over."

Lombardo shook his head.

"When I saw your Hummer in the parking lot, I thought it was a mirage. Tell me Frank, is Samantha there or are we on a conference call?"

Within the Seahawk, Frank leaned back in his chair and looked his co-pilot over.

"I'm as surprised as you are, Lombardo. She's here. In the flesh. Over."

"You're telling me she's only, what, a half hour late? Give me some proof you're actually ready to go."

Samantha leaned in to the helicopter's front glass panel and produced her middle finger. She waved it at the control tower.

"That enough proof for you, Lombardo?" Samantha said.

Laughter filled her headphones.

"You should respect your elders," Lombardo replied.

"I will, as soon as they grow up," Samantha said. "By the way, according to my watch we're running a mere seventeen minutes late. Most airlines consider that on time."

"Did you say seventeen minutes?" Lombardo asked.

"Yeah. Why?"

"Because it means I owe Frank a beer."

Samantha faced her co-pilot.

"Beer?" she said.

"*A* beer?" Frank retorted. "You mean a *case* of beer."

"Case? I thought the bet was for a single beer. Over."

"You have trouble hearing, Lombardo?"

"Only when I lose bets."

"Just what the hell are you two children talking about?" Samantha interjected.

Frank shrugged. "We had a little bet going as to how late you'd be."

"And you bet the under, right?" Samantha said. "At least someone around here has faith in me."

"Not quite," Lombardo said. "Frank thought you'd be twenty five minutes late. He came closest to the actual delay."

Samantha shook her head.

"It's good to see the extent of faith my fellow brothers in arms have in me," she said. "Good thing Uncle Sam doesn't account for every minute of *your* time."

Frank let out a laugh and hit the microphone button. "So what do you say, Lombardo? Can we get out of here or what?"

"What the hell," Lombardo replied. "See you after your vacation. Skiing, right? Break a leg."

"Ha, ha."

Frank gave Samantha the thumbs up sign and powered the helicopter's engine.

The helicopter's blades became a whirlpool that sent clouds of sand into the air. The chopper slowly lifted, soaring over and above the palm trees and the island. In minutes it was a tiny dot in the sky.

10

Michael removed the larger pieces of shattered glass while ignoring the furious blare coming from the facilities' alarm systems. The wailing began immediately after he shattered one of the cryogenic unit's glass covers and was followed by the flickering of emergency lights. Those lights flooded the laboratory like an angry red sun.

It occurred to him, only after shooting out the glass, that his actions may well have killed whoever lay inside the casket. Not from the bullet, as he angled his shot to hit glass only, but rather from the fact that the environment contained within the casket was lost.

I'll go to hell for sure if Walt Disney's tucked away in here.

Despite the attempt at levity, Michael swore. His actions, for better or worse, could not be taken back. The realization that he might well have killed someone during this mission ate at him, but he could ill-afford second guessing his moves. At this point he needed to get a good look at the casket's occupant and make his escape. Hopefully, the technicians of the base could save the frozen individual should he need –or deserve– saving.

Michael removed the last of the glass and stared inside the casket. A cold mist rose from within and he desperately waved it away.

"Dammit," he muttered. What he didn't need was more delay. Security forces were already outside the lab door, pushing at it and edging his barricade back. It was only a matter of seconds before they were inside.

"Come on, come on."

The mist cleared just a little, and Michael brought his camera up. He aimed it at the cryogenic unit's occupant as the last of the heavy mist faded.

He gasped.

Inside the unit was what appeared to be a smooth faced mannequin.

What the hell?

The mannequin's face was devoid of any human features. The thing had the shape of a naked human, but its face had no eyes, no nose, no mouth, and no ears. Wire sensors were attached to the figures' head like a halo. Other sensors were placed on the figure's chest and arms.

What the hell is this?

There was no more time to think about it. There was no more time at all. Michael snapped his last picture and ran to the air duct, to his escape. Abruptly, he stopped. Out of the corner of his eye he noticed a slight movement coming from the casket. The hairs on the back of his neck stood and a chill passed through the agent's body.

Had the mannequin just...moved?

Impossible.

The thing was nothing more than a featureless crash test dummy. Its purpose was probably to test the effectiveness of the cryogenic system and that was it. Everything. There was no way it could move on its own. No way.

Yet Michael couldn't shake a growing unease. Though he was seconds away from capture, his eyes remained on the mannequin. The featureless skin was so smooth and so perfect. *Too* perfect. What was it made of? Plastic? Porcelain? There was something about it that gave the impression it was...alive.

Another chill ran down the British agent's spine. There was far more to the thing in the casket than he could possibly guess. What had he stumbled into? What was this...thing?

No more time.

Michael hurriedly climbed into the duct and closed the grill behind him. He finished screwing in the first fastener when five guards burst into the laboratory. They carried high powered automatic machine guns and held them up, ready for use. Michael expected them to run into the room and conduct a fast search for the laboratory's intruder, but when they saw the ruptured cryogenic crypt, they abruptly stopped.

Michael watched with mounting horror as they aimed their guns at the shattered unit and the occupant within. One of the guards yelled into his walkie-talkie.

"This is a Code Red! Unit two has a breach! Repeat, unit two has a breach!"

The alarms grew silent but the flashing lights continued throbbing. The thick metal doors leading into the laboratory closed, their loud groans reverberating throughout the duct. Michael fell back as a metal panel slid over the air vent he used to gain entry into the laboratory. The panel's movement was sudden and violent. It completely flattened the detached fan unit

Michael removed to enter the lab. Had any of Michael's limbs been in the way, they would surely have been cut off with this dull guillotine.

The British agent was plunged into total darkness. Michael heard the sound of other security doors closing throughout the air duct. He wondered whether he was trapped in this darkness. Memories of the rat's decaying corpse brought a shiver.

The thought evaporated the moment gunfire erupted. The guards in the laboratory fired off a furious wave of bullets that ricocheted against the walls.

What the hell are you firing at? Michael thought. There was, of course, only one answer.

They were firing at the mannequin.

Michael leaned in close to the security panel. Sweat dripped from his forehead.

Why are you firing at them?

There came an eerie groan, the sound of thick metal ripping apart, followed by a loud crash.

Michael let out a gasp.

Had he just heard the sound of the heavy metal door leading out of the lab fall to the ground?

The intensity of the gunshots increased. The security guards within the room were yelling. Some screamed desperately for backup.

"It's not stopping," someone said.

The gunshots continued.

Something heavy smacked against the wall and just below the air duct. When it hit, it did so with a crunch and bloody splatter. There came another scream, louder still. The sound of gunfire died down.

After one last scream, the gunfire stopped all together. All grew deathly silent. Michael leaned closer to the metal panel separating him from the laboratory until his ear was pressed against it. Michael concentrated hard, trying to hear something, anything, coming from the laboratory. After a few seconds, he did. A man was crying. Between sobs, he begged for mercy. Another one, farther away, said he was out of ammo. Then came the very last words Michael would hear:

"Please don't."

After that, no one spoke.

Several long seconds passed. Michael crawled away from the metal panel. His body was shaking. Five guards entered the laboratory. They were heavily armed and opened fire on...on whatever the thing in the casket was. They fired at it with a barrage of bullets that would have taken out a small village.

Yet the guards were massacred.

Every last one of them.

Michael curled up.

What the hell did I do?

After a few more seconds of silence, he heard the sound of breaking glass. That sound was followed by the groan of more ripping metal. Though Michael couldn't be certain, it sounded like the thing he freed was destroying the other two cryogenic units. It was releasing the other two mannequins.

My God, Michael thought. *Those security guards were killed by one of those things. There are three of them now.*

Another crash.

Michael gasped as the air duct shook. The metal panel separating him from the laboratory groaned and bent backwards.

They're coming for me!

Michael furiously crawled back to his rope.

He had to get the fuck out of there.

Now.

11

The trip from Bad Penny to the Alexandria Air Base by Seahawk and at their current speed normally took a little under two hours. After a few minutes of flight, the helicopter's passengers settled down and relaxed. The newbie Alicia Cunningham and Howard Bartlett, who managed to keep as far away from her as possible, drifted off to sleep. Becky, at the far end of the compartment and crowded in by Bartlett, was quietly reading a paperback novel.

On the other side of the aisle, Dan Thompson continued to eye Jennie Light. With each passing second, he grew more and more fascinated and attracted to this quiet beauty. She, on the other hand, hadn't acknowledged his, or anyone else's, presence. She stared out the window closest to her seat and watched the beautiful early evening sky.

"Nice view," Thompson said.

Jennie nodded without turning.

Thompson was about to say something else but his eyes drifted to Howard Bartlett across from him. The soldier let out a snore.

Hope he's not listening, Thompson thought. *Then again, it's not like you were hitting it off with the ladies, either.*

Just like that, Thompson realized he was tongue tied.

What do I say to her now? How do I say it? And what...

When his eyes left Bartlett, he found Jennie Light staring directly at him.

"How about you offer me some gum?" she said.

Thompson's face turned a deep red. He leaned back in his chair and folded his arms across his chest.

Samantha took full control of the helicopter while Frank released his controls and stretched. They were just over an hour into their flight and rapidly coming up to the mainland of the United States.

Samantha stifled a yawn and scrutinized the weather report streaming on the monitor just above her controls. A strong cold front whipped by Alexandria and was barreling down the east coast. By sometime very early in the morning, it would pass through the heart of Bad Penny.

Samantha leaned back and made herself comfortable. Frank had already done so. He rubbed his face and sighed.

"When I was younger, I wanted nothing more than to be a pilot," Frank said. "It was an adventure. You went all over the world, exploring exotic lands and meeting fine young ladies. Fast forward to now. I'm a pilot just like I dreamed and I've met my share of fine young ladies." He eyed Samantha. "Don't laugh."

"Wouldn't think of it."

"So how come I feel like an over-glorified taxi driver?"

"Because that's what we are," Samantha replied. "Our job is to take people here and there and back again. Don't feel so bad. At least we get to enjoy that awesome army cafeteria food."

"You know the worst thing about all this?"

"No, but I have a feeling you're going to tell me."

"Even if I weren't in service and rich as hell and could afford my own wings, I don't think I'd fly anywhere. The older I get, the more I want to settle down. To *not* move."

"Jeeze, Frank. You're a real barrel of laughs. Someone spike your coffee?"

"It did taste a little funny."

"Sounds like you want to settle down," Samantha said. "There isn't anywhere, anywhere at all, you want to go visit?"

Frank shot his co-pilot a sidelong gaze.

"I always was curious about Sugar Tit, South Carolina."

"Sugar Tit?"

"Yeah. Small town down in the bible belt."

"You're kidding."

"Look it up if you don't believe me."

"I'll take your word for it," Samantha said. "I'm afraid to ask. Why in the world would you want to visit that place?"

"Morbid curiosity. Be honest: Now that you know there's a town named 'Sugar Tit' somewhere out there, you aren't the least bit interested in seeing what it looks like?"

"Ah! A reason to live!"

"Even in my darkest hours, I somehow find 'em," Frank said.

Static filled the pilots' headphones.

"This is Delphi calling MT-1034," came a voice through the static. "You copy, over?"

"This is MT-1034," Frank said. "We are receiving you, Delphi. We are on course with an E.T.A. of forty minutes. Looking forward to seeing you. Over."

"Be advised you have new orders, MT-1034."

"New orders?"

"You are to change course," Delphi continued. The air traffic controller's voice was all business. "New destination is Tortuga Military Base. Repeat, Tortuga Military Base. Once there, you are to land at Helo Pad 3. I repeat, Helo Pad 3. You will be briefed as to your next action following arrival. Over."

Frank covered his microphone and grimaced. He leaned against Samantha and spoke into her ear.

"Sounds like we just got fucked," he said. Frank removed his hand from the microphone. "Acknowledged, Delphi. We will proceed to Tortuga Military Base. Since we're going out of our way, can I get some info on the place? Any good bars? We got some thirsty passengers. And pilots. Over."

There was a brief pause.

"You are not, I repeat, *not* to advise your passengers of the detour," the Delphi operator said. "Once landed, you are to instruct all passengers to remain on board your craft. I repeat: All passengers are to remain on board the helicopter until further notice."

"Copy, Delphi," Frank said. "But it might get uncomfort—"

"Observe red alpha protocol," the Delphi operator added. "Over."

A deep frown appeared on Frank's face.

"Red Alpha?" Samantha asked. "What the hell is that?"

Frank motioning her to quiet down.

"Acknowledged," he said. He entered information into the central computer to his right. "E.T.A. for arrival at Tortuga Base is fifty four minutes. We will maintain radio silence until our arrival. Over and out."

Frank switched the radio off. His eyes were unfocused and distant.

"Radio silence?" Samantha asked. "What was that all about? Why don't they want us to tell the passengers about our detour? For that matter, why do they want them to stay on the chopper?"

If Frank heard the question, he ignored it. His mind appeared a million miles away.

"Frank?"

Frank faced his co-pilot.

"We're about to get a VIP."

"Oh," Samantha said. "Well, that makes *all* the difference in the world. Why the hell can't we tell our passengers about that?"

"Because those are our orders."

Samantha knew it was pointless to ask any more questions. She noted the first stars appear in the twilight. In the extreme distance she spotted the edge of the cold front heading their way. There were flashes of lightning and the last of the sun's rays faded.

Soon it would be completely dark.

The lighting danced high above, illuminating the thick clouds racing toward the Tortuga Military Base. Otherwise, night arrived silently and with it came a complete, all-enveloping darkness.

Samantha eyed her instruments and frowned. According to her GPS, they were within twenty miles of the Tortuga base. As with Bad Penny, Tortuga was also located on an island. It was stationed just off the coast of North Carolina. Unlike Bad Penny, this facility stretched over seventy five acres and featured a state of the art field and barracks as well as a sophisticated dock and berth. It housed battleships, submarines, and coast guard cutters as well as two full divisions of soldiers.

Tortuga was considered one of the biggest non-cities in the southeast. Certainly it was one of the largest military bases on the east coast of the United States. This made the inky darkness that stretched before Samantha all the more eerie. She knew the *Little Charlie* was quickly approaching the base, yet all she saw was the all-consuming darkness.

"Why can't we see them?" Samantha asked. "For that matter, why can't we see anything? I know the economy sucks, but I figured the U.S. Government could afford to pay their electric bill."

Frank ignored her question and pressed a series of buttons.

"This is MT-1034," Frank said. "Calling Delphi. Over"

"Acknowledged, MT-1034," Delphi tower replied. "We have you on radar. Please proceed to Helo Pad 3 as instructed."

"How about showing us the way," Samantha intruded. "Or do you expect us to feel our way there?"

"Helo Pad 3 is now illuminated."

Off in the distance to the north a small circle of lights came on. As promised, a concrete helicopter landing pad was visible. In its center were the numbers "03" written in bold white paint against the black tarmac.

"I guess they wanted to keep us in suspense," Samantha muttered. "We're just about on top of it."

"We have a visual of the landing pad, Delphi," Frank said. "Our ETA for touch down is ten minutes."

As the words left his mouth, a loud buzz filled the pilots' headphones. The helicopter's computer monitors streamed lines of flashing data. One monitor displayed a blood red warning.

"They're locking missiles on us," Samantha yelled. "What the hell—?"

"Attention, MT-1034," Delphi said. "This facility is under red alert. Our anti-aircraft mechanisms are armed and have targeted your craft."

"No kidding," Samantha said.

"We will not fire unless you deviate from your route. Please proceed exactly as directed. I repeat, *do not deviate from your route.* Proceed to Helo Pad 3. Over."

"Son of a bitch," Samantha spat. She instinctively reached to her left, to the controls of the anti-missile equipment. It was impossible for the *Little Charlie* to survive the base's barrage of missiles, but she felt naked without some kind of protection.

Before she reached the controls, Frank grabbed her hand.

"Don't," he said.

Frank held Samantha's hand so tight she winced in pain. Her lips quivered and a chill rolled along her spine.

"Let go of me."

Frank drew a breath and released his co-pilot's hand. There were red marks left from his grip.

"Sorry," he said.

"What aren't you telling me, Frank?"

"Nothing," he replied. "We were called to pick someone up. Other than that, I don't know what's going on."

"The hell you don't."

"Even if I did, I couldn't tell you," Frank said. "Look, we're a small transport helicopter up against the full defensive might of one of our most sophisticated military bases. Turn on any of our anti-missile packages and they might interpret our actions as hostile."

Samantha rubbed her hand. The pain lingered.

"You've got some grip," she said. "If we get out of this alive, I should take up skiing."

Frank didn't answer. Samantha sighed.

"What the hell harm could we do to one of our 'most sophisticated military bases'?"

"None," Frank acknowledged. "But we follow orders and we don't do anything provocative."

As if to prove the point, Captain Frank Masters made sure the Seahawk's approach to Helo Pad 3 was as routine as humanly possible.

The Seahawk landed in the dead center of Tortuga's number 3 landing pad. From the cockpit it was impossible to make out what lay beyond the bright lights illuminating the landing site. On the edges of those lights, however, and just outside the spreading darkness, Samantha thought she spotted a ring of vehicles and soldiers. If that was the case, their helicopter was surrounded.

Samantha clicked on the intercom switch.

"Ladies and gentlemen, this is your pilot," she said. "For the time being, I ask you to please remain in your seats."

She turned the intercom off and leaned in close to Frank.

"They think we're in Alexandria," she whispered. "We need to tell them something."

Frank nodded. Samantha turned the intercom switch back on.

"Ladies and gentlemen, I'm sorry for the extended radio silence on my part. Although we were scheduled to fly into Alexandria, at the very last minute we were diverted and ordered to land in Tortuga. As soon as we get clearance, we will resume our flight to Alexandria so please sit back and relax. We will remain on board the helicopter until we're cleared to leave. In the meantime, I'm shutting the engines down and, in a few moments, you'll be able to remove your headsets. This delay should be temporary."

So she hoped.

The crew and passengers of the *Little Charlie* sat in their places. No one from the Military Base stepped up to the helicopter and none of the passengers or crew left their seats. As they waited, whispers from the passenger compartment floated into the cockpit. Samantha's passengers wondered with differing degrees of irritation why they were being held in place. Their irritation was tempered somewhat by their conditioning. They were soldiers. They were trained to follow orders.

But after more than an hour of waiting, the occupants' patience was tested. Though none of them rose from their seats or voiced a desire to exit the craft, it was only a matter of time.

"How much longer are we supposed to wait?" Jennie Light said. Her icy blue eyes were on fire.

"As soon as we know, soldier, we'll tell you," Frank said.

Jennie Light folded her hands across her chest and shook her head. Next to and across from her, Howard Bartlett and Dan Thompson's faces remained sour. Alicia Cunningham, the newbie, could barely contain a look of growing panic. It was obvious she also suffered from claustrophobia.

"Easy," Becky Waters told her. Of the passengers, she was the least troubled with their interrupted flight. "We're on the ground. No chance of getting airsick."

Alicia smiled and nodded.

"There's that," she admitted.

After a few more minutes, the occupants of the Seahawk heard the low drone of another helicopter approaching from the north. In seconds, it roared over them. The craft's lights were off, its body invisible in the night sky. From the sound of its engines, Samantha recognized the craft as an AH-64 Apache. Fully loaded, it was one of the most fearsome attack helicopters in the world.

After passing over them, the noise from her engines receded. The Apache drifted to the east. Another landing pad a half-mile away in that direction lit up. Samantha heard a series of urgent whispers from the crew compartment in reaction to the lights.

For the second landing pad's lights illuminated the extent of personnel and vehicles surrounding their chopper. A trio of IAV Strykers, eight wheeled armored combat vehicles, were parked end to end, their weaponry pointed directly at the Seahawk. Crouched before them were at least fifty soldiers carrying an assortment of weapons, from assault rifles to automatics to, incredibly, shoulder fired RPGs. Those too were aimed at the *Little Charlie*.

"What is this?" came a voice from the rear compartment. It was Thompson. "Did we do something wrong?"

Samantha looked into the passenger compartment.

"We were told we'd be picking up a passenger," she said. "Other than that, I don't know any more than you do."

"Sit back and relax," Frank said. "If they wanted to shoot us, they'd have done so already."

"How encouraging," Bartlett said. "If this piloting gig doesn't work, you should give inspirational speech a try."

The grumbling from the passenger cabin decreased to sparse muttering. Everyone's attention was on the other illuminated landing pad. Presently, the Apache helicopter appeared. She hovered for a few seconds over the center of the distant landing pad, a metal Valkyrie itching for a fight. Then, she reluctantly descended, as if a mighty beast forced back into her cage. Her wheels touched down and the mighty rotors slowed. As soon as they stopped, the landing pad's lights shut off. Everything around the Seahawk returned to the way it was. Nothing outside of their landing pad was visible.

"This is Delphi," came a voice over the headphones. "We request Captain Frank Masters respond."

"This is Frank Masters."

"Please exit your craft but remain within a ten foot radius of her side doors. Be advised, should you deviate..."

"Understood," Frank said. He removed his seat belt and stood up. "Your boys know I'm coming out, don't they? I wouldn't want anyone to get overly excited when I do."

There was no immediate response. A bead of sweat rolled down Samantha's forehead.

"Proceed slowly, Officer Masters," Delphi replied.

"Yes sir."

Frank placed the headset on his chair. He rubbed his hands against his pants and stretched.

"Better do exactly what they say," Samantha whispered.

"It would be suicide to do otherwise."

Frank stepped past the cockpit partition and into the passenger compartment. The passengers watched as he opened the sliding door leading out of the helicopter.

"They want me outside," he told them. "Only me. Please stay where you are."

Samantha followed behind Frank. She released the step ladder and allowed Frank space to climb out of the craft. As soon as his feet hit the tarmac, he heard the sound of a car's engine. A fueling truck emerged from the darkness and parked twenty yards away from him.

"Remain where you are," came a voice over a loudspeaker.

The truck's driver exited the vehicle. He left the door open and disappeared back into the darkness.

"Please refuel your craft," the voice over the loudspeaker said.

Frank slowly walked to the fueling truck and removed a thick hose. There was no one inside the truck and no one around it at all. Alone, he dragged the hose to the Seahawk and removed its fueling cap. He then clamped the hose into the Seahawk and stepped back.

Inside the *Little Charlie*, Frank's actions were scrutinized.

"What the hell is going on?" Thompson asked no one in particular.

"Maybe it's an infection," Bartlett said. "Maybe we've been quarantined. What did they tell you?"

"Nothing," Samantha said.

"Bullshit."

"Believe what you want, private," Samantha said. "Your guess is about as worthless as mine."

"Anyone else have any ideas?" Thompson said.

For a while, the passengers said nothing. Alicia was the first to break the silence.

"Whatever it is, it's serious," Alicia said.

"Well that explains everything," Jennie Light spat back.

"Take it easy," Thompson said. "We're all a bit frazzled. I'm sure this'll be over soon."

"I may not be a seasoned veteran, but I'll tell you what," Bartlett said. "This could be a simple misunderstanding or we could be in some serious shit. But whatever's happening, you can bet it *won't* be resolved quickly."

With that, the passengers grew silent while staring out their windows. Some muttered among themselves. Samantha noted the only person who had not joined in any conversation so far was Becky Waters. She held a book on her lap but her eyes were locked on the window before her.

Samantha felt a rush of suspicion. Could Becky Waters know something everyone else didn't?

"What do you have to say, Private Waters?" she asked.

The other passengers' conversations died out and all eyes were on Becky. If she noticed the stares, she ignored them. After a few tense seconds passed, she said:

"Someone's coming."

12

He stepped out of the shadows and into the light of the number 3 landing pad.

For a moment, he stood alone.

The lights were at his back and his features were hidden behind thick shadows. Despite this, the passengers of the Seahawk saw enough of the man to know he was in his mid-forties. He was lean and athletically built. He wore a simple black suit that lacked any sort of military insignia, yet he exuded authority. He wore sunglasses in spite of the darkness and his right hand rested close to his belt. A large knife sheath was clipped to his side. Otherwise, the man appeared unarmed.

He looked the area over, noting Frank Masters and the refueling truck. After a few seconds he turned to the darkness behind him and waved.

From this darkness emerged another figure. In contrast to his partner, the man was short and squat. He had a protruding stomach and thinning gray hair. His glasses were thick and built for functionality and not vanity. In his right hand was a thin black suitcase. Immediately behind him was another man. He was considerably younger, in his early to mid-thirties, and walked with the precision of a military lifer. His suit was freshly pressed, his crew cut as crisp as his walk.

"Welcome to the party, Captain America," Bartlett muttered after seeing this third man.

The passengers stared at the three individuals and assumed they were the reason for their flight's diversion. Only Becky noted what appeared to be identical knife sheaths attached to each of their belts.

The first man, the one who most exuded authority, broke off from the group and approached Frank Masters. He raised his hand and saluted the pilot.

"How are you doing, soldier?" the man said.

"Could be better," Frank replied. If he was surprised to see the man, he didn't show it.

"You'll get back to your vacation soon enough," the man said.

"I've heard that before."

The man smiled.

"It's been a long time, Frank."

The passengers watched as Frank and the man with the sunglasses talked. Presently, they were joined by his two partners, and their conversation continued. At times it seemed cordial. At times their expressions hinted at bitterness and tension. Becky Waters, in particular, focused hard on their unheard conversation.

After a few moments, the man with the sunglasses realized their group was being watched by the *Little Charlie's* passengers. He pointed to the rear of the craft and the four moved out of sight. They remained hidden for several long minutes before emerging. Their conversation now over, Frank escorted the trio to the helicopter's entrance and climbed aboard.

"Ten-shun!" Frank said.

The passengers within the helicopter rose to their feet as the trio of strangers entered the craft.

"At ease," said the man with the sunglasses. He stood by the door and let his partners walk past him and deeper into the craft. "My name is Paul Spradlin. General Paul Spradlin. I apologize for this delay. We'll be in the air as soon as your pilot fills this craft's tanks." Spradlin addressed Frank. "Why don't you finish that up?"

Frank nodded and exited the craft.

"So the good news is we'll be leaving very soon," the man continued. "The bad news is that we're returning to Bad Penny."

Although no one within the helicopter said anything, their anger and frustration spiked.

Spradlin removed a paper from his pocket and looked over its contents.

"Before we go, we need to see who's here. Becky Waters?"

"Present."

Spradlin pointed to the man sitting beside her.

"You're Howard Bartlett."

"Yes sir."

"Alicia Cunningham?"

"Present," said the newbie.

The General faced the helicopter's opposite aisle.

"And you're Dan Thompson," Spradlin continued. He pointed to the soldier sitting next to him. "Jennie Light?"

The blonde nodded but said nothing. Spradlin turned to the woman standing next to the door.

"And, finally, Captain Samantha Aron, our co-pilot."

Samantha waved.

Spradlin folded the paper and put it away. He pointed to the short balding man who arrived with him.

"This is Doctor Evans," he said and then pointed to the younger man standing next to him. "And this is Lieutenant Alan Robinson. They're joining us on the journey back. Any questions?"

Howard Bartlett raised his hand, almost smacking Alicia Cunningham in the process.

"Permission to speak, sir," he said.

"Go ahead, son."

"Yes sir," Bartlett began. "Begging your pardon, sir, but my wife is about to give birth and I've been looking forward to this leave for over two months. If you need to get back to Bad Penny, wouldn't it be easier to leave us here so we can find our own way home?"

Spradlin shook his head.

"I'm sure every one of you had something better planned for just about right now," he said. "I sympathize. Unfortunately, leaving you in Tortuga is impossible. Our actions are dictated by circumstance and our current circumstance is this: We need to return all personnel to Bad Penny."

"Pardon me sir, but why?"

"It has to be," General Spradlin said. "Look, if everything works out, you'll be on the first flight out of there in the morning. By no later than noon tomorrow you should all be at Alexandria."

The passengers mulled this new information. Alicia Cunningham was the first to speak.

"That isn't too bad."

The sour mood lightened, if only a little. One day's delay, inconvenient as it was, was manageable. Samantha Aron, however, remained skeptical. She gazed at her three new passengers and was about to return to the cockpit when her eyes locked on Becky Waters. From the look of seriousness in the soldier's face, it was clear that she, too, felt the same sense of unease.

So much time and effort was expended to get this helicopter and its seven occupants back to Bad Penny. Returning the next day seemed overly optimistic.

At least in that, Samantha thought, *we think alike.*

Becky looked away from Samantha and out her window. Frank Masters was in the process of removing the fueling line from the helicopter. Once done, he climbed back inside.

"Finished?" Spradlin asked.

Frank nodded. He stepped past the General and into the cockpit, followed by Samantha. Spradlin wore a crooked smile and said:

"No use prolonging the agony. How about we get this bird off the ground?"

The *Little Charlie* lifted off just as the first drops of rain from the approaching front hit the tarmac. She lifted almost perfectly vertical, rising over seventy five feet before initiating a slow counterclockwise turn.

Three minutes later she passed the outer perimeter of the Tortuga base. By then the rain from the cold front was falling in sheets.

"Ladies and gentlemen," Samantha Aron said over the intercom. "This soup is just beginning. Unfortunately, it'll follow us all the way back to Bad Penny. Make sure your seatbelts are strapped in tight."

Samantha turned off the intercom. Five minutes after exiting the outer perimeter of the Tortuga base, the missile lock warnings went silent. Samantha looked out her side window and back at the base. She expected to find the many buildings illuminated and its airfield easy to spot. She expected the base to come to life.

Instead, all she found was darkness.

13

The passengers aboard the *Little Charlie* spent much of the trip back to Bad Penny in silence.

The five soldiers from Bad Penny stole glances at General Spradlin and his two companions, their eyes searching for some hint as to why they were forced into this return trip. For his part, General Spradlin offered no clues, either verbal or physical. He sat straight back in his chair, his head up and his eyes hidden behind his sunglasses. He scanned the passengers now and again, each time spending several long seconds on one or another. If the object of his gaze noted Spradlin's stare, he looked away and began the process all over again with someone else.

Sitting to Spradlin's right was Dr. Evans. Unlike his partner, the older man kept his head down and didn't seem to care much about what the other passengers were doing. If it wasn't for the fact that his body was so rigid and neither slid nor shifted in his seat, one might think he was sleeping. The last of Spradlin's men, Alan Robinson, sat next to Evans and beside a window. He stared out that window for much of the trip, his eye lids at times narrowing as if trying to see something in the distance. Considering the complete darkness outside, that was very unlikely.

In the cockpit, Samantha and Frank worked the controls of the *Little Charlie*. After thirty minutes, the chopper was in the thick of the rapidly moving cold front. The rain and wind outside were strong and battered the helicopter from side to side. Samantha pushed the chopper's speed with the hopes of eventually passing the front and building some distance between it and the chopper. She hoped to land in Bad Penny well before the front once again caught up with them.

Samantha eased back in her seat. She could barely see the stars in the sky above or the deep darkness of the Atlantic Ocean below. She scratched her chin and turned her microphone on. She set it for private communication with her co-pilot.

"You know General Spradlin?" she asked.

"I've met him a few times," Frank said.

"Is he always this...intense?"

"It's in the nature of his job," Frank replied. "But, yeah, every time I've seen him he's exactly like this."

"When was the last time?"

"A couple of years ago. He showed up at our base and needed transportation from point A to point B. It was all very hush-hush and *right now.*"

"Where did you fly him?"

A sly grin appeared on Frank's face.

"If I told you, I'd have to kill you."

Samantha nodded and didn't push. She wasn't entirely sure if Frank was kidding.

By 2300 hours, the southern edge of the front was just behind them. But it lingered behind them in hot pursuit. Heavy rain still splattered now and again against the *Little Charlie's* windshields but Samantha found the chopper much easier to handle. Frank was on the computer, pulling up weather charts and muttering instructions and up to the minute data. Samantha clicked on the intercom.

"We passed the edge of the front," she told her passengers. "But we'll slow down when we approach Bad Penny. The front will probably overtake us and things are going to get very interesting when we land. Take a moment and double check your seatbelts."

The level of tension in the passenger compartment, already high, soared. Alicia Cunningham, true to her word, turned very pale and showed advanced signs of air sickness. She held on tight to a sickness bag and kept her head down. Becky Waters put away her book and, like Howard Bartlett beside her, double checked to make sure her seatbelt was secure. She then patted Alicia on her back and offered to do the same for the newbie. Alicia accepted the help between gasps of air.

"Don't talk," Becky said. "You'll be fine. As soon as we get on the ground."

Dan Thompson followed suite, checking his belt and noting Jennie Light was pressed back into her seat. The blonde's teeth were clenched. Perhaps she too, Thompson thought, might have a touch of air sickness. He turned from Jennie and looked down the length of the cabin. Alan Robinson continued to stare out his window, while Dr. Evans' skin color was almost as pale as Alicia's. Still, he didn't look sick.

General Spradlin, the last person seated in the row and nearest to the cockpit, removed his seat belt. He grabbed the overhead hand rail and got to his feet. He took a couple of steps and stopped at the cockpit's entry.

"How much longer?" he yelled. His voice just managed to pierce the maddening shriek of the helicopter's engine.

"We've got a little less than an hour left, General," Frank replied.

"Thank you," Spradlin said. He returned to his seat.

When he was gone, Frank activated his microphone.

"You look hungry, Samantha," he said. "How about some chili? Or maybe some yogurt?"

Samantha's lips curled into a sneer.

"That sounds like a dare," Samantha said. "Or at least the makings of a bet. How about it, Frank? That case of beer Lombardo owes you to whichever one of us *doesn't* get sick on this flight."

"What if neither of us gets sick?"

"Then we share, like you should have done to begin with," Samantha said. "You wouldn't have won your little bet without me in the first place."

"I wouldn't have the bet at all if you were a little more punctual."

"Point taken."

"What if we both get sick?"

"*You* might get sick," Samantha said. "I won't."

The *Little Charlie* suddenly banked to the right. Samantha held tight on the controls until the chopper leveled off. Frank smiled.

"Stacking the odds in your favor?"

"You know it," Samantha said. She allowed the chopper to drift to the left, then right. Frank let out a laugh.

"It occurs to me we made the wrong bet," Frank said. "We should bet on which of our passengers makes it through this trip without hurling. We're experienced pilots; we're supposed to have stomachs of steel. The people back there may not appreciate this weather quite like we do."

"Loser cleans up the mess?"

"There you go," Frank said.

"Winner gets the beer," Samantha added.

"Fine."

Samantha chuckled before shaking her head. The moment of levity was over, and her thoughts returned to General Spradlin.

"So what did you say to the General back at Tortuga?"

"Nothing much," Frank replied.

"You spent a pretty good amount of time talking to him. I'm assuming it wasn't about the weather."

"No," Frank said.

Samantha shook her head.

"Don't tell me. If you say anymore—"

"Yeah."

There was a heavy finality to the single word answer.

Don't ask any more questions.

The front's fringes, gorged with sharp gusts of wind and sheets of heavy rain, whipped around the Bad Penny military base. Ghostly trees, their forms barely visible in the night, swayed and lashed against each other. The only road leading through the military town was, with the exception of a single HUMVEE parked in the center of that road, deserted. Fluorescent lights flickered through random windows of buildings along the road, their illumination faint in the stormy night.

The landing pad on the south end of the island, similarly, was not immune to the increasingly harsh weather. Palm trees danced wildly on the edges of the pad while rain splattered against the control tower's windows.

Inside this structure, metal shutters clanked as the winds increased. Radio equipment lined the other side of the room and from one of the speakers came the low hum of static. An ashtray loaded with cigarette butts sat beside the radio equipment. Smoke rose lazily from one of the butts.

The sound of static increased, until it was like a whine of screeching metal. This sound was replaced by a distinctly human voice.

"This is transport MT-1034," Frank Masters said. "Do you read me, Bad Penny?"

In the hallway outside the room, a file cabinet lay overturned. Its contents, paper and navigational charts, were scattered across the floor. Mixed in with the papers were shards of broken glass.

"I repeat, this is transport MT-1034. Do you read me Bad Penny?"

The control room was alive with lights. They flashed and blinked, following a well-established routine. Below them, the loose sheets of paper, alone or bunched together, danced in the wind. When it momentarily died down, the paper's dance was over and they settled back onto the floor.

"Lombardo, are you there? Please respond."

A shadow flicked over the radio's control panel. A muddy hand reached for the microphone.

Aboard the *Little* Charlie, Frank and Samantha wondered why they weren't getting a response from Bad Penny. Frank sighed and gave the radio another try.

"I repeat, this is Transport MT-1034 calling Bad Penny. We are—"

"MT-1034 this is Bad Penny. We read you loud and clear. Please proceed with landing protocol. Over."

"Lombardo? Is that you?" Samantha said.

There was a long pause, punctuated by the crackling on the radio.

"Affirmative."

"Where were you guys?" Samantha said. "Taking a nap?"

More static.

"We read you," Lombardo said.

"No one believes in working the night shift," Samantha muttered.

Frank smirked. He pressed the microphone button.

"We're coming home earlier than expected, Lombardo," Frank said. "Can't always get what you—"

"We have you on radar and will see you soon," Lombardo said.

Samantha glanced at Frank. She leaned in close to his ear.

"Something's wrong," she said. "More so than usual. Did someone kick Lombardo's dog?"

Samantha activated her microphone.

"Hey, Lombardo. You remember your bet with Frank?" Samantha asked. "He's coming for it."

"Bet?" Lombardo said after a long pause.

"The beer, dummy," Samantha replied. She frowned. "You don't remem—"

"Over and out."

The radio signal went dead.

"Well, that didn't help," Samantha said.

"You know Lombardo," Frank said. "He *really* hates paying off debts. Especially when they involve large quantities of liquor."

"I suppose."

Though she said nothing more, Lombardo's reply rattled Samantha. Instead of talking to an old friend, she felt like she was talking to a total stranger. She stared forward, into the darkness of the night, and wondered exactly what she would find back at Bad Penny.

As she pondered that question, Frank eased into his seat and, very casually, thrust his left hand into his jacket pocket. Samantha did not notice his movements. Just as casually, Frank removed his hand from the pocket. In it was a small black remote control device. On the device were two buttons, one red and one black.

Frank eyed the device for a few seconds. Finally, he pressed the black button. He then placed the control on the counter where Samantha couldn't see it.

He made sure to keep his fingers as far away from the red button as possible.

In the passenger compartment, General Spradlin stretched. He looked down at his belt and a small black beeper clipped on it. The beeper was vibrating. General Spradlin pressed a button on it and the vibrations stopped. He casually eyed the passengers and removed his headset before turning to Doctor Evans and motioning for him to do the same.

Doctor Evans complied and General Spradlin leaned in to whisper something into the elderly man's ear.

Almost all the passengers paid little attention to General Spradlin's actions. Even under the unusual circumstances they found themselves in, there seemed nothing untoward about the General talking to one of his partners.

But one of the passengers, Becky Waters, watched with interest as General Spradlin whispered to his elderly partner. She watched General Spradlin's lips, catching the movements and forming the words he was speaking in her mind. As she did, her eyes opened wide. When General Spradlin was done talking, she had to force herself to look away.

She had to force herself not to shake.

14

The wind and rain were growing in fury around the Seahawk. Samantha and Frank fought hard against increasingly sluggish controls. The front had once again caught up with them as they slowed for their approach into Bad Penny.

"Winds are coming from the west," Samantha said as she adjusted to the latest burst. "I'm bringing her around."

"Yeah," Frank replied. His left hand held down the two-button remote control. He glanced at it, for only a second, to make sure his fingers weren't anywhere near the red button. He frowned before unbuckling his seat belt and getting to his feet.

"What are you doing?" Samantha asked.

"Got a cramp," he muttered and stretched. He rubbed his leg with his free hand.

"Great timing," Samantha yelled.

"It's a skill," Frank said.

"I could use a hand here."

"That sounds mildly perverse," Frank replied. "I have the greatest faith in your piloting skills, Captain Aron."

Samantha shook her head. Her eyes returned to the weather display. She pressed down on the intercom button.

"Passengers, this is your pilot. I know I'm starting to sound like your mother –at least to those who have a mother– but if you haven't done so already, please make sure you're buckled in real tight. This stuff is only going to get worse."

Samantha shut off the intercom.

"That goes for you, too, Frank. Get back to your seat."

Frank did as told. He laid his small remote unit back on the control paneling. A burst of lightning flooded the cockpit and was followed by a thunderous crack. The passengers gasped as the helicopter veered wildly to the right.

Samantha swore as she fought the sluggish controls. It took several seconds for her to level out the chopper.

"Call Bad Penny," Samantha said. "Tell them we're coming in as fast as we can."

Frank hit a switch.

"This is MT-1034 calling Bad Penny," Frank spoke into his microphone. "We are on final approach, coming in from the northwest side of island." Frank's eyes returned to the remote unit. He tensed. "Eta for landing is eight minutes. I repeat, eight minutes. Over."

Frank and Samantha waited for a response. None came.

"I repeat," Frank said. "This is MT-1034. We are on approach from the northwest side of the island. Eta for landing is eight minutes. Please acknowledge."

Again there was no response.

"Don't know why I bothered getting out of bed today," Samantha muttered. She pressed her microphone button.

"Bad Penny, this is MT-1034," she said. "Do you read me, Lombardo? Where the hell are you?"

As with the previous calls, there came no reply. Another burst of lightning, this one from farther away, illuminated the cabin. The helicopter lurched forward.

"What the hell is wrong with those guys?" Samantha said.

"I wish I knew," Frank replied.

"If this is their idea of a practical joke, it's not fucking funny."

Samantha slammed down on the radio button.

"When this is over," she said. "I'm having a real heart to heart with Lombardo and the rest of those boys."

She shook her head and focused on her controls.

"At least we're nearly home," Frank said.

He saw the fringes of the coast of Bad Penny in the near distance. In seconds the *Little Charlie* would be over land. Frank's thumb hovered over the red button of the remote control. He knew what he had to do when they reached the coast.

Frank's thumb now rested on the red button. A simple push and it would happen.

Rain splattered against the windows, streaking down and away. More lightning followed.

The coast was very close now. Very close.

Frank braced himself. There was another burst of lightning, followed by another crash of thunder. Frank rubbed his thumb along the edges of the red button. They were almost over the coast. Almost. Almost.

Now.

Frank closed his eyes tight and pressed down on the button. In that very instant, another loud crash filled the body of the helicopter. The craft shuddered and lights flickered across the instrument panel. The helicopter lurched forward into a steep descent.

Frank flew out of his chair. He hadn't replaced his seat belt after stretching. His right knee slammed against the chopper's control panel. There was a ghastly crunching sound and Frank screamed in pain. The two-button remote slid from his hand and fell to the floor.

Frank grabbed his injured knee. Blood poured out of the wound.

"We've been hit!" Samantha yelled. If she noticed her partner's injury, she didn't dwell on it. Instead, her complete attention was on regaining control of the craft. It was falling. *Fast.* She switched on the radio.

"Emergency," she yelled. "This is the MT-1034. We're going down! We're going down!"

The helicopter fell at a steep angle. In the passenger compartment, the passengers grabbed their loose possessions. Some screamed, one cried. Complete panic enveloped the area. All save for General Spradlin and his men, who held on tight to their hand rest and gritted their teeth.

In the cockpit, Samantha pulled at the yoke.

"Answer me, Bad Penny!" she yelled. "Goddamned lightning hit us!"

As before, there was no response.

"Fuck you too, Lombardo," she spat. She hit the intercom button. "All passengers, brace for impact. We're going down."

The helicopter swayed violently in the heavy rain. Thick smoke flowed from near the helicopter's rear rotors. More flashes of lightning burst around the wounded craft. Her angle of descent, however, leveled.

Samantha felt a trickle of blood in her mouth. She wiped it away.

"Better," she muttered, pleased to have regained some control of her craft. She again hit the radio switch. "This is MT-1034," she said. "Mayday, Mayday! We're going down, northwest corner of Bad Penny. Anybody, Mayday!"

Still no reply.

"This just isn't our day!" she yelled. She turned to her side and spat out blood. It hit the floor and mingled with other drops of blood. Curious at this sight, she looked up. For the first time, she noticed her co-pilot. His face was pale and he held on to his bloody right knee.

"Frank?"

Frank gritted his teeth and managed a ghostly smile.

"Forgot to put on my Goddamned seat belt," he muttered. "Don't worry about me. Get this bird down in one piece."

"Easier said than done," Samantha replied. "We need to find a clearing and I can't see a fucking thing."

"Two o'clock," Frank said, his voice was hoarse. "Small area. Better than nothing."

Samantha leaned forward and looked in that direction.

"I don't see it."

"It's there," Frank assured her.

Samantha eased the controls to the right. The helicopter shuddered. The engine sounded increasingly ragged.

"I hope you're right," Samantha said. "If we're lucky, we've got maybe thirty seconds before the engine gives up."

Samantha pushed the controls forward and sent the *Little Charlie* on an easy descent. The tops of the palm trees thrashed against the chopper's landing gear.

"I'm still not seeing it," Samantha muttered.

"It's there."

Samantha shook her head. The chopper moved forward at a crawl, and for a moment Samantha considered coming to a complete stop and descending straight down. The forest, however, was thick with tall palm trees. Going down in this dense area could be fatal. The whirling rotors would splinter when they hit the trees. Shrapnel would fly in all directions, with a high likelihood at least some of it would slice through the body of the chopper and into whichever unfortunate occupant was in their way. If the fuel tanks ruptured, there was a risk of a fire or explosion. Even ignoring all that, there was the danger of the fall itself. The physical effects on a human body falling anything more than two stories straight down could be devastating.

No, Samantha realized, she would have to hope Frank was right and there was a clearing coming up.

For the sake of her passengers, for the sake of everyone, she hoped he was right.

15

The clearing appeared.

Even though her complete attention was on the terrain below and she kept the helicopter's forward speed at a crawl, she very nearly overshot her target.

"Good eyes, Frank," she said.

Samantha turned the helicopter clockwise, allowing for a more comfortable fit into the tight, empty space.

"We're going to make it, Frank."

Frank Masters nodded. The pilots smiled but, as the chopper descended, the controls grew increasingly sluggish. The vehicle's engine rattled noisily and the acrid smell of burnt rubber and oil filled her interior. The computer panels before Samantha flashed, all desperately seeking her undivided attention. Each and every one of them warned of imminent, catastrophic failure.

Samantha slid her tongue along her lower lip. She felt a painful, jagged cut just inside her mouth that oozed blood.

Bit your lip, did you? She thought. *If that's the worst injury I come away with, I'll take it.*

"We're going to make it," Samantha muttered. "We're going to fucking make it."

She pushed the intercom button and said, in an even, steely voice: "Brace for emergency landing."

In the passenger compartment, the Bad Penny passengers glared out the windows. They saw very little of the outside world thanks to that same rain and darkness that inhibited Samantha's perceptions. All on board, however, felt the helicopter's slow descent. General Spradlin stared forward, eyeing the various passengers, his face a mask of neutrality, as if the events of the moment were already in the past and the results a foregone conclusion.

While the other passengers tried to contain their panic, Becky noted the General's cool demeanor. She met his neutral stare with one of her own. They watched at each other for what seemed a lifetime before Becky looked away. Unlike General Spradlin, she really was scared.

Very much so.

The fear Samantha felt, on the other hand, was dissipating by the moment. Despite the increasing loud metallic groans coming from the chopper's engine, they were a little over thirty feet from the ground. The landing might be a little hard, Samantha knew, but everyone would walk away from this.

She eased the chopper's throttle, decreasing the rotor velocity and torque. The chopper lowered. Twenty feet. Ten.

Samantha managed a smile.

They would make it. They would—

A chilling groan came from the tail section of the helicopter. In that moment, the rear blades split off, slicing a jagged line across the lee side of the chopper. Despite Samantha's best efforts, the *Little Charlie* spun in a wild circle. The chopper's tail smashed against several palm trees and the body of the helicopter dropped the final ten feet like a rock.

It hit the jungle floor with a loud crash, sending sparks and smoke throughout the craft's interior.

Samantha, her entire body numb with pain, nonetheless reached for the controls and quickly hit a series of switches. The *Little Charlie's* engine coughed one final time before dying. The clipped rotors above her slowed. In moments, they would be still.

"We made it," Samantha whispered, as if speaking this truth too loudly might invalidate it. Nonetheless, she looked out the front window to make sure. When she saw the ground, she let out a relieved breath. "We made it."

She unbuckled her belt and reached to her right, to grab a small fire extinguisher fastened to the side of the control panel. She stood up and eyed her co-pilot, who was still in his seat, his hands pressed against the bloody injury on his leg.

"I should try to reach Bad Penny again," she said.

"Don't bother," Frank replied between gasps. His voice lowered to a whisper. "Something's happening."

"What?"

"I'm not sure," Frank said. "We'll talk when we're out of here, OK?"

Samantha considered Frank's cryptic words. *If I didn't know you better...*

"OK."

She helped Frank up and, with his arm around her shoulder, helped him out of the cockpit and into the passenger compartment.

Samantha was relieved to see her passengers were getting to their feet and moving around.

"Any injuries?" she asked.

No one replied, but Samantha nonetheless gave each passenger a quick look. A couple of passengers reached for their luggage.

"Forget all that shit," Samantha yelled. "Someone grab Frank and get him out of here. Everyone else, reach under your seats and grab all the first aid kits or emergency flashlights. If you don't find any, don't waste time searching. This bird might still go up and everyone needs to be off."

General Spradlin rushed to Samantha's side and took Frank from her arms. Samantha handed him her fire extinguisher as well. Spradlin glanced at her co-pilot's injury before addressing Samantha.

"You need to get out, too," he said.

"There's another first aid kit and a PCOM in the cockpit," Samantha replied. She licked her bloody lips and added: "Now get your ass moving. Sir."

General Spradlin pulled Frank through the passenger compartment. The outer hatch was already open, and Alicia Cunningham and Dan Thompson stepped out. Samantha hurriedly returned to the cockpit.

She fell to her knees beside Frank's chair and reached for the compartment below it. She pulled out two cases, one white and filled with first aid supplies, the other a dark green metal box with black letters labeling it a PCOM, or portable communicator. The device was, essentially, a military cell phone. Samantha checked to make sure it was in its case within the box before getting back to her feet. As she did, she noticed something on the floor. It was a small black rectangular object. It lay next to her co-pilot's foot pedals. Had something fallen off the control panel? Samantha frowned. No, the object looked cheap, like a small novelty flashlight, the type usually found on the end of key chains, not a part of a Seahawk's sturdy control panel.

Samantha grabbed it. The object was plastic and had two buttons, one black and one red. It was no flashlight. If anything, it resembled some kind of remote control, the type you use to open a garage or turn on a TV or...

Samantha's suppressed a gasp.

...or something you use to set off an explosive.

For several seconds, Samantha remained on her knees, staring at the object in her hand. *The only way it could be here is if Frank had it on him and dropped it. And if Frank had it...*

Samantha shook her head.

Later, she thought.

She pocketed the remote control and returned to the passenger compartment. She was the last person still aboard the helicopter.

The passengers gathered a safe distance away from the downed Seahawk. They flashed lights in Samantha's direction and the pilot followed them until she joined the group. They were all there, huddled together under a swaying palm tree.

"Didn't any of your mothers tell you it's not safe to stay under a tree during a thunder storm?" Samantha said.

Doctor Evans let out a laugh.

"It would be quite ironic to survive this crash only to die of electrocution," he said. "Quite ironic."

The passengers glared at Samantha and the Doctor. Dan Thompson's teeth were chattering. His hands were thrust tight around his midsection. Doctor Evans noted his discomfort.

"How are you, soldier?"

"Fall knocked the shit out of me," Thompson replied. "Otherwise, I'm alive." He noted the wrecked craft. "Who the fuck am I to complain?"

"That goes for all of us," General Spradlin said. "With the possible exception of our co-pilot."

Samantha walked to the center of the group. Sitting on the jungle floor and propped up by the palm was Frank Masters. His face was pale, his leg a bloody mess.

"Oh, Frank," Samantha said.

"You should see the other guy," he said.

"I'm not going to lie, it's pretty bad son," General Spradlin said. "Doctor Evans should take a look."

"I don't think that's necess—," Frank began.

"Of course it's necessary," Spradlin said.

"Sir, I really don't think—"

"Cut the macho bullshit," Samantha said.

"I don't need him."

"What the hell's the problem with you men?" Samantha hissed. "You face bullets for your country but when it comes to seeing a Doctor, you're jelly."

"Begging your pardon, General," Doctor Evans intruded.

"Yes?"

"I'm a scientist, not a medical doctor," he said. "There's very little I know about treating injuries."

"You're all we have," Spradlin replied. He turned back to Frank. "You have no problem with him giving you a look, do you?"

Frank relented.

"Fine," he said.

"I hope I don't make things worse," Doctor Evans said.

The elderly man grabbed a first aid box from Alicia Cunningham and opened it. He removed a pair of scissors and carefully cut away a strip of Frank's pant leg. When he was done, the injured knee was exposed. The skin around the knee was torn and bloody. Shattered bone ripped through that skin.

"It's broken," Doctor Evans said.

"What a surprise," Frank said. He let out a weak laugh.

"How did this happen?" Spradlin asked.

"I broke it when the lightning hit the chopper," Frank replied. The smile on Frank's face disappeared. "If it hit."

"What do you mean, *if* it hit?" Howard Bartlett said.

Frank's jaw tightened.

"We made it down safely and are only a couple of hours walk from home base," Frank said. "We should be glad, right?"

No one said a word. They had Frank's undivided attention.

"Well, that's where you're wrong," Frank continued. "Someone's been jamming our communications."

"What is he talking about?" Howard Bartlett said. He looked at General Spradlin. "What's going on here?"

Dan Thompson pulled the soldier back.

"Easy," he said. "General?"

The remaining passengers all faced General Spradlin. The General reached for the PCOM case Samantha held. He opened the metallic green box, removed the PCOM device, and accessed the code for Bad Penny. After dialing, he pressed it to his ear.

"This is General Spradlin calling Bad Penny. Do you read, Bad Penny?"

His only answer was static.

"This is General Spradlin calling Bad Penny," he repeated. "Do you read me, Bad Penny?"

More static. General Spradlin frowned and pressed several buttons. He switched the device to a general communication mode.

"This is General Spradlin of the U.S. Armed Forces. Does anyone out there read me?"

They waited several minutes, but there was no response.

"Nothing," General Spradlin finally said.

"Same as I got," Frank said. His eyes drifted to his wound. Doctor Evans was wrapping the injury in gauze. "Someone, *anyone* should have answered your calls. From the east coast of the United States to any of the islands, someone should have replied."

"He's right," Samantha agreed.

"How long have we been jammed?" General Spradlin asked.

"We were talking to Bad Penny maybe five minutes before we crashed," Samantha said. "After that, we got absolutely nothing."

"But even that transmission was strange," Frank said.

"Strange? How so?"

"We were talking with a man named Lombardo at the Bad Penny control tower," Frank said. "Captain Aron and I've known him for a few years now. We've talked to him hundreds of times before. But the guy I talked to while on approach to Bad Penny...that guy sounded like Lombardo, but he sure as hell didn't *talk* like Lombardo."

"What do you mean?" Alicia Cunningham asked. "You think it wasn't him?"

"He sounded distracted," Samantha said.

"It was more than that," Frank said. "He didn't remember the bet."

"Bet?" General Spradlin asked as he put the PCOM device back into its carrying case.

"Nothing important," Frank said. "Silly stuff. But something he should have remembered. Only he didn't."

"If it wasn't this Lombardo guy you were talking to, then who was it?" Alicia persisted. "Why would anyone bother to fake you guys out?"

"That's the million dollar question," Frank said.

"Maybe we're overthinking this," General Spradlin said after a few seconds. "Maybe this device is just malfunctioning. Do we have any other communication device? Any at all?"

"Other than the chopper's radio and that PCOM, none with us right now," Samantha said.

"What about cell phones?" Doctor Evans asked. "Anyone have any?"

"Bad Penny forbids personal cell phones on base," Jennie Light said.

"That's that," General Spradlin said. He shook his head. "We've been through a hell of a lot in a very short amount of time. The good thing is that we survived the crash and are close to the base. Once we get there, we'll figure the rest out."

His words did little to ease the passenger's worries. Some of the passengers, in fact, looked even more worried. But if General Spradlin noted the darkening mood around him, he didn't show it. He patted Doctor Evans on his shoulder.

"How's our patient?" he asked.

"He needs to get to a clinic, quick," Evans said. "Best I can do is immobilize and bandage the leg. Needless to say, he won't be able to put any pressure on it."

"We'll have to carry him."

"On the plus side, we've got plenty of pain killers," Doctor Evans said. "The trip to Bad Penny shouldn't be too uncomfortable for you, Captain Masters. I'm assuming there's a stretcher somewhere inside the chopper?"

"Yes," Frank said.

"Good," General Spradlin said. He eyed the chopper. The smoke coming from her engine had lessened considerably. "Do you suppose it's safe to return?"

"If she hasn't blown yet, there's a good chance she won't," Samantha said. "But we shouldn't push our luck."

"Good advice," Spradlin said. He pointed to Alan Robinson and Samantha. "You two come with me. Let's get that stretcher."

General Spradlin, Alan Robinson, and Samantha Aron stumbled across the field and to the helicopter while the others waited behind. Spradlin led the trio, his flashlight cutting through the darkness like a missile. Soon, they stood before the still smoldering wreck of the *Little Charlie*.

"Hello again," Samantha muttered. The Seahawk was a cranky old thing, but reliable. Even in the end.

Alan Robinson wiped rain from his forehead. It continued to come down heavily, punctuated by distant bursts of lightning.

"Shine the light over here," Robinson said. He pointed to the crumpled tail section of the Seahawk. Because of the way she landed, it rested only six feet from the ground. A still smoking basketball-sized hole ripped through the otherwise smooth metal plate that made up her body. Samantha leaned in to take a look. She noted the serrated edges at the point of impact protruding outwardly.

"Allow me," Robinson said. He brushed past Samantha and ran his hand around the outer hole.

"Give me the light," Robinson said. Spradlin handed him the flashlight. Robinson aimed it into the hole and continued his examination.

As he did, Samantha reached into her jacket pocket and grabbed the black remote control device she found in the cockpit. She bit her already swollen lip, cursing silently as she did, and wondered if she should tell General Spradlin about the device she found in the cockpit. Her mind was a whirl of conflicting thoughts. The remote control device could have been used to detonate a small explosive, something capable of creating the hole in the tail section. If this was the case, it meant Frank, her co-pilot and longtime friend, was the one who brought the chopper down.

But why?

The frown on Samantha's forehead deepened. She pulled the device out of her pocket and took a step toward General Spradlin. She had to tell someone. And if she couldn't trust a General, who could she? She opened her mouth and was about to speak.

"We got some good news and some bad news," Robinson said. He pulled away from the tail section and approached Spradlin.

As he did, Samantha put the remote control back in her pocket.

Maybe later.

"Give me the good news first," Spradlin said.

"The damage to the tail section wasn't too bad," Robinson said. "There are some scorched wires and frayed contacts. With the right equipment, it wouldn't take more than a couple of hours to fix all that up. That is, if the chopper hadn't clipped that palm tree and gotten twisted around."

"Are you criticizing my landing?" Samantha said.

"No offense, Captain. It could have been better."

"We're alive. It could have been a hell of a lot worse."

"What's the bad news?" General Spradlin intruded.

"That damage wasn't caused by lightning," Robinson said. He pointed to the hole. "Someone fired upon us."

Samantha shook her head.

"We didn't get any missile lock warning."

"It wasn't a missile that hit us," Robinson continued. "I'm thinking we were hit with a high caliber projectile."

Samantha closed her mouth. She held the remote control device tight. Spradlin took the flashlight from Robinson and shined it on the hole.

"We were a slow moving, very big target."

"Yes sir," Robinson said. "So either we got real lucky and the people shooting at us thought they did more damage to the chopper than there actually was..."

"Or?" Spradlin said.

"Or they didn't want us dead."

"What are you implying?"

"Let's assume that Captain Frank Masters was right and an imposter was sending radio messages from Bad Penny," Robinson said. "This impostor tells our pilots everything is fine and they continue their standard, predetermined route to the Bad Penny landing pad. Even if the message and the messenger sounded odd, there's little reason to do anything but follow landing protocol. What else could they do? There's enough fuel in the chopper to get to the base's landing pad but not enough to to turn around and return to Tortuga. The impostors jam our communications at the last possible moment, just as we're on final approach. By this time, we're close enough to them so they can take their shot."

"Go on," General Spradlin said.

"So here we are, suspicious but not suspicious enough, coming in from the northwest and following a standard flight plan. Our hidden enemies are set up and ready to take their shot. They do so."

"And we go down," General Spradlin said.

"Bad Penny is covered almost from tip to toe on the north end with dense forest," Alan Robinson continued. "How convenient this clearing just happens to be close enough to use for an emergency landing."

Samantha Aron felt chills run down her spine.

Frank spotted the clearing. I couldn't even see it until we were on top of it...

"Maybe they figured we'd be injured enough so we had to land here," Robinson continued. "If that's the case, I'd lay odds our friends are approaching, maybe even surrounding us. All while we're standing around, talking."

"You got quite an imagination, soldier," Spradlin said.

"Let's hope it's not too fanciful, sir."

Spradlin faced Samantha.

"Get me that stretcher," he said.

The trio entered the helicopter and walked to her rear compartment. Bolted to the wall and behind the last passenger seats was a stretcher. Samantha removed the bolts holding the stretcher and released it. She then returned to Spradlin and Robinson.

"How about weapons," Spradlin inquired. "Do we have any on board?"

Samantha laid the stretcher down.

"We're equipped with four M-16's and three .45's," she said. "They're stashed in the rear vault."

"Can you get them?"

"Gladly, sir," Samantha said. She reached into her jacket and pulled out a small ring of keys. "We've only got a couple of spare clips."

"Let's hope they're enough."

16

When Spradlin, Robinson, and Samantha returned to the passengers, they were met with startled glances. The passengers immediately noticed the weapons they carried and wondered why they were necessary.

General Spradlin stepped into the center of the group.

"I'll make this short and sweet," he said. "We examined the helicopter's damage. We have reason to suspect it was not caused by a natural event."

"What caused it?" Howard Bartlett asked.

"Gun fire," Alan Robinson said.

The passengers grew very quiet.

"We have reason to believe we were brought down by persons unknown and for reasons unknown," Spradlin continued. "There's also the possibility we were crippled just so we would land in that clearing. If so, we're not safe staying here. We need to get moving. Right now."

Spradlin pulled the two M-16 rifles he was carrying off his shoulder and handed them to Bartlett and Thompson.

"Each of you take one," Spradlin said. He turned to Robinson, who was also carrying two M-16s. Robinson handed one of them to Spradlin. "Robinson and I will carry the remaining rifles. Captain Aron?"

Samantha reached into her jacket and pulled out two of the three .45s she was carrying. She handed them to Becky and Jennie.

"That's all we've got," she said.

Spradlin faced Doctor Evans and Alicia Cunningham.

"That leaves you two," he said. "Private Cunningham and Doctor Evans, let's get Captain Masters strapped down on the stretcher. We're not far from the base, but given the darkness and the jungle terrain, this trip will not be a cakewalk. I anticipate it will take us just under two hours to make it to Bad Penny. To keep everyone fresh, we'll carry Captain Masters in one hour shifts. You two will carry him first. When your shift is done, you will be given weapon duty while someone else carries him."

"Yes sir," they replied in unison.

"Doctor, please keep your eye on him," Spradlin said. "It's up to you to make sure he remains well."

"I'd love to, General. But I'm not a medic."

"Look at this as a chance to broaden your horizons," Spradlin said. He pursed his lips and again addressed the entire group. "This situation is very fluid, ladies and gentlemen. Perhaps in examining the helicopter we've misinterpreted something and we're suffering from an overabundance of imagination. Regardless, we need to be on our toes. You are soldiers of the U.S. armed forces and as such, you're trained for this sort of situation. Keep your eyes and ears open. Be on the alert for anything, but for God's sake, do not shoot at shadows. I'm of the opinion that the safest places on Earth one could be in are United States military bases. As luck would have it, we've got one not all that far away. Let's move out."

As they penetrated deeper and deeper into the jungle, the wind and rain eased.

The cold front passed, leaving behind a chilly air. By the time the group reached a small inlet ringed with knotty mangroves, the rain had completely died out. With the clouds gone, a quarter Moon shone down on the jungle floor. Though it was still dim, the group no longer needed to rely entirely on their flashlights to see their way.

No one spoke. Alan Robinson held point, while Howard Bartlett and Dan Thompson brought up the rear. In the dead center of the group were Doctor Evans, Alicia Cunningham, and the injured Frank Masters. Samantha Aron walked close to General Spradlin, her face filled with doubt and concern. She desperately wanted to tell the General -anyone- about the remote device she found, especially after Spradlin's companion offered his theory for the *Little Charlie's* crash.

As the minutes passed, she became convinced Robinson was purposely lying. He *had* to know the damage to the helicopter's tail was not caused by gun fire. Just looking at it, it should have been obvious the damage was caused by an explosive device planted within the tail itself.

That being the case, the situation she and the others were in was even more dangerous than it at first appeared. Before entering the helicopter back on Tortuga, General Spradlin, Doctor Evans, Alan Robinson, and Frank Masters talked on the tarmac. Were they planning the manner in which to bring the helicopter down? If so, was Frank Masters the invisible hand, via that remote control device, for doing the deed?

One thing in particular stuck in Samantha's mind: The Clearing. Alan Robinson was right; the clearing was the only place on the north side of the island where they *could* have landed. And Frank spotted it. At the time, his discovery of the clearing seemed a Godsend. Now, it appeared pre-planned.

Sinister.

Samantha took a deep breath.

She couldn't keep this information to herself, but if Robinson was General Spradlin's right hand man, he too might have known about this from the beginning. If that was the case, then the General was in on this as well. If he was, who could she trust? She looked back at the other passengers, then forward again. Other than Frank, Samantha didn't know anyone in this group well enough to trust them. Could one or more of them be in on this? Even worse, could *she* be the only one out of the loop?

And then the biggest question: Why go to all this trouble and risk so many lives along with expensive military property to land just outside Bad Penny's base? What purpose could there be for that?

What exactly is going on here?

The weight of the .45 in her hand was a comfort, but she was out gunned and, for all she knew, there might be others just beyond the nearest palms watching and waiting for their chance to move in. To move in and...

"It's been close to an hour," General Spradlin said. He was looking at Alicia Cunningham. The newbie looked exhausted. "Let's take a break."

Alicia Cunningham and Doctor Evans laid the stretcher on the ground. General Spradlin walked to their side.

"How are you two holding up?"

"Fine sir," Alicia said. Despite her words, she was out of breath and tired. It wasn't easy carrying this weight through the slick jungle ground. "At least the rain is gone."

"How about you, Doctor?"

"I can go on a little more, if needed," Evans replied.

Spradlin nodded but said nothing. His attention was on Frank.

"What about you, Captain Masters?"

"Hurts when I laugh," Frank replied and winced. "That's my life. One big comedy."

"Get some rest, Frank. You need it."

Samantha listened intently to the exchange between General Spradlin and her co-pilot.

"They look real cozy," she whispered. There was a rustling from behind her, and Samantha found Becky Waters standing close by. Her hands were in her pocket and, like the others, she was wet from head to toe. Becky leaned against a tree. Her eyes were on Samantha, daring her to elaborate on her thoughts.

Samantha's first instinct was to walk away. There was little reason to talk to the soldier, much less tell her what was on her mind. But she didn't move. Neither, however, did she say anything. After a while, Becky spoke.

"You've got a good eye for details," she said. Her voice was as low as Samantha's.

"What do you mean?" Samantha whispered back.

Becky crouched down before the inlet, as if resting from the walk.

"Nothing," she said. "Just making conversation."

"If you have something to say..."

"Easy, Captain," Becky offered. "I didn't mean to offend."

Samantha stole a quick glance at Becky and noticed that, beneath the outwardly calm features of her face, there was a layer of worry.

"I'm the one who should apologize," Samantha whispered after a few seconds. "It isn't every day you crash land."

"I should hope not."

There was a brief silence before Samantha spoke.

"Have you ever had the feeling you were stuck playing...playing a game? A game you could barely make out?"

Becky didn't reply. She turned away from the inlet and looked deep into Samantha's eyes.

"I've noticed things," Samantha continued.

"Like?"

"Like that General Spradlin gave all the big weapons to the men and stuck us with the handguns."

"Big guns for big boys," Becky replied. "Nothing all that sinister about sexism."

"You know what I'm talking about."

For the next few moments the two were silent. After a while, this silence became uncomfortable. Becky leaned down close to Samantha.

"I know what you're feeling," she said.

Samantha felt a sense of relief.

"If I tell you something, do you promise you won't tell anyone else?"

"I don't know," Becky replied. "Depends on what you have to say."

Samantha grimaced.

"Never mind," she said and stood up. Samantha walked away.

Becky sighed. She followed Samantha.

"OK," Becky said. "I promise I won't tell anyone else. What do you think is going on?"

Samantha grasped a twig from a tree. She motioned Becky a little farther away from the group.

"I took some courses in projectiles and explosives at Southern Command," Samantha said. "Our instructors had us test impact craters and bullet holes and all kinds of fun shit like that."

"And?"

"I'm not saying I'm a genius at this particular science," Samantha said. "There's a reason I became a pilot instead. Anyone who's read a Nancy Drew book can tell you most of what I learned."

"Nancy Drew investigated explosive impacts?"

Despite herself, Samantha let out a chuckle.

"Maybe in the later books," Samantha said. "All right, consider this: Someone's house is burglarized. It doesn't matter what was robbed, but something was taken, and when the house is examined, the police find that one of the first floor windows is broken. Everyone figures that's the way the bad guy got into the house. Only when Nancy Drew or the Hardy Boys or the fucking Bobbsey Twins investigate, the clever little fucks realize there's something suspicious about that broken window. You see, the shattered glass from the window was found lying on the *outside* of the house. But the only way that happens is if someone inside the house smashed the glass out."

"I think I read that book," Becky said.

"So our junior detectives conclude the theft was, literally, an inside job.   Someone who had access to the house was responsible for the theft and, to muddy the waters, smashed that window to make it *seem* like the bad guy came in that way."

"Go on," Becky said.

"Now we move up to bullet impacts," Samantha continued. "Like the shattered glass, damage at the point of impact tends to leave an indentation protruding *into* the target. If the bullet has enough force to exit the target on the other side, we'd find an outward burst there. On the other hand, if, say, explosives were planted inside an object like, say, the tail of a helicopter and detonated, we would see evidence of an outward burst on either side. No indentations."

"Which is what you found."

"It's the *interpretation* of what we found that bothers me."

"Which was?"

"When we got there, General Spradlin's man, Alan Robinson—"

"Captain America," Becky said.

"Captain America takes a few seconds to look over the damage and concludes we were hit by something. I head over there, to see what he's looking at, and tell him we didn't have any missile lock warning and therefore couldn't have been brought down that way. As I'm examining the damage, he tells me we were hit with a high caliber projectile, probably fired from some kind of rifle."

"But you see the glass was on the outside of the house."

"Exactly. Something inside the helicopter's tail blew *out*. It had to be a bomb. A very small one, but big enough."

"You didn't tell General Spradlin?"

"Of course not," Samantha said. "I think Robinson was saying all that shit about projectiles for my benefit."

"General Spradlin knew?"

"I think so."

"That means we can't trust either of them."

"Or Doctor Evans."

Becky nodded.

"It gets worse," Samantha said. "There was at least one more person in on this."

"Who?"

Samantha removed the remote control from her jacket pocket and showed it to Becky.

"I found this on the floor of the cockpit, just under my co-pilot's chair."

Becky Waters looked at the object.

"It's a remote control? What for—"

Becky didn't finish her thought. She drew a sharp breath.

"I think Frank used this to detonate the charge that brought the helicopter down," Samantha said. "He was the only one allowed outside the chopper on Tortuga. I think he planted the device when he was refueling the chopper. He detonated it when we were close to the clearing. "

"So the entire crash was...was planned?"

Samantha put the remote control back in her pocket.

"That's what I think."

Becky let out a low whistle.

"Am I crazy?"

For a second, Becky said nothing. Then...

"I think you're right."

"I may be, but why take such a risk?" Samantha said. "Why make us crash land on the north side of the island? Why not let us land at Bad Penny? There's no logic to any of this."

Becky rubbed her hands and blew into them to warm up. She said:

"When I was a little girl, one of my best friends was deaf. She tried hard to teach me to read lips. I never fully got the hang of it, not like her, but I'm not too bad at it, either. For most of the trip, General Spradlin and his men kept their mouths shut. But they talked a few minutes before the chopper was...was struck down. They were saying strange things, things that didn't make sense."

"Like?"

"Alan Robinson asked if everything would work out, that he was afraid there would be injuries. General Spradlin told him not to worry, that he had faith the plan, whatever it was, was sound."

"That's all?"

"No," Becky replied. "He said another two words, not even a minute before the chopper was hit."

Becky stared deep into Samantha's eyes.

"He told Captain America to, and I quote 'hang on'."

The rustling of leaves in the wind died down until almost all was silent. Samantha felt the chill in the air and couldn't help but shudder.

"Fuck."

Some twenty feet away from them were General Spradlin and Alan Robinson. They were talking in hushed tones, just like Samantha and Becky. Their backs were to the group.

"What the hell are they up to?"

"General Spradlin said the safest place in the world we could be in is a military base," Becky said. "But if you're right, and he and his men orchestrated the downing of our chopper, then maybe they didn't want us to get there. At least not by conventional means."

"What do we do?"

"I don't know," Becky said. "Breaking away from this group is useless on an island this size. There aren't a whole lot of places we could hide for any extended period of time. Besides, we'd eventually have to go somewhere, and the only place we could go..."

"...is back to the base," Samantha said. "Maybe...maybe he doesn't want us to get there at all. Maybe he wants to get rid of us."

"Why? What could we have done that requires that type of drastic action? Other than you and Frank, we're a bunch of low level privates. None of us is worth all this."

Becky pulled out her .45 and released the ammo clip. She removed a cartridge from the clip and showed it to Samantha.

"And then there's this. If they wanted to get rid of us, why give us weapons? I know we don't have the big guns, but we can defend ourselves. If General Spradlin meant to do us harm, he could have come up with any excuse to keep all the weapons for himself and his boys."

"You're right," Samantha said. "And there's one other thing."

"What?"

"Captain America could have also told me back there, when we were looking at the chopper, that we were hit by lightning," Samantha said. "It was what we all thought happened in the first place. By saying we were attacked, he puts us on alert. General Spradlin and his boys *want* us to think we're in danger. He wants us to be ready. I think they *want* us to be able to defend ourselves."

"So the General and his boys sabotage the chopper and bring us down," Becky said. "Logic suggests he's up to no good and means us harm. But the fact that he's armed us and warned us of danger argues *against* this. None of it makes any sense."

"We make terrible Nancy Drews," Samantha said and, despite the tension, laughed.

Becky joined in and shook her head. The laughter died.

"Whatever is going on, it has to be about Bad Penny," she finally said.

"Maybe someone's taken over the base?" Samantha said.

"Who would do that? The Bahamians?"

"Maybe the Cubans."

"Come on. There isn't a nation within hundreds of miles with either the reason, the skills, the manpower or, most importantly, the *balls* to do something like that. And even if there was and even if they did, you think the U.S. fuckin' A. can only muster ten soldiers to deal with their invasion force?"

Samantha and Becky thought some more. They drew blanks.

"Damned if I know what's going on," Becky said. "I'll tell you this much: We'll find out soon enough. I'll keep an eye on General Spradlin. See if I can read any more whispers to his men. Until then, or until he decides to tell us what this is about, the best we can do is keep our eyes open."

"Agreed," Samantha said.

"Good. Let's get back to the group. If we hang together too long, the others might start talking."

"You're not my type," Samantha said.

Becky's right eyebrow arched up.

"You learn something every day," she said.

17

Alan Robinson fiddled with his rifle, checking and rechecking her individual components with robotic precision. His movements were quick and, at times, almost frantic. General Spradlin laid his hand on Robinson's shoulder.

"Easy, soldier," he said. "You're making the others nervous."

"They should be," Robinson replied. His voice was very low.

"True," General Spradlin said.

"We're behind schedule."

"Behind?" Spradlin replied. "By now you should know how these games are played. Any schedule we had was, at best, nothing more than an optimistic guess."

"But if we take much more time…"

"More time? We could have ended this before it began."

"The final option?" Robinson said and shook his head. "Brass disagreed."

"They almost always do."

Alan Robinson eyed his commanding officer.

"And you're making the best of a bad situation?"

"I always do."

Robinson chuckled.

"If you don't mind my saying so, you're one cold blooded bastard, sir. Just how much humanity is left inside there?"

"Enough to know when it's time to cut your losses," Spradlin said.

"We need to find out what happened," Robinson continued. "It's the only way we'll improve."

"You saw the satellite images that came in after Bad Penny went dark," Spradlin said. "It's not too hard to figure out what happened."

"We need details."

"All right, Lieutenant, I'm all ears. What do you recommend we do?"

Robinson pointed to Frank Masters.

"We should leave the injured pilot behind. It's too dangerous—"

"I won't leave anyone behind," Spradlin said. "Especially Captain Masters."

Robinson gazed in the direction of Frank Masters, lying on the stretcher. The pilot was sleeping.

"You're keeping an eye on him?" Robinson asked.

"I'm keeping an eye on everyone," Spradlin said. He was silent for a few seconds before a smile appeared on his lips. "They've given you a nickname, you know."

"Nickname?"

"Captain America."

"Captain America?" Robinson said. "Could be worse. Did I ever tell you what they called you back at Vostok?"

"Do I want to know?"

"No. Not really."

"Those Russians were never ones to hold back. On anything. I miss a couple of them. Fucking bloodbath."

Robinson wiped sweat from his forehead.

"Let me scout ahead and see what, if anything, is coming our way."

"I don't like the idea of breaking the group up."

"Beats the hell out of walking straight into Bad Penny. Unless, of course, you want a repeat of Vostok."

Spradlin thought about that.

"How long have we worked together?"

"Too fucking long."

"These missions require great care. The first mistake..."

"I know," Robinson said.

General Spradlin leaned in closer to Robinson.

"Perhaps we can make use of our time for effectively," Spradlin said. "You're taking along some company."

"Wouldn't have it any other way," Robinson said.

A small smile appeared on Spradlin's face. It disappeared the moment he faced the rest of the helicopter survivors.

"Private Waters and Thompson, could you please come here?"

Becky Waters half turned. Samantha walked behind her.

"Good luck," Samantha whispered.

Becky offered the co-pilot a slight nod. She and Dan Thompson approached Robinson and General Spradlin.

"Yes sir?" they said in unison.

"Colonel Robinson, allow me to formally introduce you to Private Waters. Her record is exemplary."

"Pleased to meet you," Becky said. Though her voice was calm, the inference in General Spradlin's words was clear: *If he knows my record, he knows everyone else's. Just how much did you prepare for this sudden trip?*

Robinson nodded but did not respond to Becky's greeting.

"Private Waters is considered something of an expert in survival skills," Spradlin continued. "She has an affinity for tracking and camouflage. Private Thompson has also passed the tracking courses with a rating of 'superior'."

"Terrific," Robinson said.

"While the others are resting, you will join my first officer on a recon mission," Spradlin said. "I want you three to check out the next mile of terrain. Keep your eyes open but do not, I repeat, do not engage with any individual or individuals out there, be they hostile *or* friendlies. At this point in time, and until we reach Bad Penny, we have to assume anyone and everyone in this forest outside our group is a hostile and therefore responsible for bringing us down. If you see anyone, you high tail it back here, understood?"

"Yes sir," Becky and Thompson said.

"You understand what we are doing is not a training exercise, right?" Robinson said. "Are we clear?"

"Yes sir," Becky and Thompson said.

"And you?" General Spradlin asked Robinson.

"Couldn't be clearer, sir."

"Then get going."

"Follow me," Robinson said.

With that, the trio wandered off into the forest. Once gone, Spradlin returned to the group. He stopped next to Frank Masters and Doctor Evans. The pilot's wound was freshly bandaged but a faint ring of blood seeped through, staining the otherwise immaculate white surface. Spradlin again stared into the forest, where Robinson and the two passengers disappeared. If he was thinking anything at all about the departed trio, he didn't say.

Howard Bartlett ignored General Spradlin movements and, for what felt like the millionth time, stared at Jennie Light. He'd already stuck out with Becky Waters (*stuck up bitch*) and Alicia Cunningham (*too damn green...it's like trying to date a pre-schooler*) and knew the chopper's pilot had an MP boyfriend (*that's all I need when I get back to Bad Penny, have an MP breathing down my ass*), which left him with Jennie.

He shook his head. Perhaps it was the rush of adrenaline, the fact that they survived what seemed like certain death, that he now felt so damn...horny. That and the fact that Jennie Light was an absolute knockout, easily one of the prettiest women he had ever seen.

You say that about all of them, don't you?

Bartlett stifled a laugh. And why the hell not? This is life. There is no dress rehearsal. You go through this ride once, so why not make the best of it and have all the fun you can?

Bartlett smiled. The direct approach was always the best. It might not always work, but it worked often enough. He slowly approached Jennie Light's side.

Keep it subtle, don't look too damn desperate.

It took a few minutes, but between the time General Spradlin ordered the group to rest and shortly after he sent out his scouts, Howard Bartlett found himself standing beside Jennie Light. Like him, she too was soaked. Her short blonde hair hung limp just above her shoulders in stark contrast to the well groomed strands she had on board the helicopter. He didn't see her shake, but he could tell she was miserable. A pretty girl like her wasn't used to these conditions.

I'll warm you right up if you give me a chance.

"Some shit we're stuck in," Bartlett said. "Can't wait to get back to the barracks and take a warm shower."

"What's the matter? You got something against freezing cold rain?"

Bartlett managed a relieved grin. Anything short of her telling him to fuck off was progress.

"About as much as I like gum," he said.

"That makes two of us," Jennie offered. She smiled.

Bartlett let out a laugh. More progress. He motioned to the forest.

"You know," he said. "The more I think about this, the more I think it's all bullshit. They say we were shot down and the General's forcing us to slink around the forest like Hansel and fucking Gretel. What if he's wrong? What if it *was* lightning that brought us down? No one showed me any piece of solid evidence to suggest otherwise."

"What type of evidence do you need?"

"I don't know. Shrapnel. Hell, a bullet fragment. Anything."

"You got a point," Jennie said. She leaned against a palm and ran her hands through her soggy hair.

"They're wasting our time," Bartlett continued. "I'm sure of it."

"The military wasting our time," Jenny replied. Her voice was cool yet playful. "What's the world coming to?"

The grin on Bartlett's face broadened.

"All this sitting around is getting on my nerves, you know? We could be doing other things, moving along."

"Yeah."

Bartlett looked from side to side. The conversation was going fine. Better than fine. It was time to play his hand.

"What say we head out, do a little reconnaissance of our own?"

"Why would I want to head out into the forest? Especially with you?"

Bartlett's smile remained on his face. It was time to bring out the big guns. While making sure no one saw him, he reached into his jacket pocket. He produced a bottle of vodka and gave Jennie a peek.

"It's a pint," Bartlett said. "I'm willing to share."

The sight of the vodka produced a slight but noticeable change in Jennie Light's face.

"At the very least, we warm ourselves up," Bartlett continued. "It's better than sitting around doing nothing."

"And much better than chewing gum," Jennie said and giggled. "How the hell did you smuggle that into Bad Penny?"

"Professional secret," Bartlett said. "You coming or what?"

"Sure," Jennie said. "But we can't just walk away."

Bartlett offered Jennie a wink.

"Leave that to me."

Bartlett left Jennie and approached General Spradlin. He offered the General a salute.

"Yes, Private?" Spradlin said.

"Begging your pardon, sir," Bartlett responded. "You sent your man ahead for the purpose of reconnaissance."

"Yes I did," Spradlin said.

"Sir, perhaps we should also worry about what lies behind us," Bartlett said. "If a hostile force brought us down, they may be tracking us as we speak. It would be wise to check. To make sure."

Spradlin thought about this for a few seconds, a pause much longer than Bartlett was comfortable with.

"I could go out and get back in no more than fifteen minutes, sir."

"I won't let you go alone."

Bartlett fought hard to suppress a smile. That's exactly what he was hoping the General would say.

"Agreed," Bartlett continued. He made a show of looking around at the other soldiers in the camp. "Private Alicia Cunningham is a nice officer in training. However, at this point she lacks the experience for recon."

"Yes," General Spradlin said. "And Doctor Evans should stay with the injured pilot."

"I would take Captain Aron," Bartlett continued. "However, while I have no doubt she's an excellent pilot, I'm not so sure she'll be an asset in the forest."

"Which leaves Private Light and me," Spradlin said.

Bartlett held his breath. This was it. Make or break time.

"You should stay here, sir," Bartlett said. "You're our senior officer. You need to coordinate our actions, not risk yourself on recon."

Spradlin thought some more. He nodded.

"Private Light it is," Spradlin said. He removed his M-16 from his shoulder and handed it to Bartlett. "I'm not sure what might be out there, Private, but if we are in danger, you'll need maximum protection. Give this to Private Light. Tell her to give Private Cunningham her .45."

Bartlett took the rifle. He once again suppressed a smile.

You did it. You got exactly what you wanted. Some alone time with Jennie Light.

"I'll get going, sir," Bartlett said. He offered a sharp salute. General Spradlin didn't reciprocate. Instead, he leaned in close to the soldier and said:

"She's an attractive girl."

"...sir...?"

Spradlin's face drew to within inches of Bartlett's.

"This isn't a high school field trip," Spradlin said.

Bartlett mustered as much indignity as he could and said:

"Sir, I'm a married man. I have a pregnant wife."

"Who no doubt misses you a little more than you miss her," Spradlin fired back. "You've got fifteen minutes."

Bartlett managed another salute. It was far less crisp. He returned to Jennie Light's side and handed her the M-16. He told her to give Alicia her .45.   When Jennie was done with the exchange, Bartlett muttered:

"Let's go."

General Spradlin watched Privates Bartlett and Light walk away from the clearing. He said nothing as they disappeared into the bushes. He eyed the portable communication device lying on the floor in front of him and considered his next action. After several long seconds he grabbed it and stepped into the middle of the makeshift camp.

Alicia Cunningham sat to the side, her arms wrapped around her, trying to keep warm. Even from a few feet away, he could tell her teeth were chattering. Doctor Evans remained crouched over the injured Frank Masters, and Samantha Aron watched the two while sitting on a fallen palm that lay a few feet away. Everything seemed tranquil.

Spradlin let out a sigh.

"We'll rest another fifteen minutes," he said. "If the others aren't back by then, we leave. They'll have to catch up."

His words hung in the air like a poison cloud. The remaining passengers didn't reply. They hardly noticed as General Spradlin walked off after Howard Bartlett and Jennie Light.

18

The jungle was thick with trees and bushes. Alan Robinson peered between leaves, trying to see as far ahead as he could. Now that the cold front had passed, the clear night sky was visible. A half-moon gave off enough light to see a dozen or so feet ahead.

Dan Thompson and Becky Waters carefully followed Robinson's lead. Becky Waters paid particular attention to their sides, while Thompson watched their back. All eyes were wide open, taking in everything.

It was ten minutes since they left the camp, and Thompson figured they were no more than a fifth of a mile from the others. Slogging through the thick jungle, especially with a man on a stretcher, and especially at night while trying not to make too much noise, would not be easy. Without thinking, Thompson reached into his chest pocket. He placed a cigarette in his mouth.

"Put that away," Robinson hissed. "You want someone to spot us?"

Thompson was startled by Robinson's words. Even more so when he realized what he was about to do.

"Fucking bad habit," he said as he grabbed the cigarette. "I'm sorry sir."

Robinson ignored Thompson's apology. Instead, he addressed Becky Waters.

"You got our bearings, Private?"

Becky stared at the night sky, identifying the constellations.

"Yes sir. Proceeding due south. Right on track."

Robinson nodded. He and Becky continued forward. Thompson stared at the unlit cigarette and shrugged. He tossed it to the ground. His action was detected.

"Jesus Christ, Thompson," Robinson said. "Pick that up. Let's not give our enemies a trail to follow us by."

"Yes sir," Thompson stammered. "I...I'm sorry sir."

Robinson's anger eased almost as quickly as it first appeared.

"Take it easy son," Robinson said. Though his tone was casual, it retained authority. "You're not thinking enough. Remember your training. Let things come naturally."

Thompson swallowed. A stiff wind flared, sending the palm leafs swaying.

"Yes sir," Thompson repeated.

Robinson motioned for the two to follow him. Becky laid her hand on Thompson's shoulder and offered him a supportive nod. She stepped past Thompson and followed Robinson into the brush.

Thompson let out a breath and reached down to pick up his discarded cigarette. A deep frown crossed his forehead.

"Fucking idiot," he chastised himself while straightened up. The unused cigarette lay like so much garbage in his hand. It was water logged and crumpled from the fall. There was no way he could smoke it later.

Useless, Thompson thought. *Just like me.*

The thought added to Thompson's exasperation.

"Only a year more," he muttered and moved forward. During the past year, he thought about whether it was worth it to re-enlist. Sometimes, the idea was appealing. But that desire shrunk with each passing day. Thompson crumbled the soggy cigarette into a ball and slipped it into his pants pocket. He pushed a branch to the side and continued forward. In the near distance, he could make out Robinson and Becky.

He shook his head.

How fucking condescending of you, laying your hand on my shoulder, he thought. *Like I really needed the fucking sympathy.*

Thompson's mind was so clouded with anger that he didn't see the shadowy form until it was far too late.

As if by some dark magic, it materialized right in front of him. Its arms moved so fast Thompson wasn't entirely sure they had.

The Private tried to scream, to alert the others of this sudden threat, but he couldn't open his mouth.

His jaw felt like pudding, wobbly and wet. Confused and horrified, Thompson reached up to feel what had happened to his face.

The shadowy form snapped his neck before the soldier realized his lower jaw was completely gone.

19

Alan Robinson came to a stop. Becky Waters followed suite a few feet behind him. She realized, just as Robinson had, that Thompson was no longer following behind them.

"Where is he?" Robinson said. He raised his M-16.

"I don't know," Becky replied. "Do you want me to—?"

"No," Robinson said. "Not alone."

The two retraced their steps, working back to where they last saw the missing soldier. Their trip was short, but each step they took without finding the missing Private raised their fear that they would never find him.

"Thompson?" Robinson whispered as loud as he dared. "Where are you?"

There was no reply. After a few more seconds of searching, Robinson stopped and shook his head. They had already passed the last place they saw him.

"Colonel?" Becky said.

She pointed at the jungle floor. Almost buried under the damp leaves and grass were three cigarettes. Robinson picked one up.

"They're dry, for the most part," he said. "They're Private Thompson's."

Robinson continued to look around, but Becky noted his movements were slow. It appeared Robinson wasn't so much searching for the missing soldier as he was bracing for an attack.

"We have to move on," Robinson finally said.

"What about Thompson?"

"Either he's headed back to camp or somehow passed us by," Robinson said. "If he headed back to camp, we'll find him there. If he passed us by, we'll find him on the way to the base."

"He didn't pass us," Becky said. "And he's not the type that would go back to camp alone."

"What exact type is he?"

"The type that doesn't show enough initiative to do anything on his own. Not without telling us."

"Your file said you could read people's lips. Can you do the same with people's minds, Private?"

Becky swallowed her surprise as best she could. *What don't these people know about us?*

"Just enough to know when I'm being fed stories."

To Becky's surprise, Alan Robinson let out a laugh.

"What do you think happened to him?" Becky asked.

Robinson didn't answer. Instead, he shrugged, as if it that were answer enough.

"Sir, he's one of ours," Becky insisted. "We can't just write him off and hope everything works out later."

"I don't know what happened to him," Robinson said.

"Begging your pardon, sir, but that's a load of bullshit."

"You've got something more you want to say, Private?"

"Plenty, sir," Becky replied.

"Good. Keep it to yourself. This isn't the time or the place."

Even as the words left his mouth, Robinson froze. Very, very slowly, he motioned to the bushes in front of them. Though there was no wind, the bushes moved.

"We've got more important things to worry about," Robinson whispered.

Howard Bartlett stepped through the brush with a swagger. To the greenery around him, he acted as though he were king of this particular jungle.

His M-16 dangled off his shoulder and his clothing were drying nicely even in the chilly air. A smile brightened his face. He was walking behind Jennie Light, and he was enjoying the hell out of that view.

"It's just you and me now," he said.

Jennie Light gave Bartlett a sour look.

"The only reason I agreed to this little field trip was because I could use some warming up," Jennie said. "And by that, I don't mean anything more than that drink you've got."

The smile on Bartlett's face grew. He reached into his jacket pocket and pulled out the pint of vodka.

"By all means, fair lady," he said and handed the liquor to Jennie Light.

She unscrewed the cap and took a sip. Her lips compressed, her eyes closed. She nodded.

"Now we're talking," she said.

"I'm here to serve."

Jennie eyed Bartlett. He was staring at her and doing a bad job at containing a growing lust.

"Tell me, Bartlett—"

"Call me Howard."

"Tell me, Bartlett, you really think there's nothing to this? Getting redirected to Tortuga and taking on a trio of spooks before getting shot the fuck down?"

"Oh, something's going on all right," Bartlett said. "But I'll bet all this shit we've been through is about those spooks and not us. As soon as we get back to the base, we'll be debriefed and sent on our way. An hour or two of misery and we're fine."

"You're very optimistic."

"Always."

"Well I'm not," Jennie said. "So do me a favor, keep your eyes on everything *but* me. I'm not about to risk my life because you're feeling an itch."

Bartlett let out a laugh.

Fifteen feet away, hidden behind the brush, General Spradlin heard Bartlett's laugh. He eased forward and kept his body low to the ground. Spradlin estimated he was no more than fifteen feet away. In this dense jungle and at night, fifteen feet might as well be a hundred miles. The two soldiers he was following wouldn't see him, but he made sure he was close enough to keep track of them.

"Don't worry, princess," Bartlett said. "I'll get you to your castle in one piece and I won't let myself get distracted. Afterwards, when this is all done, we go out. I know a real nice restaurant in Coconut Grove."

"Do I have a say in this matter?"

"As long as what you say is 'yes'."

"No problem," Jennie replied. "We go to town while your wife takes care of the newborn. You don't think she'll mind, do you?"

Bartlett let out another laugh. Spradlin, still hidden behind the bushes, bristled. Not only was Bartlett a fool, he was a very *loud* fool.

"That can be our little secret," Bartlett said.

"Do you even have a wife?"

"Certainly," Bartlett said. "She's nice and fat and pregnant, just waiting for me to get back to her."

"Really? Here I was thinking all that was just talk and you were hoping the General would feel enough for your sorry ass to let you go."

"I knew it couldn't hurt," Bartlett replied.

Jennie Light screwed the cap back on the vodka and tossed it to Bartlett.

"Thanks for the drink," she said. "Time to get back. I've had enough of your company."

"So has my loving wife," Bartlett said. He cradled the vodka. "You want to know the truth? All right, here it is: She and I are done. I've been stationed five different bases over the past year. I can count on one hand the number of times I've been with that bitch during that time, so forgive me if I'm a little suspicious about my loving, devoted wife's pregnancy. Odds of that kid being mine aren't all that great. Either way, it doesn't matter. Last time I talked to her, she said she was seeing a lawyer. I figure I'm heading home to sign the divorce papers."

"Why would anyone want to lose someone as precious as you?"

"At least I'm honest," Bartlett said. "Besides, I'm not such a bad guy. Give me a chance and I'll prove it."

It was Jennie's turn to laugh.

"You're so full of shit," she said. "How much of *that* was true?"

"All of it," Bartlett said. He raised his right hand. "Scout's honor."

Jennie Light motioned to the bottle.

"Give me some more of that," she said.

The smile on Bartlett's face returned. He once again handed her the vodka.

General Spradlin eased in closer. He saw the two soldiers clearly now. He watched as Howard Bartlett handed Jennie Light the vodka. By the tone of her voice and her posture, it was clear the two were getting along a little better.

But General Spradlin wasn't interested in their fraternization. If there was ever a bad time for that...

"About that restaurant in the Grove," Bartlett said as Jennie Light took another shot of the liquor. "The place is open air, practically on the water. It's got a real European vibe, if you know what I mean."

"Sounds great. I'll expect your invitation the moment your divorce is finalized."

"Come on," Bartlett said. "Why wait? Life is short. You should enjoy every second."

"Now that's a real original line. I'll bet you used it on your wife back in the day."

"Come on."

"I thought so."

"Look, Jennie, we go out, have a couple of rounds, maybe even a few laughs. What's the harm? It'll be on my dime any—"

Bartlett didn't finish his thoughts. The smile on his face disappeared and he straightened up. His entire body tensed.

"What is it?" Jennie said. She drew her handgun and looked around.

In the bush, General Spradlin also tensed. He clicked his gun's safety off. He was ready to rush out.

"What is it?" Jennie repeated.

Bartlett leaned in close to Jennie Light, his lips only inches away from her ear. They quivered.

"I know your problem," he whispered. "You have a boyfriend, right?"

Jennie Light pushed Bartlett away. The mischievous grin returned to the soldier's face. Jennie shook her head and thrust the gun back into her pant pocket.

"You're a riot," she said. Despite her anger, Bartlett noted a small grin appear on to her face as well. The vodka and his persistence were working their magic.

"I showed you mine, I figure you show me yours," Bartlett said in mock innocence. "Don't make me spin my wheels if you're committed."

"Of course," Jennie retorted. "Why would I even think of doing that?"

"Are you with someone?"

"That's none of your business."

"C'mon," Bartlett said. "Make nice. If you and I were to go out just one time, it wouldn't hurt anyone. No hassles, no hang-ups, and all the honesty you can handle. Don't tell me you aren't tempted even a little? We have a great meal and some drinks and afterwards, I rub your shoulders and I'll even let you rub mine. If you play your cards right, I'll let you rub me all over."

This time, it was Jennie Light whose face turned from mirth to seriousness. Bartlett noted the change in her face. He continued to smile, hoping to find another crack in the ice, but her expression remained dead serious. Her eyes scanned the bushes to the north. Her hand returned to her gun, still tucked in her pocket.

"What is it?" Bartlett whispered.

Jennie Light said nothing. Her gaze shifted, this time to the north east. She noted a dip in the ground some twenty feet away. Runoff from the rain had formed a puddle of mud. Beyond it was the darkness of the jungle. Jennie Light moved down the dip and approached the puddle, stopping only a foot away from it. In the evening gloom it was a miniature pool, dark and eerie. Jennie crouched down close to the puddle's edge.

"What?" Bartlett whispered. His hands were on the M-16. He brought the weapon up and aimed it in the direction Jennie Light was looking.

Jennie Light motioned Bartlett to her side. The Private followed Jennie's lead and also crouched down, stopping next to her.

"What time is it?" Jennie Light whispered.

Bartlett blinked several times.

"What the hell kind of question is that?"

"What time is it?" Jennie repeated. Her voice was strong, impatient.

Without thinking, Bartlett lowered the rifle and looked down at his wristwatch. As he did, Jennie Light spun around and, with all her might, pushed the crouching soldier.

Howard Bartlett fell in a heap into the puddle of water and mud.

General Spradlin watched Bartlett fall. Though his face remained impassive, a small grin worked its way to the corner of the General's mouth.

Jennie Light stood up and took a step back to savor the results of her handiwork. Howard Bartlett sat on the ground, confused, muddy, and soaked.

"What the *fuck*?" he yelled.

"I'll tell you what time it is, you fucking creep," Jennie Light said. "Time to get back to camp."

Bartlett gasped, incredulous at what Jennie had done. Jennie walking away but paused in mid-stride.

"Coming?" she said.

Bartlett's face turned bright red. He rose from the muddy puddle and gripped his weapon. As he staggered from the filth, one of his boots remained stuck in the mud. He couldn't move without losing it.

Jennie let out a laugh but belated realized she had pushed the Private too far. He screamed in fury and gripped his weapon. Jennie couldn't believe what she was seeing. Would he actually fire at her? Jennie let out a shriek and ran, right into the arms of General Spradlin.

"G...General?" she said and stepped back.

Behind her, Bartlett lowered his weapon. The fury in his face dissolved into embarrassment. General Spradlin examined the two, his face cold granite.

"You've had your fun," he said. "Let's move."

Howard Bartlett wiped the mud from his face and swore.

I'll get you, he thought. *I'll get you, but good.*

There would be plenty of opportunities. They were still a few miles from Bad Penny and moving slower than a fucking turtle.

Yes, there would be *plenty* of opportunities.

Bartlett reached down and pulled at his stuck boot. The mud was like a suction cup. It held the boot in its grasp and wouldn't let go.

"For fuck's sake," Bartlett muttered. He was a complete mess, muddy and wet and furious. He heard someone giggle. It was her.

Laugh, bitch, Bartlett thought. *The last laugh would be—*

Bartlett froze. The giggle came from in front of him. Jennie Light and General Spradlin were behind him.

"What the hell?" he said.

The giggling stopped and the bushes before him rustled.

"Who's there?" Bartlett said.

The bushes rustled some more. Something was moving very fast. It crashed through the vegetation and was coming directly at him.

"What the fuck?!" he yelled. He grabbed for his weapon but his hands were slick from the mud and he didn't get a good grip of the M-16. His mind barely registered the sleek black form explode out of the jungle.

It was the last thing he would ever see.

20

At the makeshift camp, the remaining passengers of the *Little Charlie* killed time, oblivious to what was happening outside their private little world.

Doctor Evans adjusted the bandage around Frank's leg for the fourth time before getting up and stretching.

"Damn arthritis," he muttered.

Sitting a few feet away from them was Alicia Cunningham. Her short brown hair was, like her clothing, mostly dry. Her army fatigues returned to their original light green color. Despite all this, the poor girl looked miserable and lost.

Doctor Evans walked to the girl's side.

"How are you doing?" he asked.

"Not so good," Alicia replied. She tried, but failed, to stop shivering. It was difficult to tell if this was the result of the cool temperature or the situation.

"We're close to home," Evans said. "Very close."

"I hope we get there soo...soon," she said through chattering teeth.

Doctor Evans sat beside her.

"We'll make it," he said. "After everything we've been through, we damn well better."

Alicia nodded but the worry remained in her face. Her entire body shook.

"Don't take this the wrong way," Doctor Evans said. "But if you'd like, we can warm each other up a bit."

Alicia looked at Doctor Evans. For a second she stared at his face, at the lines on his forehead. She let out a frightened little laugh.

"On any other day, I'd say that was the clumsiest pick-up line I'd ever heard," she said. "Today...today I could really use the company."

Doctor Evans put his arm around her shoulders. Alicia leaned into the Doctor's body. As she did, she heaved. She took a series of sharp breaths and, when she couldn't contain herself anymore, let out a loud sob.

Samantha Aron, seated on a toppled palm a few feet away, watched Doctor Evans huddle with Alicia. After the newbie starting crying, she could no longer look. She sympathized with the young soldier. Things had gone to hell quickly and only now, a short while after the crash, was her mind beginning to process all the events leading to now. Even so, the others had adjusted far better than the newbie.

She shouldn't be here, Samantha thought. The pilot looked at Frank. Her co-pilot was sleeping. His breathing was deep and every now and again he let out a soft snore. It was almost drowned out by Alicia's sobs.

Almost.

Samantha gritted her teeth and walked to Frank Masters' side. Though his face was placid, his skin was pale. His eyes twitched now and again. If he was sleeping, he was dreaming.

Hope you're having one hell of a nightmare, Samantha thought.

Of the people aboard the *Little Charlie* when she crashed, Frank was easily the worst off. But, unlike Alicia, Samantha found it hard to muster any sympathy for the man she once thought, not so very long ago, a friend and confidant.

What did you do? Why did you do it?

He knew what all this was about –the deviation to Tortuga, the crash landing– and he kept it to himself. He kept it from *her.*

She had a stray memory of sitting with Frank in the Bad Penny Cantina and sharing a couple of drinks. They were talking and, more often than not, laughing at some silly joke. Toward the end of their stay, Frank introduced Samantha to a very shy officer who he said was desperate to meet her. His name was Warren Bligh.

Samantha remembered rolling her eyes and biting her tongue. Her first instinct was to tell Frank to mind his own fucking business. But she played along, knowing there was no way she and that army rat would ever find anything in common. Besides, her focus was on her career. She neither wanted nor *needed* anyone. Samantha figured the conversation with Warren would be a royal pain and in the end she'd be polite yet firm in letting him down.

Funny how things don't work out the way you planned.

To Samantha's surprise, Warren proved a sympathetic soul. The two clicked like old lovers, and a very good phase of her life, up through today, began. Each day she was with Warren was special in its own way, and each time she had to fly out of Bad Penny she missed the hell out of his company. Since then, every time she made that trip and looked over at her co-pilot, she realized just how thankful she was for introducing Warren to her. From that moment on, she realized Frank was someone she could count on. Someone she could trust.

You were the big brother I never had.

The anger within Samantha bubbled up.

Yeah, right.

She grasped the remote control in her pocket. Her grip was tight, so tight she had to force herself to release the device, lest it shatter in her hand.

The truth is I don't know you at all, Frank. I never did and probably never will.

"You going to stand there all pissed off or are you going to tell me what's on your mind?" Frank muttered.

Samantha took a step back and controlled her surprise. Frank was awake, looking up at her. After taking a few seconds to compose herself, Samantha leaned down closer to the injured pilot.

"Why did you do it, Frank?" she asked.

From somewhere behind her, Samantha heard Alicia's sobs.

"*How* could you do it?"

"What—?" Frank began. Before he could complete his question, Samantha pulled the small black remote control device from her pocket and held it before his face.

"Where did you find it?" he asked.

"On the cockpit floor."

"Must have dropped it when I smashed my knee," Frank said.

"Must have," Samantha repeated. "Colonel Robinson lied about us being shot down. We weren't shot down. We were sabotaged. An explosive device was planted in the helicopter's tail. A device set off by a remote control unit. *This* unit. You set off the explosive, didn't you?"

For a second it looked like Frank might plead innocence. For only a second. He closed his eyes and nodded.

"There's more to this," Frank said.

"I'm listening."

Frank took a few seconds to collect his thoughts.

"I've known –*knew*– General Spradlin for many years. All the way back to Desert Storm. He was something of a legend around our team. Back then, we were all green and scared shitless while he was in total control. He calmed us down, trained us hard, and had us ready to fight. When it was time for us to do so, we didn't hesitate. Thanks to him, we came through."

"That's all really fascinating, Frank, but even if General Spradlin is the reincarnation of Washington, Grant, Patton, *and* Eisenhower, it doesn't explain why the fuck you sabotaged the helicopter."

Frank sighed.

"Isn't it obvious?" he said. "General Spradlin ordered me to."

The words hung in the air like fallout from a dirty bomb. Though Samantha strongly suspected it, hearing it confirmed so bluntly took the wind out of her. For several seconds, neither Frank nor Samantha said anything.

"He tells you to sabotage a U.S. military helicopter loaded with personnel and you just go ahead and do it?"

"The explosive wasn't strong enough to destroy the—"

"How the hell did you know?" Samantha said. "What if Spradlin miscalculated? What if his little bomb wasn't quite as little as he thought? What if you didn't find that clearing like you were supposed to?"

"You knew about that, too?"

"It didn't take all that long for everything to fall into place," Samantha said. "At first I was so fucking thankful you spotted that clearing I didn't bother to think *how* you knew it was there and why you could see it from such an impossible distance. You knew where it was and you knew where we were so all you had to do was set off the charge at the right time and at the right place and point out where we needed to land."

"I'm a soldier, Samantha. What else could I do? General Spradlin's my commanding officer. Whatever he tells me to do, I fucking do."

"Come on, Frank, don't feed me the old 'I was only following orders' bullshit."

"He's my superior."

"And *he's* got a bunch of superiors above him. If you're ordered to sabotage a very expensive piece of military equipment and put the lives of soldiers in jeopardy, shouldn't you have taken at least a few seconds to double check his orders?"

"When? You were there. We had no time."

"That's bullshit and you know it," Samantha said. She shook her head. "Let me get this straight: We get diverted to Tortuga and, while we're being treated like lepers on that landing pad, you're called out under the pretext of refueling the chopper."

"It wasn't a pretext," Frank said. "That's all I was going to do."

"And while you're out there, General Spradlin and his boys show up and have their chat with you."

"That's when he gave me the orders," Frank said. "Colonel Robinson left the explosive and the remote next to the refueling pump. He's the one that told me where to place the charge."

"Go on."

"General Spradlin said if I place the explosive exactly where Robinson told me to, the device would cause enough damage to force us down, but not enough to blow us out of the sky."

"Why did he want you to do this? Why did the General want us to land in that clearing?"

"I don't know, Samantha, I swear. I asked, but he didn't tell me why he wanted this done, only that I had to do it."

"And instead of telling General Spradlin and his boys to check themselves into the nearest mental ward you say 'Sure, why the fuck not'."

Frank lay back down and closed his eyes.

"I thought I knew you, Frank," Samantha continued. "I thought you were one of the smart ones. I was so fucking wrong. You've got everyone staring at shadows, scared shitless, when the boogeymen are right here, walking among us."

Samantha could no longer look at her partner. Alicia's cries continued. They felt like knives digging into her brain. Involuntarily, Samantha hands balled into fists. There was one last question she needed to ask. One final question before she could no longer stomach the sight of Frank ever, ever again.

"Back when we were ordered to land at Tortuga, the central operator told you to observe red alpha protocol. What the hell is that?"

"It's...it's an old code, from the original Desert Storm," Frank said. "It means some really nasty shit is about to go down."

21

Colonel Alan Robinson and Private Becky Waters stood eight feet away from the rustling bush and aimed their weapons at it. Robinson's grip on his weapon, however, was not as tight as Becky's.

Through the corner of her eye, she noticed Robinson held the rifle with his left hand only. His right hand dropped to the knife sheath strapped to his belt. Robinson unclipped the sheath's top strap, exposing the knife's dull grey handle. Robinson slowly pulled the weapon from its holster.

Becky was confused by Robinson's actions. How was a knife better protection versus an M-16 rifle? Why would Robinson think of using it at all?

Becky's body tensed. She alternately watched the bush and Robinson's knife as he pulled it out. Now fully exposed, Becky was surprised to find the weapon's body was entirely black instead of the expected shiny silver. Nonetheless, it looked very sharp and high tech. Was the blade made of some kind of sophisticated ceramic?

No.

The knife Robinson carried was the size and had the general shape of a machete but a sharper point. *It was created for stabbing as well as slashing.* Though she was hardly an expert in ceramic knives, Becky knew that while they retained their cutting edge far better than metal knives, they were also brittle. They were good in a kitchen but not as good as offensive weapons, especially if you were trying to slash through bone.

Therefore, the blade Robinson carried was probably not made of ceramic. If it wasn't, then what was it made of?

Robinson eased up next to the bush. He locked eyes with Becky and, soundlessly, mouthed "One". Then "Two".

Becky leaned closer to the bush, forgetting about the strange knife for the moment.

"Three," Robinson said.

Becky and Robinson jumped to either side of the bush. To their surprise, a man in a fetal position lay on the ground. He was dressed completely in black. His face was stained with black grease paint, most of which had rubbed off. The skin below, in stark contrast to the camouflage paint, was a very pale white. The man looked to be in his mid-twenties or very early thirties. He had a lean, athletic build. Before him and lying on the ground was a small black backpack.

"Do you recognize him?" Robinson said. Becky noted Robinson lowered his M-16 and held the eerie black knife close to the stranger's head.

"What?" she asked, confused by Robinson's question.

"From Bad Penny, soldier. Have you seen him before?"

"No sir," Becky replied. "But I couldn't swear…"

"You don't need to," Robinson said. He released the M-16 and moved in closer to the intruder.

"What the fuck?!"

When they heard Howard Bartlett scream those words, Jennie Light and General Spradlin spun around.

General Spradlin's mind whirled. He watched in horror as a black humanoid *thing* burst like a living nightmare from the bushes behind Howard Bartlett. Leaves and branches flew in all directions. The figure ignored the havoc and lashed out. Its right hand slammed with incredible force into Bartlett's face. General Spradlin heard a grotesque crack before the two bodies fell into the muddy puddle. Water splashed at Jennie and Spradlin's feet.

Upon hitting the muddy water, Bartlett's body went limp. The creature nonetheless continued its attack. It slashed at the soldier's neck, almost severing head from body and staining the muddy water until it was a deep red. The creature's head, like its body, was sleek and formless. It moved back and forth, taking in its surroundings while the creature's arms made sure Bartlett was beyond giving any resistance at all. Every one of the creature's movements was precise, mechanical.

Robotic.

Once done examining its surroundings, the creature turned its attention to the wrecked body of Howard Bartlett. It took only a few seconds to look its victim over and assure itself that he was indeed dead. Then, the creature's formless head turned a full one hundred and eighty degrees until it settled on Jennie Light and General Spradlin.

For several seconds, the dark attacker held still. The features on its face vibrated. After a few seconds, an opening –a mouth!– formed on its jet black face.

"I know a real nice restaurant in Coconut Grove," the dark shape said. Its voice was garbled and the words sounded like a mechanical grunt. The inflection, however, was recognizable.

"Sir?" Jennie Light whispered.

"Easy," General Spradlin said.

"The way I figure, the odds of that kid being mine aren't all that great, you know?" the creature continued. The second attempt at speech was much clearer than the first. The mechanical edge was almost gone. "Look, Jennie, we go out, have a couple of rounds, maybe even a few laughs. What's the harm?"

Jennie Light's hand came to her mouth.

"What...what the hell is this thing?"

Spradlin grabbed Jennie Light by her arm and pulled her toward him. As he did, the PCOM slipped from his hands and fell to the muddy ground. It slipped down the incline, stopping at the edge of the puddle.

Its motion caught the creature's attention.

The creature released Howard Bartlett and stood up. It walked to the edge of the puddle and leaned down close to the PCOM.

Bartlett's body, no longer pinned down, floated to the surface of the muddy water. Despite the mud and filth, Jennie and Spradlin saw what remained of Bartlett's face. It was caved in and unrecognizable. Tissue and bone fragments oozed out of the destroyed skin that had once been nose, cheeks, and forehead. His left eyeball was gone. His right eyeball floated on the water beside his head, connected to his shattered face by a line of viscera.

The creature finished its examination of the PCOM and walked out of the puddle. It stepped on the device, flattening it.

Spradlin's grasp on Jennie Light's arm tightened.

"Run," he yelled.

22

Alan Robinson and Becky Waters stood at either side of the darkly dressed man. Robinson released his M-16 and allowed it to hang loose on his shoulder. He had both hands on the long black knife.

If you aren't going to use the M-16, you could give it to me, Becky thought. *Maybe he's not so much Captain America as he is Tarzan.*

Still, Becky felt that if the black blade was, to Robinson, a more powerful weapon than the M-16, then her puny .45 handgun was less than worthless.

"Who are you?" Robinson asked the man in black.

"Sir," Becky Waters said. "General Spradlin told us not to engage—"

The man on the ground looked up. His eyes were wide with terror.

"Please don't hurt me," he whimpered.

"He's British," Robinson said. The accent was strong.

Robinson's eyes drifted to the man's backpack. It was open and a miniature camera protruded from its top.

"Who are you?" Robinson repeated.

"The man's in shock," Becky said.

"Maybe," Robinson muttered before bending down to reach for the backpack.

Robinson pulled it close to his body and reached inside. Along with the camera he found a pair of binoculars, a small rectangular box, and a Heckler & Koch .45 with a silencer/flash suppressor. Robinson smelled its barrel. It hadn't been fired.

"Any I.D.?" Becky asked.

"None," he said. "Given his gear, I didn't expect any. See this?"

Robinson pointed to the binoculars.

"They look like a typical pair of binoculars, right?" Robinson said. "They're not. See the buttons on the side? Digital image enhancement and intensification. Night vision."

Robinson put the binoculars back and pulled out the camera. He looked it over.

"This might tell us what we need to know about this gentleman," Robinson said. "Mini digital, no brand name or identification. I'm guessing it takes some very high definition photographs and video. Likely has some kind of connectivity, should you need to send out your images."

"What was he taking pictures of?"

Robinson turned the camera over.

"Don't know," he said. "Camera's got no LCD screen. I'll have to get its memory card to a computer to see whatever it was he took."

Becky pointed to the small metal box.

"And that?"

"SOS," Robinson said. He slid the front of the box open, revealing a small button. "Short range transmitter, waterproof, fireproof, damn near explosive proof. Allows you to tell whoever's on the receiving end you're in trouble."

"Which is why he's also got a handgun," Becky said. "Not your typical lost tourist gear, I take it?"

"Not by a long shot," Robinson replied. "What we have here is a British Special Forces operative."

"Special Forces? You mean a spy?"

"Yes."

"For the British Government?"

"I don't know many Cuban nationals who talk with a strong British accent."

"What is he doing here?"

"I'll tell you what he wasn't doing: Taking pictures of the island's native flora and fauna."

"He's spying on Bad Penny?" Becky said. "He's spying on *us*?"

"Of course."

"Maybe I'm not up on current events, but aren't we supposed to be allies with the British?"

"No 'supposed to be' about it," Robinson said. "We are allies, but that doesn't stop us from sniffing around each other's playgrounds now and again."

"Sniffing around?"

"Call it verification. Making sure everything's going fine and we're still pals and all."

"Is everything going fine?"

Robinson shrugged.

"What's going on at Bad Penny?" Becky asked. "Did it have something to do with him?"

"That I don't know."

"The hell you don't," Becky said. "Ever since you, General Spradlin and that Doctor came aboard our helicopter, we've been strung along like puppets. You know a hell of a lot more than what you're saying."

"That'll be all," Robinson said. The tone in his voice meant it.

Robinson pocketed the Heckler and Koch, closed the backpack, and handed it to Becky. The private took the offered backpack and stared at it. Though she tried, she could no longer contain herself.

"General Spradlin knew the helicopter was going to be hit," she said.

Robinson shook his head and grinned.

"How long did it take you to figure that out?"

Becky was surprised by Robinson's lack of surprise.

"I know," she said. "And so do others in the group. We may not have all the facts, but we're not idiots either."

"I never thought you were," Robinson said. "Look, this'll all make sense, eventually. You'll just have to trust me when I say what we're doing here is the right thing, and that this guy may have the answers to many of my questions."

He reached down and grabbed the intruder under his left arm. "For now, how about we shelve this discussion until—"

Robinson's thought remained unfinished. When he tried to lift the man in black he found him an immovable object. The man was virtually welded to the jungle floor. Robinson let out a yell and tried to jump away.

He was too late.

The man in black's left arm snapped against his body, pinning Robinson's hand in place. The figure tightened its arm some more, sending crushing forces at either side of Robinson's trapped hand. Robinson gasped as the sickening sound of breaking bones filled the area. Despite his agony, Robinson faced Becky and yelled:

"Get out of here!"

Becky, however, stayed in place. Spurts of blood flowed from Robinson's crushed hand. She couldn't let him suffer. Becky lifted her gun and aimed it at the figure in black's lowered head.

"Let him go!" she screamed.

The figure stirred and Becky stepped back.

"I mean it!"

The figure stirred again. Its head, facing down and away from Robinson, turned at an impossibly sharp angle to look directly at her before coming face to face with Robinson. The figure's face was still for only a second and then, as if it were made of living clay, shifted. Skin stretched and bubbled. The figure's cheekbone rose and its forehead lengthened. Eyebrows and hair turned from black to brown. Wrinkles appeared under the thing's eyes. Its face changed...

Changed until it looked like Robinson!

The thing stared at its counterpart's face, as if checking to make sure every line and wrinkle were in their proper place. Yet there was a noticeable difference. The color of the real Robinson's skin was more natural than the shiny plastic in his counterpart. In spite of this, it was real enough to fool anyone. At least for a little while.

"I asked you a question," the thing said. Like its skin, the voice was also artificial. "Who are you?"

The thing paused for no more than a couple of seconds.

"Who the hell are you?" it repeated a second time. The mechanical edge wasn't as noticeable.

"Go," the real Robinson gasped.

Instead of doing so, Becky walked up to the unreal Robinson and aimed her .45 at the thing's forehead. She fired twice at point blank range. The bullet splattered against its head, sending the thing lurching to the side. It fell to the ground, taking the real Robinson with it.

Once on the ground, the thing convulsed and released Robinson from its grip. Becky grabbed and pulled the wounded man up. She assessed his injured right hand and found it was completely crushed. There was no way it could ever be repaired.

"Let's go," Becky yelled.

Alan Robinson nodded weakly.

"Thank you," he said.

It would be his last words.

The creature reached up as Robinson rose. It grabbed the Colonel by his neck and, in a flash, pulled him down. Becky again heard the repellant sound of bones cracking and knew Robinson was finished. The creature had done to Robinson's neck what it did to his hand.

"You son of a bitch!" she yelled. She aimed the .45 at the creature's face and fired over and over and over again. Pieces of the creatures face chipped away, revealing an oozing dark matter just below the surface of the plastic skin. One of the bullets smashed into the creature's right eye, collapsing it. The creature sank back and rolled away, coming to a stop almost exactly where Robinson and Becky originally found it. It lay face down and remained very still.

Becky sank to her knees beside Robinson. She felt a rising nausea.

Easy. This isn't the time to let emotions get the best of you.

She checked Robinson's body to verify what she already knew. The creature squeezed the Colonel's neck to less than a third of its size. His spinal cord was nothing more than bone chips and powder. It was a wonder the man's head remained connected to the rest of his body.

Becky removed Robinson's M-16. She laced the weapon's strap around her shoulder and removed the Heckler and Koch from Robinson's belt. Next to it was Robinson's sheath and knife. Becky stared at the odd weapon, and started to pull it off.

As she did, she sensed movement to her side.

Becky fell backwards. She watched in horror as the creature rose, its face still marred by the shots from her .45. It appeared disoriented and was looking around. Looking for her.

Becky didn't let it do so for long.

She fired at the thing with the Heckler and Koch. The fearsome gun's bullets ripped into the creature's chest and face. While they weakened the integrity of its face, the bullets from the Heckler and Koch tore through what remained. Strange green and black fluids poured from the gory facial wounds. The creature's mouth opened and it let out a hideous scream before sliding back down and falling into the brush.

It lay still.

Very cautiously, Becky approached the creature's side. Her weapon's entire clip spent, she put the Heckler and Koch away and grabbed the M-16. She nudged the creature with the barrel of the rifle. It did not move.

"Stay the fuck down," Becky growled.

Without turning away from the creature, she took a several steps back. She reached down and felt for Robinson's corpse, then slid her hand to his black knife. She removed it from its sheath and examined it.

The knife was surprisingly light, far lighter than any metal blade of similar size and dimension. The blade's black surface remained a complete mystery to her. It looked like it was made of some kind of stone rather than metal. She strapped the knife to her side and stole one final glance at Robinson.

"I don't know what you were up to," Becky said. "But you didn't deserve this."

Becky shook her head.

"Nobody deserves this."

She got to her feet and, after taking one last look at the creature, ran toward the camp.

If she had stayed only a few more seconds, she would have seen the creature's left arm twitch once again.

23

The distant sound of gunshots echoed throughout the makeshift camp site. Frank Masters sat up and winced.

"What the hell?" he yelled.

Samantha was on her feet. She and Alicia Cunningham, the only two left in the camp carrying weapons, drew their .45's. They looked in the direction of where the shots originated, and realized it was coming from where Becky Waters, Alan Robinson, and Dan Thompson had ventured. The first series of shots was closely followed by a second. The echoes of that second volley faded and a dark, brooding silence descended over the campsite. No one spoke, no one moved. It was as if they were frozen in amber.

The quiet lasted only a few seconds.

The bushes opposite from where the sound of gunfire originated rustled. The people in the camp did an about face. Someone crashed through the bush and was heading directly toward them.

Samantha raised her gun at the shadowy forms and peered down the barrel. In the corner of her eye, she could just make out Alicia Cunningham. The newbie held her gun at her side, as if a cowboy of the wild-west, ready to draw. The muscles on her thin arm flexed with tension, then shook with fear. Her eyes were also on the disturbance, yet they nervously shifted back and forth.

Samantha felt a bead of sweat roll down her cheek. Alicia might be armed, but she doubted the newbie was ready to fight. It was possible she might fire blind and hit a friendly.

Screw that. She might hit me.

The disturbance in the bushes drew closer, and closer.

"Take it easy, Alicia," Samantha muttered. A dull burn grew in the pit of her stomach.

Take it real easy.

The bush the two faced crashed apart and, for a fraction of a second, Samantha's finger tensed on the gun's trigger. In the next fraction of a second, she released the trigger and in a flash reached over and pulled Alicia's gun hand down.

Standing some twenty feet away and exiting through the forest was General Spradlin.

"Don't shoot!" Samantha commanded.

Alicia neither fired nor fought Samantha off. Belatedly, Samantha realized the newbie was so overwhelmed as to be useless.

Immediately behind General Spradlin came Jennie Light. The blonde soldier's head swiveled back, to look in the direction from where they had come. Her hands were locked around the M-16.

The two stopped in the center of the camp.

"Where's Bartlett?" Samantha asked.

"Dead," Light replied between gasps. She shook from fright. "Some...creature..."

Spradlin grabbed the rifle from Jennie's hands and aimed it at the bushes.

"It's following us," he said.

"It...it sounded like him," Light babbled. "It talked like him! It...it was all black...all black."

General Spradlin faced the camp's occupants.

"Doctor Evans, Officer Light, grab Captain Masters. We're moving out."

Jennie Light stumbled to Master's side. She grabbed one end of the stretcher while Doctor Evans grabbed the other. They roughly hoisted Masters up. The injured pilot winced.

"We're going that way," General Spradlin said, pointing in the direction Waters, Robinson, and Thompson had gone. "We need to make it to the base. Fast."

All at once there was movement throughout the camp. General Spradlin maintained a close watch on the bush he just exited. His eyes were locked in, searching for any movement at all. There was none. He took a second to look back at the camp and see the progress of his soldiers. He found Alicia Cunningham standing still in the middle of the maelstrom. She was shaking. She was still frozen in place.

"Don't just stand there, Private Cunningham," General Spradlin said. "Get moving."

Alicia didn't respond. Her mouth hung half open. Beads of sweat glistened on her forehead. Her eyes turned, very slowly, toward Spradlin. Her eyes were dilated. She was in shock.

"Alicia, you need to get moving," Spradlin repeated. His voice was softer.

Alicia remained in place.

"Please move," he whispered.

No response.

"Soldier? *Move!*"

As the words left his mouth, the bushes before the two exploded. A dark shape tore through the green, its movements incomprehensibly fast.

General Spradlin barely had time to react before the dark shape clipped him. The wind was knocked from General Spradlin and he collapsed to his knees. The creature's forward momentum sent it directly into Alicia Cunningham. Alicia's frail body was slammed into the ground and pinned under the dark shape.

The creature ignored Spradlin and the rest of the group and turned its full attention to Alicia. As if it had all the time in the world, the creature sat on her stomach, its muddy arms holding hers down. There was no fight in the newbie. Alicia's face was a pasty white, her eyes a blank. The creature stared at her for a second, confused by her lack of fight. Alicia blinked. Some color returned to her face. Despite the creature's dark skin, it had the face of Howard Bartlett. Alicia recognized him and was confused by this similarity. It looked like Howard Bartlett, but it clearly was not him.

"Please," she pleaded. "No."

The creature's head tilted. The familiar features of Howard Bartlett disappeared. The creature's face compressed. Empty sockets formed where there should be eyes. The emptiness was filled with black ovals. Hair appeared on the thing's head. Lips formed. They opened, mimicking Alicia's facial movements.

"Please," the thing repeated. Its voice was mechanical, distorted. Almost, but not quite yet, emulating Alicia's voice. "No."

The right side of Spradlin's body was on fire. It felt like he ran full speed into a fire hydrant. He looked around at the creature and Alicia.

"Oh no," he said.

Spradlin dropped the M-16 and reached for the knife he carried in its sheath around his waist.

Just as he did, another figure burst through the bushes behind the General. Spradlin turned toward the sound. In his mind, he thought this was the end. Taking on one of these creatures was near impossible. There was no way he could fight two.

His despair instantly evaporated. It wasn't another creature coming through the bush: It was Becky Waters!

She ran past Evans, Light, and Masters. In her hand was Robinson's black blade.

The creature didn't notice or care about Becky's approach until it was too late. With one mighty thrust, she slid the blade into and through the creature's back. Its tip exited out of the creature's chest.

The thing stared at the black blade's tip, curious but not noticeably disturbed by this sudden inconvenience. Its right hand rose, touching the blade, examining its surface. When it was done, its mouth opened. A low, eerie electronic howl filled the camp site.

The creature's head abruptly spun around and stared at its attacker. It's newly formed mouth opened, revealing a set of razor sharp, nightmarishly black teeth.

Becky stumbled backwards, startled by the creature's reaction. As she did, she released the blade's handle.

And at that very moment, all hell broke loose.

A loud hiss emanated from the creature's wound. A loud energy crackle followed. Steam rose from the creature's body as an incomprehensibly strong burst of electricity pulsed through it. The creature moaned as pieces of its body erupted and cracked. Its smooth shape almost melted under the extreme electrical assault. The black teeth, so terrifying only a second before, turned to ash.

Poor Alicia remained in the thing's grip. The electrical current running from the creature's body bridged the gap between them and shot directly into her body. Alicia shook and convulsed. Smoke rose from her eyes and the sickening smell of burnt flesh filled the campsite. Alicia's body stopped shaking long before the creature finally collapsed at her side.

Becky watched it all in growing horror. The creature was dead. So too was Alicia. The black knife, the cause of all this, was all but gone, turned into flickering ash.

"I killed her," Becky muttered. The horrible truth just a couple of feet away. "I tried to save her—"

"She was dead already," Spradlin muttered. "She...she didn't suffer."

Becky got to her feet. She looked at her right hand, the one that had held the blade. It was red and singed. Had she not fallen away from the creature, she too would have—

Becky swallowed hard. She lowered her hand and again looked at the remains of the creature and Alicia. It was hard not to stare.

The others in the group hadn't moved throughout the attack. Only now, after the danger was past, did they rustle. Doctor Evans motioned to Jennie Light to lay the stretcher carrying Masters down. Jennie did as told and remained at the injured pilot's side.

Doctor Evans stepped past Becky and leaned down to examine Alicia. He gently brushed ash from her face. Her skin was blackened. Smoke rose from her mouth and the dark holes which had been her eyes.

Doctor Evans touched Alicia's neck. He felt for a pulse, perhaps hoping that, by some miracle, what appeared so obvious to everyone in the campsite somehow wasn't. Doctor Evans' hand remained on Alicia's neck only a couple of seconds. Finally, inevitably, he lowered his head and closed his eyes. He then faced Becky. His expression told her all she needed to know.

Becky felt a strong wave of nausea. She closed her eyes and stayed still for a few seconds while the feeling passed. When her eyes opened once again, she was again looking at the lifeless remains of Alicia Cunningham. The newbie. She hardly knew her.

From somewhere seemingly miles away, she heard General Spradlin say something.

"You saved us."

If the words were meant to offer solace, they barely registered. Becky straightened up and eyed the remaining members of the group. Doctor Evans was still crouched next to Alicia. Jennie Light and Frank Masters were together at the edge of camp. Samantha Aron leaned against a tree, her face ashen.

General Spradlin reached for his M-16. It was on the ground, where he had thrown it. Becky Waters saw him throw the gun to the ground when the creature burst through the bush. He dropped that fearsome weapon so he could grab his black blade. The exact type of blade Alan Robinson had. The one Becky had taken from Robinson's remains. The one she used to kill the creature.

The one that also killed Alicia.

Anger burned bright in pit of Becky's stomach. She tried to hold it in, to let it dissipate. It didn't. She reached for the Heckler and Koch at her waist. She pulled the weapon out and, in a sudden, furious motion, ran to General Spradlin's side and grabbed him by the neck. She thrust the gun's barrel against the General's head. It took considerable effort on her part to not pull the trigger.

"It's time we talked, General," she said. She was surprised by how calm her voice sounded.

Spradlin remained very still. The other members of the group froze. Spradlin locked eyes with Doctor Evans and shook his head very slightly. Doctor Evans nodded in silent acknowledgement.

"Yes," Spradlin acknowledged. "We should talk. If we are to survive this day, we need to. But first, tell me where Robinson and Thompson are."

"What do you think?" Becky said.

General Spradlin eyes narrowed. For a fleeting second she saw...sadness in the General's eyes.

"Was it...?" the General asked.

"Quick enough."

General Spradlin closed his eyes. His body sank a little.

"Where did you get that handgun? It's not one of the models we had on the helicopter."

"Nothing escapes you," Becky said.

"Force of habit. What happened?"

"We lost track of Thompson."

"Lost track?"

"He was behind us one minute, gone the next. We headed back to find him and instead found a man lying on the ground. At least he *looked* like a man. He talked with a British accent."

"You were told not to engage—"

"I know that," Becky yelled. "But your man Robinson got real interested in the guy's backpack and must have forgotten all about your orders. After searching through his gear, and given his accent, Robinson figured he was a British agent sent her to spy on Bad Penny."

"He...he probably was."

"But it wasn't human. It crushed Robinson's hand...it...it crushed his neck."

"How did you get away?"

"I blasted the shit out of that thing."

"Shot it?"

"With this very gun," Becky said. "Bastard ate all twelve rounds."

"The full clip?"

"Yes. The full—"

Becky was about to say more when she realized she had already said too much. She swore before lowering the unloaded gun from Spradlin's head.

"As I said before, nothing escapes you," she muttered and put the weapon away. "Yeah, I emptied the full clip into the creature. Every fucking cartridge this gun had."

General Spradlin faced Becky. She expected him to yell at her, to tear her apart. At the least, charge her with insubordination.

Funny, how regulations frown upon officers threatening Generals. Especially with handguns.

Instead of yelling, General Spradlin surprised her by saying:

"Then it's not dead."

He eyed the other members of the group.

"We need to move."

"What do you mean it's not dead?" Becky asked. "Between the Heckler and Koch and the .45, it took over twenty shots point blank. How the fuck could it *not* be dead?"

Spradlin picked up his M-16 and grabbed Becky by the arm. He led her to the remains of the creature and Alicia. Spradlin gave the creature's body a gentle kick.

Incredibly, the very soft blow caused the charred remains of the creature to crumble into little pieces. The pieces dissolved into a fine black dust which blew away in the breeze.

"That's what one of these creatures looks like when it's dead," Spradlin said. "In a few minutes, these ashes will be gone. Nothing will be left, including the knife you used to kill it. All that'll remain is Alicia Cunningham's body."

The others in the group stared at the blowing ash.

Spradlin walked over to Jennie Light, Frank Masters, and Samantha Aron. Doctor Evans left Alicia's body and followed behind. As he passed Becky Waters, he laid a sympathetic hand on her shoulder.

"The General wasn't kidding, you saved us all," Evans said.

"Yeah," Becky said. "I'm a real hero."

She turned away from Alicia's remains and noted who was left in the group. It was then she realized there was one other person missing.

"Where's Bartlett?"

"He didn't make it, either," Jennie Light said.

"What happened?"

Jennie folded her hands across her chest and shivered.

"That thing you just killed got to him."

"We've already lost four members of our group?"

"Looks that way," Samantha said.

Becky ran to General Spradlin's side.

"General, what exactly are our odds of getting out of this alive?"

"None at all, if we stand around and talk," General Spradlin said.

"What do we do... what do we do about Alicia's body?" Samantha asked. "We can't just leave her here."

"For now, that's all we can do," Spradlin said.

"But..."

"We'll come back for her," Spradlin added. "For her and Bartlett and...and anyone else. We owe them that much."

They moved slowly through the deep brush, zigzagging around trees and rocks and other obstacles. In front of Becky Waters were Jennie Light and Doctor Evans. They carried Frank Masters on the stretcher. In front of them walked General Spradlin. His hand was firmly on the handle of his black blade and only loosely on the trigger of the M-16.

Samantha Aron noted Becky's stare.

"Bullets only slow them down?" Samantha asked.

"You heard what the man said."

"General Spradlin and Doctor Evans have those blades."

"Yes they do. And we get the guns."

"Think they're willing to trade?"

"Would you?"

Samantha closed her mouth as a burst of cool air stirred the leaves around them. The humidity made her sweat, the cool air made her shiver.

"It'll be morning soon," Samantha said. "At least we won't be jumping at every shadow."

Up ahead, General Spradlin came to a stop. He headed back to the group and addressed Becky directly.

"Is this the way you and Robinson came?"

Becky looked around. She spotted crushed stalks and a pair of snapped branches.

"Yes sir," she said. "Shouldn't be too far from where...where Colonel Robinson..."

Becky didn't finish her thoughts and General Spradlin didn't push. He addressed the rest of the group.

"As I said before, the creature Lieutenant Waters faced is still alive."

Spradlin reached for the handle of his knife and pulled it out enough for everyone to see the black blade.

"Barring an overwhelming pummeling by high caliber bullets or being blown up, the only way to effectively kill these things is by using this blade."

"What exactly is that thing?" Jennie Light asked.

"We call her the lightning rod," General Spradlin said. "She's made of a special alloy that slips through these creature's skins. Microcircuits within the blade scramble their system. The end result is a massive short circuit."

His eyes were on Becky Waters.

"All the other weapons we carry, as you no doubt have surmised, at best only slow the creatures down," Spradlin continued. "Lest there remain any confusion, these creatures are machines. The reason they resist bullets is because they have a self-repairing technology hardwired within them. Provided any injury they receive isn't too grave, it can take them anywhere from a few minutes to a few hours to fix their wounds and becoming fully functional. They are programmed to show no mercy to their intended targets. The fact that Private Waters escaped the creature she encountered proves she did some damage. But when it repairs itself, it will hunt us down. It might even bring along help in that cause."

"There are more of them out there?" Jennie Light asked.

"The one that killed Private Cunningham and Bartlett came from the north. The one Private Waters encountered was farther to the south. There's little doubt the two attacks were caused by different creatures. If there are two, we have to assume there might be more. We have to assume the worst."

"Where did they come from?" Becky asked.

"Later," Spradlin said. "Right now, let's focus on getting this other creature or getting to safety."

"Do you have any more of those fancy blades?" Samantha asked.

"Just the two," Spradlin replied.

"Terrific," Jennie said.

"If you slow them down even a little, it may be all the time we need," Spradlin said.

Becky pulled the M-16 from her shoulder. The others checked their weapons. A thick silence hung over the group.

"We can make it out of here," General Spradlin said. "But only if we work together."

Another breeze kicked the brush around the survivors of the *Little Charlie*. General Spradlin offered no other words of encouragement. There was little point.

In silence, they continued their trek south to Bad Penny.

It took them another five minutes to reach Colonel Robinson's body.

His corpse lay just as Becky remembered. Robinson's neck was twisted and shattered, crushed by the creature's steel grip. Robinson's eyes remained open, staring up at the sky. No more than a couple of feet away, the brush was trampled down.

This was where the creature fell. This was where Becky last saw it.

"It's gone," Becky said.

"So it is," General Spradlin said as he leaned next to Robinson's body. His hand settled gently over the soldier's face. He closed Robinson's lifeless eyes and bowed his head.

"You were like a son to me," Spradlin muttered. He offered no prayers or comment. Instead, he got back to his feet and faced the group. His expression was stone, unemotional and unreadable.

"The base isn't too far away," Spradlin said.

He walked off into the bush.

24

They stumbled through the darkness, hoping with each passing minute to finally see lights from the base coming through the trees. Lights that indicated Bad Penny was finally within range. They used their flashlights only sparingly, out of fear of attracting those things. But doing so slowed them down even more. An hour passed and their progress was minimal. Fear gave way to frustration and exhaustion.

Doctor Evans and Jennie Light carried Frank Masters. Samantha Aron and Becky Waters covered the rear while General Spradlin continued on point. Since seeing his dead partner, General Spradlin's mood turned pitch black and he talked very little with the others. Now and again he slowed to see how everyone was doing, but in general he was forced to wait for the others to catch up.

After an hour and a half of stumbling in the darkness, he had the group come to a full stop. He turned his flashlight on and examined each of the members of the group. They all looked exhausted. Frank Masters remained in the stretcher. He too looked completely spent.

"I would suggest taking another break, but that didn't go so well for us the last time," General Spradlin said. "Anyway, the base can't be too far away."

Despite the cooler temperatures from the passing front, sweat filled General Spradlin's forehead. He leaned against a tree and looked around. There wasn't much to see. The darkness swallowed the forest around them.

"Private Light, I'll take over for you," General Spradlin said.

Jennie Light pointed to Doctor Evans.

"What about him? He might need some relief, too."

"He's stronger than he looks," General Spradlin said.

"So am I," Jennie Light countered.

"I have no doubt you are," General Spradlin said. He eyed Doctor Evans and nodded. Doctor Evans nodded right back.

Jennie Light allowed General Spradlin to take the stretcher's rear handles. Spradlin and Evans continued along into the forest.

Jennie Light shook her head and watched as the trio of men walked off. Becky Waters and Samantha Aron approached her side.

"Let's move, soldier," Samantha said.

"Yeah, let's do that," Jennie Light replied. "Men."

"What's that?"

Jennie Light pointed to the trio of men and sniffed.

"Ever study psychology?" she asked.

"Why?" Becky Waters replied.

"I read somewhere that when a group of animals are in a stressful environment, they flock together. The group is stronger than the individual."

"We're all together in this right now," Becky said.

"Yeah, but the men are over there and we're over here."

"Groups within groups," Samantha Aron said. "What does that tell you?"

"It tells me there isn't a whole lot of trust among us. Either that or the men have mother issues. I wish I had studied more than just Freud."

"Two of the men know what's going on while we women haven't a fucking clue," Becky said.

"All three of them know more than we do," Samantha added.

"All three?" Jennie said. "You mean your co-pilot...?"

"Knows plenty."

"What?"

Samantha shook her head.

"Are you holding back?" Jennie said. "Even now?"

"Look, they arranged our crash landing, OK? They sabotaged the chopper. They forced us down."

"Holy shit," Jennie said. "I had no fucking idea. I guess that makes us the odd women out."

"Three of us together?" Becky Waters said.

"Groups within groups."

"Why not?" Jennie Light said. "Charlie's fucking Angels."

"Feeling any better?" General Spradlin asked Frank Masters when he stirred.

The pilot eyes fluttered open. He grimaced and shrugged.

"You escorting me to the dance?"

"For the last mile," General Spradlin said.

"I can think of better dates."

"So can I. I asked you a question, Captain. You feeling any better?"

"No real change."

General Spradlin nodded. He eyed Doctor Evans and the Doctor returned the gaze. Unspoken messages were passed between them in that instant, and General Spradlin turned his head to see the remaining three members of his group.

The women were a few paces behind, whispering to each other. He had a good idea what they were talking about. If he were in their place, he'd do the same. Forming connections. The group is stronger than the individual.

General Spradlin fought off a chill at that final thought.

The outer perimeter of the Bad Penny Military Base was marked with a thick chain link fence. Time and the inevitable wear left rust and withered leaves intertwined within their structure. Despite this, she remained sturdy.

The group arrived at the fence just as the sun's first rays rose in the east. It was looking like the beginning of a beautiful day.

None of the survivors of the *Little Charlie*, however, noticed or cared about the weather.

They leaned against the fence and were careful to remain well hidden in the ample bush. They were just north of the main barracks. It seemed like several lifetimes had passed since the last time they were here.

In spite of the early morning hour, the weary group expected to see plenty of activity within the base. They expected to see groups of soldiers engaged in early morning drills and senior staff members drifting in and out of the barracks, clipboards in hand and a stern looks across their faces. They expected to see the odd soldier marching south, toward the mess hall, eager for an early morning meal.

But they saw no such movement. They saw nobody at all. All was deathly quiet.

The base looked completely deserted.

"What the hell happened here?" Samantha asked no one in particular. "Is everyone...is everyone gone?"

"I don't know," General Spradlin said.

No one spoke for several long seconds. Despair hung in the air like a thick fog.

"We need to find a way in," General Spradlin said.

"Too bad the chopper didn't carry bolt cutters," Jennie Light said. She pulled at the fence and found it wouldn't give. "We'll have to climb over."

"No need," Becky said. She pointed to a portion of the gate some thirty yards away. It was a hinged entry that was slightly ajar.

"How inviting," Frank Masters mumbled. He sat up in the stretcher. His face was bone white.

"Let's move," Spradlin said.

The group silently approached the entry point. Once there, they noticed a heavy padlock lying on the ground. The hinge had been neatly sliced through.

"Could the creatures do this?" Samantha asked.

"I don't think so," General Spradlin said. "There would be no need for subtlety on their part. They'd just rip it right off."

"What about the British spy?" Becky said.

"More likely," Spradlin admitted. He thought about this for a moment before turning to Becky. "Tell me more about him."

"He was another creature," Becky said. "What more is there to tell?"

"The creatures are chameleons," Spradlin said. "Though it might not seem like it based on your experiences so far, their primary function is to emulate people."

"Why?"

"So they can pass themselves off as someone else. Very helpful when your goal is to infiltrate."

"Then the creature we found never was a British spy?"

"On the contrary, I suspect there was a British spy on the island," Spradlin said.

"Why?"

"There is absolutely no reason for that chameleon to adapt a British disguise unless the creature saw the spy first hand," Spradlin said. "Therefore, my guess is there was a very real British spy infiltrating Bad Penny. This spy ran into one of these things and, after it killed him, it assumed his identity. It's probably why Robinson let down his guard. He was just as surprised and intrigued to find a British subject on American grounds as you were."

"He was curious," Becky said.

"Curiosity," General Spradlin spat. "You know what it did to the cat."

Becky Waters offered the General the British spy's backpack.

"And you aren't curious?"

General Spradlin considered the backpack.

"Other than the handgun, what did he find?"

Becky Waters looked inside the backpack.

"Binoculars, a camera, some kind of radio device."

"What were his conclusions?"

"Robinson said he was SIS," Becky said. "I asked him why our allies were spying on us. He said that even though we're allies, we like to sniff around in each other's back yards now and again, to make sure everything was the way it ought to be. Something like that."

"How poetic," Jennie Light said. "You guys live in an interesting world."

"You don't know the half of it," Spradlin said.

"Do we spy on the Brits?" Samantha asked.

"Let's just say it would be foolish to blindly trust everyone's good intentions." Spradlin said.

General Spradlin was silent a few seconds. He nodded.

"The SIS officer's presence here might certainly explain things."

"Like?"

"Like how the creatures got out," Doctor Evans said.

The women's eyes shot toward Doctor Evans.

"We didn't create them," General Spradlin said. "But we had a few of them locked up on the island."

"You know what they are?" Becky Waters spat. "With all due respect, General, are you going to tell us everything or do we beat it out of you?"

General Spradlin smiled. The smile vanished quickly.

"Perhaps it is time," General Spradlin said. "The information you're asking about is top secret. Very few people outside of the military's highest command know anything about these...these *things.*"

The wind died down and the leaves stopped rustling.

"The fact is that we don't quite know what they are, not entirely," he continued. "We've been trying to figure that out for many years now."

"By sniffing around other's back yards?" Becky asked.

"It's a little more complicated than that."

"Enlighten us," Jennie said.

"The gathering of intelligence is like playing a game of poker in the dark," General Spradlin said. "Not only are your opponents' cards hidden, so too are your opponents. Sometimes you have to show your hand a little before they show theirs. The trick is making them show you *more* than you show them."

"What the hell does that have to do with anything?" Jennie said.

"What I'm getting at is—"

The General abruptly stopped talking. He crouched low to the ground and motioned for everyone to do the same. All eyes followed General Spradlin's stare.

In the distance, on the main road leading to the heart of the base, a single dark figure appeared from within the shadows of a barrack. It looked like a man. It carried a limp form over its shoulder. The form was familiar.

"It's Thompson!" Becky Waters whispered.

She tightened her grip on the M-16.

"We have to save him!"

General Spradlin grabbed Becky's shoulder and held her in place.

"Don't you dare move."

Becky squirmed under Spradlin's tight grip. Spradlin released her. Becky remained in place. Barely.

"It's just one, General," she said. "Thompson might still be alive."

General Spradlin shook his head.

"You saw what it did to Robinson," he said. "Do you really think it treated Thompson any differently?"

Becky's grip on the rifle loosened. She drew a deep breath.

"What about the base? There are over three hundred people stationed at Bad Penny."

General Spradlin didn't reply. Samantha shook her head.

"You can't be serious?" she whispered. She thought of her lover, Warren. The man it took such effort to leave behind for what turned out to be the last flight of the *Little Charlie*. Was he still alive? "You don't think *everyone's* dead, do you?"

"We'll see soon enough," Doctor Evans said.

"Where's the creature taking him?" Jennie Light asked.

"I don't know," Spradlin replied. He sat on the ground.

"How many of those creatures did we have?" Becky asked.

"Three."

"Three?" she repeated, incredulously. "You're telling me just three of these things were enough to silence an entire base?"

"That's how many we had locked up."

"Below the shed?" Samantha said.

"How did you know about the shed?"

"Too many people were guarding something that didn't look like it was worth guarding at all."

General Spradlin thought about that.

"Good eyes, Captain," he said. "Maybe that British Special Forces agent saw the same thing you did."

"He freed them...?"

"It's certainly possible" General Spradlin said. "At this point, he's the only wild card in this whole situation. It was less than one hour after your departure from Bad Penny that we received word the base was dark."

"That's why your helicopter was diverted to Tortuga," Doctor Evans said.

"You thought one of those things was on the chopper?" Becky asked.

"It was a possibility," General Spradlin said.

"And if you were certain?"

"We'd have blown you out of the sky."

"Why bring us back?" Samantha said.

"We needed a quick reconnaissance of the base. We needed people who knew their way around the island. We're on point, folks. We're the ones drafted into figuring out what exactly is going on here and, yes, if someone might still be alive."

"On the plus side, one of the creatures is dead," Doctor Evans said.

"Therefore there are at least two left," General Spradlin said. "The big question is where we go from here."

"You don't know?" Jennie said.

"I know the basic layout of the base," Spradlin said. "You're here to fill the gaps."

"Where do you want to go?" Becky said.

"We're going to work our way through the base, to see what shape it's in and verify its status," General Spradlin said. "Along the way, we look for survivors. We move straight south to the control tower by the helicopter pad. I lost the PCOM back in the jungle, so we also need to find some kind of communication gear. If we don't find any in the base itself, there's sure to be some in the control tower, which is where I'm guessing the creatures' jamming equipment is, too. Once we disable that equipment, and provided we find some kind of radio gear, we call in the marines."

"We'll be exposed," Becky said.

"That's inevitable. We'll start with the barracks. They're clustered close together. It shouldn't take long. What comes next?"

"The general supplies."

"There might be communication equipment there," Samantha said.

"Then?"

"The cabins," Samantha said. "Then there's the gym and a couple of offices."

"Toward the south end of town is the Mess Hall," Frank said. "It's a big, sturdy structure. Brick and mortar. It's withstood a couple of hurricanes and is the strongest building on the island. If anyone's left alive in this base, they'll be barricaded there."

"Good," General Spradlin said. "We'll take no more than twenty minutes on the barracks and the offices. From there we move to the Mess Hall."

The soldiers nodded.

Gingerly, General Spradlin reached for the fence gate and pushed it open. He ducked behind the bushes after the gate was open. Long, silent seconds passed. There was no movement from within the base. The creature carrying Thompson had long since vanished down the road.

"OK," Spradlin said. "Let's move."

The group stepped into the base.

In back of the barracks was a small parking lot. To the south, the start of the town's main road. Becky Waters knew it well. It snaked to the south until eventually reaching the beach. She ran that course every morning.

Jennie Light walked beside her and kept very close. General Spradlin walked a few feet ahead of them. Behind them were Samantha Aron and Doctor Evans. They carried Frank Masters.

General Spradlin paused before the edge of the trees. There were over fifty feet of open ground between them and the closest barrack building.

"We need to move very fast," General Spradlin said. "Ready?"

Grim faces stared back at him. He didn't expect an answer.

"I'll go first," he continued. "I'll stop at the building closest to us and cover you. We search through them one at a time."

"It would be quicker if we split up," Jennie Light said.

"We're not splitting up."

"Yes sir."

"I'll go first. Captain Aron and Doctor Evans, you follow. Private Waters and Light, I want you two to cover them."

"Yes sir," Becky and Jennie said.

"Any questions?"

There were none. General Spradlin nodded and crouched down low. He scanned the open area before him to make sure there was no movement coming from either the barracks or the road.

"Here goes nothing," he muttered.

He was off, sprinting as hard as he could. For several agonizing seconds, he was fully exposed. There were no trees to cover him, no shadows to disappear into. He knew that if the creatures attacked, he stood no chance.

Yet there was no alternative.

He breathed heavily, realizing this was the fastest he had run in a very long time. Despite his speed, the barracks seemed so very, very far away.

For several agonizing seconds he felt like he was in a nightmare, running from unseen enemies but not actually moving. A bead of sweat rolled down his neck and fell to the ground. His breathing grew heavier and his legs ached. But he was nearly there. With one last burst of energy, he reached the rear wall of the nearest barrack building and crouched down. He welcomed its shadow.

General Spradlin took several seconds to catch his breath while searching for any threat. He spotted none. If anyone saw him sprint to the barracks, they hadn't reacted.

General Spradlin wiped more sweat from his brow. He looked back into the trees and deeper into the forest beyond. The rest of his crew was barely visible. He motioned for them to come.

General Spradlin waited several tense seconds for Captain Aron and Doctor Evans to emerge.

"Come on," he muttered.

There was the sound of someone breaking through the brush and General Spradlin's eyes locked in on the edge of the forest.

Samantha Aron emerged. She held on to the stretcher. Frank lay on it, flat. His eyes were closed and his hands were tight against the stretcher's side. He was holding on for dear life. At the rear of the stretcher was Doctor Evans. He tried his best to keep up with Samantha.

They moved much slower than General Spradlin and were therefore exposed for much longer. Spradlin watched helplessly as they made their way slowly –too slowly– through the empty area and to the barrack. There was panic on Samantha's face, heightened by every long second it took to make this dash.

"Hurry up," General Spradlin whispered. He gritted his teeth with such force his jaw hurt.

In his mind he pictured things hiding in the shadows or behind the windows of the barracks. These things were watching them all, sadistically, waiting to pounce.

"Hurry up," he repeated.

He kept his left hand on the trigger of his gun. His right hand held the black blade's handle. They were getting closer, and closer.

They were still exposed.

General Spradlin wanted to leave his hiding place and run to them, to try to somehow hurry them to safety. But he couldn't leave. He had to be ready, in case the creatures attacked.

They were closer. Samantha was gasping for air. Frank looked up, to see where they were going, to see how far they traveled.

"Hurry," Spradlin said, out loud.

Samantha heard him and ran harder. Doctor Evans had to adjust his grip on the stretcher and, in doing so, nearly fell over. Frank lay back and closed his eyes.

They entered the shadows of the barracks and, like magic, were at General Spradlin's side. Samantha Aron and Doctor Evans breathed heavily. They laid the stretcher down. Samantha wiped sweat from her face. The General waved his weapon at the various shadows around him, just in case one of them came alive.

None did.

"Good job," Spradlin whispered.

"I need to work out more," Doctor Evans replied between gasps.

"After this, I'll stick to the big cities," Samantha said.

General Spradlin stared into the forest. He waved to Becky Waters and Jennie Light.

It was their turn.

Together, Becky Waters and Jennie Light ran past the forest edge and into the empty field. They moved very quickly and followed a straight path. Their motion was furious, the concentration on their face absolute. They moved quicker than General Spradlin, yet were nonetheless just as exposed. General Spradlin watched in mounting horror. His jaw hurt from clenching it so tightly.

"Come on," he whispered.

The others around him shared his fears. They silently urged the two runners on.

"Move!" Samantha muttered. Her fists were clenched; her eyes wide open in fear.

Inexplicably, halfway through the run Becky Waters slowed. Jennie Light, unaware of this, kept going. She left her fellow soldier behind.

"What are you doing?" General Spradlin hissed.

Becky Waters looked toward General Spradlin, Samantha Aron, Doctor Evans, and Frank Masters. Jennie Light scampered behind the barracks and was at General Spradlin's side. It was only then she realized Becky Waters wasn't with her.

"Where is she?" Jennie asked. She noted everyone was staring at the open area she just ran and looked in that direction. She saw Becky standing in the clearing, completely exposed. The Private wasn't moving at all. Her eyes were locked on one of the barrack buildings.

"What the hell?" Jennie Light called out. "Becky, get your ass—"

"Stay here," General Spradlin said.

He ran to Becky Water's side.

"What are you—?"

"Look," Becky Waters said and pointed.

General Spradlin followed Becky's finger.

The survivors of the *Little Charlie*, all but Becky Waters, ran so quickly past this clearing that they failed to notice a series of scrawls painted on the east side of one of the farther barrack buildings. The scrawls made up a single word. The word was written in red.

The word was written in blood.

"My God," General Spradlin said.

He grabbed Becky by the arm.

"I saw it," he said. "Let's go."

He pulled her past the empty field until they joined the others.

"What happened?" Jennie Light asked.

"Nothing," General Spradlin said. "Let's search the barracks. Quickly."

Becky Waters knew that this search was a useless task. She shivered when she thought of what was written on the barrack wall.

Welcome.

25

"**What happened back** there?" Samantha Aron asked. "I thought you spotted them."

"We didn't," Becky Waters replied. "They knew we were coming this way."

"We can't be sure," General Spradlin said.

"Of course we can. Who else would leave that message for us?"

"Message?" Doctor Evans said.

"It's on the other side of this very barrack. Those things knew we'd arrive here. The attacks in the forest were some kind of sick game. They were having some fun with us, but they wanted us here."

The group left the shadows and walked to the other side of the barrack. They stared at the message.

"Maybe this isn't about playing games with us," Jennie Light said after a while. "Maybe they're suspicious."

"Suspicious?" Doctor Evans asked. "About what?"

"About us," Jennie Light said. "Think about it: A military base goes dark, and the government decides that rather than send in the full might of the military, they choose to send in this small, barely armed group." Jennie Light paused and pointed to General Spradlin. "They think we're up to something. I think they're right."

Becky Waters and Samantha Aron also faced General Spradlin.

"What she says makes a lot of sense, General," Becky said. "What aren't you telling us?"

"Come on, General," Samantha implored. "Tell us you didn't come all this way just to watch us get butchered."

"Tell us what you know," Jennie Light insisted.

General Spradlin shook his head.

"Right now, we search for survivors," he said. "If there are any."

The barracks on Bad Penny consisted of three very plain one story metal pre-fabricated buildings. Housed inside each building were five rows of twenty cots. In the first building, everything was neat and tidy. The beds were made and all appeared to be in its place. Personal items were stored in their bags and laid out in the middle of each bed.

There was no one to be seen.

General Spradlin, Samantha Aron, and Becky Waters conducted the search while Jennie Light and Doctor Evans moved Frank Masters on the stretcher. They remained at the rear of the group.

"Let's go to the next building," General Spradlin told his group.

They quietly moved to the next structure. Inside, General Spradlin found almost everything the same as the first barrack. All was in order and all items were in their place, except for one thing. There was a black toiletry bag sprawled on the floor, its contents spilled. There was a bottle of shaving cream, a razor, and a toothbrush lay beside the bag.

"It's like everyone just got up and left," Becky Waters said.

"I expected some signs of struggle, something," Samantha added. "Anything."

"Let's move on," General Spradlin said.

They examined the remaining barrack and again found little evidence of struggle. Even more worrisome, they found neither corpses nor survivors. How was it possible three of these creatures could so thoroughly take over this base? And where were the soldiers? Where was everyone?

Samantha though about that as they searched the final barrack. She thought she had an answer.

"It was dinner time when we left," Samantha said. "Most of the soldiers were heading from the barracks to the mess hall."

"That might explain why we see no signs of anyone," Becky said.

General Spradlin nodded.

"The supply shed is next," he said. "Let's check it out."

They found the supply shed's doors ajar and swinging in the light breeze. The place was always kept under lock and key, given the supplies within.

General Spradlin was the first to enter the small building. It took only a few seconds for his eyes to adjust to the dim light within. When he did, he was shocked by what he found.

Or, rather, what he *didn't* find.

The supply shed consisted of an entry/waiting area. A wire mesh kept visitors separated from rows of shelving that normally were filled with weapons, communication devices, clothing, paper, and toiletries.

The shelves were completely bare.

"My God," Becky Waters said. She was right behind General Spradlin.

"I take it this room carried some supplies at one time?"

"Yeah," she said. "Too many, if you ask me."

"Not anymore," Doctor Evans said. "No chance we'll find another PCOM here."

"No," General Spradlin said. He walked back to the shed's exit.

"Let's go to the Mess Hall."

The group walked along the main road. They kept to the shadows and whatever brush they could hide behind. Along the way, they passed a single HUMVEE parked beside the road. The driver door was open. Jennie Light examined the vehicle's interior as the group drew close to it.

"Our first sign of a struggle," she whispered.

The driver's side window of the HUMVEE was shattered and glass littered the vehicle's insides. Severed wires dangled below the steering wheel. Becky Waters examined the damage. It was minor. She popped the hood open and checked the engine. It looked like someone had taken a sledge hammer to it.

"There's no way to get this running," Becky said.

"Then we continue walking," General Spradlin said.

The group left the HUMVEE and headed down the road. After a short while, they could just make out the roof of the three story tall mess hall.

Samantha swallowed. They were also feet away from the cabins. Feet away from the where she left Warren last night.

Please, she thought. *Please still be alive.*

But whatever optimism she tried generating dissolved as they approached. As with the barracks, the cabins were eerily silent. There were no lights, there were no people. The individual buildings looked completely untouched. There was no debris or signs of struggle.

It was more than Samantha could take.

She broke away from the group and ran to her cabin.

"Wait!" General Spradlin yelled.

But the Captain wasn't listening. She reached her cabin door and found it ajar. She disappeared inside.

"Private Waters, come with me," General Spradlin said. "Doctor Evans, Private Light, get off the road and wait for us to return."

General Spradlin and Becky Waters cautiously walked to the cabin's entrance. They stopped at either side of its door.

"Samantha?" General Spradlin whispered into the cabin.

He received no response.

Spradlin sighed.

"Let's go," Spradlin told Becky Waters before heading inside.

The inside of the cabin was very small. The bed was unmade but otherwise everything appeared to be in its place. A shirt and pair of pants hung on a chair. The closet door was ajar, revealing more clothing. A book lay on the night table.

"Samantha?" General Spradlin called out.

He heard a sound coming from a door at the rear of the structure. He motioned for Becky Waters to stay close as he approached that entry.

From where he stood, General Spradlin saw a glass shower door. It was closed. There was water gleaming on the shower's floor, dripping from the shower itself.

"Samantha?" he whispered.

He heard someone take a breath. He pulled his black blade from its holster and gritted his teeth. He entered the bathroom.

Samantha Aron stood beside the toilet. In her hands was a white shirt. She was staring at the sink. A cup on the sink held two toothbrushes.

"Samantha?" General Spradlin repeated.

Samantha Aron didn't look back. She shook her head and sobbed.

"He's not here. No one is here. Everyone's gone."

General Spradlin slid the black blade back in its place but held on to its handle.

"People don't just disappear," he said.

"Then where are they?"

General Spradlin placed his free hand on the pilot's shoulder.

"That's what we're going to find out," he said. His voice was gentle and surprisingly caring.

Samantha's body shook as she let out another sob. When the emotion passed, she nodded. She wiped the tears from her eyes and gently folded the shirt before laying it on the sink.

"Let's do that," she said before stepping past General Spradlin and Becky Waters and heading out of the cabin.

26

The base was silent.

The base was dead.

And to the survivors of the *Little Charlie,* it felt like they were walking over her corpse.

The light breeze again kicked up. In the distance, a door creaked. The sound came from the direction of the mess hall, now fully visible from the road.

"The east side entrance," Jennie Light pointed out.

The door was ajar and the early morning breeze played with it like a cat with a mouse. It creaked open before gently swinging shut.

The group silently approached the building. As with the rest of the base, there was no one around and there were no signs of struggle. Private Waters, however, noted one oddity: The electrical lines to the building were cut. She pointed this out to General Spradlin.

"There was no electricity in the barracks, either," Becky said.

General Spradlin motioned for the rest of the group to stay before approaching the swinging door. Doing so meant he was forced from the camouflage of the bushes. The morning sun was high in the sky and illuminated everything not hidden in shadow.

General Spradlin quickly approached the thin metal door. The mess hall windows, dark and impenetrable, silently stared back at him. The metal door let out another loud creak, like a siren beckoning a sailor.

Sweat rolled down Spradlin's face. The sound was in his head and warned the creatures he imagined were lurking in the dark places all around him.

Spradlin's hand lay on the black blade's handle. He reached the Mess Hall door, took a very deep breath to calm his nerves, and grabbed it. For a moment, the infernal screech ended. The silence, however, proved even more unnerving. Spradlin looked around, convinced this silence was a sign of coming disaster. He remained still for several long seconds.

Nothing moved, nothing stirred.

Spradlin's focus returned to the door and the Mess Hall. He stared into the darkness beyond the door and could detect no motion within. The rays of the sun penetrating the building's east side windows illuminated the furniture within. Normally, the chairs and tables were arranged in neat rows. Here, they were littered about as if they were victims of a tornado. Chairs were shattered and tables were flung about like leaves in the wind. Dark marks were spread all over the floor.

Blood.

There it was, mingled in with the destruction, the first evidence of the furious struggle between the personnel of the base and the creatures.

This is where they made their last stand, General Spradlin thought. *This is where many –maybe most– of the three hundred soldiers died.*

But where were the bodies?

Spradlin motioned to the others in his group to join him. He entered the Mess Hall and held the door while they stepped inside. Samantha was the last to enter.

"My God," she said.

The others were just as incredulous with the destruction around them.

"At least they fought back," Jennie Light muttered.

Becky Waters noted a large puddle of blood by a wall. Whoever was the source of the blood, he –or she– had been dragged away. The blood stains led to the double doors separating the mess hall from the kitchen.

"Do you smell that?" Samantha said. "Something's burning."

General Spradlin quietly closed and locked the side entrance door. The later action almost made him laugh. This simple door lock would hold back one of those creatures for maybe two seconds. Three if they were lucky.

"Private Light and Doctor Evans, put Captain Masters in the east corner," Spradlin said. "When you're done, watch this door. Doctor Evans, stay with Captain Masters. Private Waters and Captain Aron, please come with me."

Becky and Samantha accompanied General Spradlin the length of the floor and to the double doors at the rear of the Mess Hall. From a distance, they appeared intact. As the trio approached, they noted scrapes and more dark splatters.

General Spradlin leaned against the doors and listened for anything coming from the kitchen beyond. He heard nothing. He removed the knife from its sheath and handed his M-16 to Samantha.

"There may be survivors," he whispered. Then, in an even more silent voice, added: "But there might not be."

General Spradlin's attention returned to the door. It had no lock and was meant to swing freely in or out, allowing Mess Hall staff easy entry and exit into the kitchen. General Spradlin laid his free hand flat on the door and gently pushed. The trio stepped inside.

It took a few seconds for their eyes to adjust to the dim lighting. It took another full minute for their minds to comprehend what they were seeing.

Between forty or fifty bodies were thrown into a bloody pile. Most of them were ripped to shreds. One of the stoves was left on and one of the bodies, now charred to a crisp, roasted over the open gas fire.

For several seconds the trio stood before this scene of carnage, their minds trying to make some sense of it.

"My God," Samantha said.

General Spradlin stepped over several corpses and turned the stove off.

"I knew something was burning," Samantha said while fighting back the urge to throw up.

She eyed the bodies, recognizing a few faces, people she came in contact with while at the base. Many of them she had transported here. Despite their familiarity, they were casual acquaintances at best.

All but one.

Through the bloody mound she spotted Warren. Despite the blood caked across his face, his features were remarkably intact. Below his neck, however, was evidence of the creature's deadly handiwork. There was a softball sized hole in Warren's chest. The cavity extended right through and beyond his heart. His death was instantaneous.

This was the only thing Samantha could be grateful for.

Samantha could no longer control herself. She fell to her knees before her lover's body and grabbed his hand. It was very cold.

"I'm so sorry," she said. "So sorry."

General Spradlin and Becky allowed the grief stricken pilot her privacy. General Spradlin motioned for Becky to search the east side of the kitchen while he headed west. More bodies were littered at the corners and the two searched through them for weapons or anything they could use against those things. But the victims of the Mess Hall slaughter were, with the exception of kitchen knives and other cooking utensils, woefully unarmed. They had come that past evening for dinner. They were not prepared for a fight to the death.

Becky's dark mood turned even bleaker. The confrontation they had with the creatures proved how fearsome they were and the bodies that lay before her proved, as if there could be any more doubt, there was no way their small group could take them on.

Killing the chameleon back in the forest represented the faintest flicker of hope. After seeing the welcome sign on the barrack and the carnage within the mess hall, it was clear this initial victory was nothing more than blind luck.

They have something in mind for us, she thought. *Something special.*

She stopped and let her fear and anger work its way through her body. She heard Samantha crying and thought, at the very least, she didn't have any loved ones among the dead. Despite three years of service, she always kept to herself and remained independent, to the base as well as the military. Perhaps, she mused, to the world itself. Nobody to worry about and no one worrying about her.

Another lie, Becky thought.

Because she did care. She cared deeply. For herself, of course, but also for the others in this small group. For the rest of the world. What would happen if these creatures got away from the base? What if they made it to the mainland? Could they multiply? If so, could *anything* stop them?

They were chameleons, General Spradlin said. They were designed to fit in to crowds and infiltrate. What if one or more of them entered a nuclear facility or a missile silo? What was to stop them from setting off a nuclear device and ridding the world of *all* humanity?

So concerned was Becky with these thoughts that she nearly missed the old man's body. Even then, her eyes were drawn to him because his bright white lab coat stood out against the standard green military fatigues of the other victims. The man appeared to be in his late sixties. He had a white goatee and probably had white hair on his head. However, Becky could only guess that was the case because the man's skull had been ripped off. Exposed brain tissue attested to the fact that he, like the others here, was most certainly dead. But that was not what held Becky's attention.

Tied to his belt was a familiar large knife sheath.

Fuck me, Becky thought. She spun around and found General Spradlin on the other side of the kitchen, focused on his search. Samantha remained kneeling beside the corpse of her lover.

Becky's attention returned to the sheath. She reached down and tugged at it. Her hands trembled with excitement. Could the man have been carrying another of those black blades? Could she get that lucky?

Becky pulled harder. She needed to free the corpse.

The man in the white lab coat was wedged under a pair of bodies. From the look of things, those victims were as young and green as Alicia Cunningham. Becky swallowed hard. She rolled one of the bodies away. This gave her better access to the belt and holster.

She grabbed and pulled at it. She was frantic, knowing that at any moment General Spradlin would notice her actions. What would he do if he found out she had a blade? Would he take it away from her? No. It was hers. She wouldn't let the General have it. She'd keep the blade for herself and...

The holster was empty.

Becky let out a breath. After the euphoria of the find, she felt utterly defeated. Finding another black blade represented hope. Finding another black blade meant she could fight those things. It meant she could once again be independent, self-reliant.

No longer. She was just another of the survivors in the group and dependent on General Spradlin or Doctor Evans and their weapons. She could not take on the creatures. Not on her own.

"Lieutenant Waters," General Spradlin called out from the other side of the room.

Becky rubbed her face and composed herself. She turned, fearful that the General had spotted what she was up to. She was relieved to see his back to her. He was in the other corner of the kitchen, kneeling before one of the corpses. Becky walked to his side.

"Take a look at this," General Spradlin said.

Becky leaned down next to Spradlin. The corpse lying on his stomach before them appeared to be like the others, with one big exception. The corpse's shirt was ripped and, instead of skin, his chest was made of shiny silver.

"What the hell?" Becky muttered.

"It's quite heavy," General Spradlin said. "Help me turn it over." He reached down and paused. "If it moves, even a little bit, run. Fast."

Becky nodded. The two grabbed the corpse's side and, with a mighty thrust, turned the body over.

When they did, they both jumped back. Instead of a bloody face, the corpse sported a grinning, shiny metal skull. The creature's hands were filled with gore. Bullet holes littered the creature's midsection. All those things were quickly ignored. In the center of its chest, protruding like a mighty sword, was a black blade!

Spradlin let out a sigh of relief. Becky stared at the weapon, the expression on her face muted. Only seconds before, she wanted so desperately to find this weapon and here it was.

"It came from the old man," Becky muttered.

"What?" General Spradlin said.

"The blade. It came from the old man."

"Which old man?"

"Back there," Becky said and pointed to the corpse in the white lab coat.

General Spradlin looked over and saw the man she was pointing at. From this distance, his lab coat was even more evident.

"He's dead," she said. "Just like the others."

General Spradlin's eyes remained on the old man. Sadness appeared just below the surface of his face.

"You knew him, didn't you?" Becky said.

"Yeah," Spradlin said. His one word response hinted at a very long history. Longer, perhaps, than the one he had with Alan Robinson.

"He went down fighting," Becky said. "He had a holster. I'm guessing this blade was his."

"It was," General Spradlin said. His attention returned to the creature. "Killing this...thing...might have been his very last act."

General Spradlin grabbed the blade by the handle. He pulled at it, hard, but it wouldn't budge.

"Let me help," Becky said.

General Spradlin paused. Surprisingly, a smile appeared on his face.

"Sometimes I forget I'm not alone," General Spradlin said.

"No one is ever alone."

"So says one of the most independent soldiers stationed on this island."

"I may keep to myself, but I'm here to help."

General Spradlin nodded.

"Thank you."

Together, they pulled at the blade's handle. They gritted their teeth and used all their strength. After much effort, the blade shifted ever so slightly before sliding out of the creature's chest. Both General Spradlin and Becky Waters stumbled backwards.

"Damn," Becky muttered. She released the handle of the blade and allowed General Spradlin to examine it. The blade was smaller than the one either General Spradlin or Doctor Evans carried, but made of the same black ceramic-like material. It appeared intact. Neither the blade nor the creature had crumbled to ash.

"This thing is different from the one we killed back in the jungle," Becky said.

"It's a robot," Spradlin said. He shook his head. "I suppose when you come down to it, they're *all* robots. But the thing we encountered in the forest, that's a true chameleon. They're the...primary...creatures. They've been known to create these clunkier units to aid them in whatever tasks they're up to. Near as we've been able to tell, they function primarily as servants to their masters. As such, they're far simpler in design and capacity."

Spradlin closely examined the blade.

"They're also much easier to kill, even with standard weapons. The blade does the trick, too."

Spradlin touched the blade's surface with his free hand.

"As you've guessed by now, several of my people were stationed here, working at Bad Penny," he continued. "Given the unique threat we're facing, trusting your fellow man or woman is not the...easiest thing to do."

General Spradlin let those words die in the still air. He leaned in close to Becky.

"You've used the blade already, and that makes you more special than you know," he whispered. "The chameleons act like humans in many ways, but they have never –*ever*– destroyed one of their own. That's why I know of everyone here, you're the one I can trust, Private Waters."

The blade was at his side, hidden from view. He handed it to Becky.

"Take it," he said. "Hide it. Keep it to yourself, just in case."

Becky felt a pang of guilt.

"You're sure about this?" Becky whispered.

General Spradlin smiled.

"In this line of work, I'm never sure about anything," he said. "Remember, the creatures are chameleons. They can substitute themselves for anyone in this group. Anyone."

Becky Waters felt a chill pass through her body.

"Do you mean?!"

"Don't jump to conclusions," General Spradlin said.

Becky slowly nodded. She took the blade and hid it at her side and under her shirt.

"When are you going to tell us what we're dealing with?"

General Spradlin wiped the sweat from his forehead. Instead of answering Becky's question, he motioned her to follow him. The two walked to Samantha's side.

"I'm sorry for your loss, Captain," he said. "But we have to move on."

Samantha released Warren's hand. Reluctantly, she rose to her feet.

"Thank you, sir," Samantha said.

"For what?"

"For giving me a chance to...to say goodbye."

General Spradlin laid a hand on Samantha's shoulder.

"Let's get back to the group," he said. "It's time I explained everything."

27

It took them a half hour to barricade the doors leading into the mess hall. They placed tables, chairs, and whatever other heavy furniture available against those doors until they were sealed tight. The mess hall windows were too high off the ground to effectively barricade but, fortunately, they were framed with metal security bars.

General Spradlin examined these bars as wearily as he did the barricades. The others knew what he was thinking. If any of those creatures attacked, the barricades would hold them off, at most, only a few minutes. Worse, they might hinder their group should they need to make a quick escape.

By the time they were done with their work, the morning sun fully illuminated the interior of the Mess Hall. Waves of heat radiated from outside and there would be no air conditioner relief. The place was turning into an oven. By midday, if they survived that long, the mess hall would be unbearable.

After setting up the barricades, the group rested. General Spradlin's mood, they noticed, grew progressively darker. Becky worried the carnage in the kitchen had shaken the General. Though he was familiar with these creatures, perhaps only now he realized the odds of their survival was very slim.

When their work was done, the group huddled in the mess hall's southern corner. Samantha, Jennie, and Becky took turns peering through the windows and searching for any sign of outside movement. Doctor Evans continued to attend to Frank, while General Spradlin sat next to the injured pilot. After several long minutes of silence, the General spoke.

"You're a good soldier, Frank. I'm sorry I got you into this."

The hours since the crash had weakened the co-pilot. His features were very pale. Despite this, he grinned.

"T...thank you sir."

Spradlin lowered his head. His hands slipped to his side.

"I appreciate the patience you've shown up to now," General Spradlin continued, this time addressing the entire group. "You're owed an explanation for what is going on, and its time you got it. First thing's first. We were not shot down."

General Spradlin paused to examine his audience's reaction to those words.

"By the lack of surprise on your faces, I'll assume you figured this out on your own. On Tortuga, I ordered Captain Masters to plant an explosive device near the helicopter's tail. It was designed to damage but not destroy, the craft. Truth to tell, it was my intention all along to land in that clearing and walk to Bad Penny."

Frank Masters squirmed in the stretcher.

"I'm...sorry," he whispered to the others.

"There is no need for you to apologize, Captain," Spradlin said. "You were following orders. Your actions were entirely my responsibility."

General Spradlin let out a sigh.

"I'm sure you're wondering why I chose to engage in such a reckless action," he continued. "The answer, by now, should be obvious: Had we landed at Bad Penny, those things would have attacked us. We'd have flown right into a massacre and our bodies would have joined the others. Now I know you all have questions and I know you want answers. Now's the time to give them to you."

General Spradlin paused and collected his thoughts.

"I said this before and I'll say it again: The information I'm giving you is classified. Apart from the President of the United States, my group, and I, there are only twelve other people in the entire world who know what I'm about to tell you. The things that attacked us, that massacred the soldiers of Bad Penny, we've known about them for quite some time. We call them Automated Chameleon Units, or ACUs. As you've seen, they have the ability to change their shape, skin color, and voice to approximate anyone they come in close contact with. The units require time to adequately perform these actions and this skill is far from perfect. You can tell you're dealing with an ACU because their skin almost always has a plastic sheen. To put it bluntly, it's a little *too* perfect. Of course, by the time you realize this, it's too late. There are other ways to tell the difference between them and us, but those methods aren't as practical. X-Rays, CAT scans, or MRIs will reveal them, but try to get one of those things to sit down to take *any* of those scans. Other ways of telling the differences involve long term contact and careful observation. The ACU's do not need food or drink. They do not require air to breath, and they don't sweat or smell like humans."

"So they are robots?" Jennie asked.

"Not entirely. They're hybrids. Their skin, despite the plastic sheen, is indeed organic. It stretches and twists and conforms to whatever it is the creature is trying to replicate. It's like a living, breathing costume draped over the machinery that makes up their inner workings. And this is the best part: Not only can this layer of organic skin replicate the look of another person, if the creature spends enough time with the subject it is emulating, the skin can be altered to replicate the individual's DNA."

Once again General Spradlin paused. The group was dead silent as the implication of this revelation sank in.

"In our modern society we use machines both large and small," Spradlin continued. "We've got aircraft carriers, cars, refrigerators, televisions, you name it. In most machines, there are essential as well as non-essential components. If you were to remove a car's lighter, lights, seats, and stereo, it would still function. If, however, you were to slice this same vehicle in half, right down the middle, it becomes a useless piece of metal. In the case of the chameleons, their internal mechanisms operate...differently. You cut them in half or into thirds and, if the pieces are close enough and they're given a little time, they will repair and reintegrate themselves into what they were before."

Skeptical stares were directed at General Spradlin.

"Have you heard of nanotechnology?" he said. "No? It's a relatively new field of science. Just about everything society has created can, over time, be made smaller. In some cases, like with cell phones and computers, this is highly desired. Nanotechnology involves the control of matter on a microscopic scale. We've already managed some strides in that area. You've probably seen images of tiny needles poking into cells. This was just the start. For years, the scientific community has researched how to go about working with objects on a cellular level. To that end, they have theorized about the possibility of creating nano-robots. As the name implies, these robots would be so small that the only way to see them is through a microscope. Their use, particularly in the field of medicine, could be tremendously beneficial."

"How?" Jennie Light asked.

"With the aid of nano-robots, there might come a day in the future when invasive and therefore potentially dangerous surgeries become a thing of the past," Doctor Evans said. "In this future, a Doctor who discovers their patient has, say, a congenital heart defect or a cancerous tumor could inject a swarm of pre-programmed nano-robots into the patient's blood stream. These machines then swim through the patient and eventually reach the tumor or heart defect. Once there, the robots can do anything they were programmed for. They could dissolve blockages or burn and cut tumors apart. All within the confines of the patient's body and all done without cutting our patient open."

"But, like most technologies, there are other far less benevolent uses," General Spradlin said. "What if, instead of creating a nano-robot that attacks a tumor, it is instead programmed to block an artery?"

"Microscopic assassins?" Samantha said.

"Why stop there?" Doctor Evans added.

"Exactly. If you can create nano-robots that swim through a person's body, why not create nano-robots capable of infiltrating and sabotaging equipment? And why stop there? You could create a nano-robot capable of swimming through telephone or electrical lines, one that could infiltrate buildings or computer hard drives for the purpose of spying on unfriendly governments or businesses. You could disable vehicles, from cars to aircraft to nuclear missiles. The possibilities are truly endless. Which brings us back to the chameleons. As I said before, their outer layer consists of organic flesh. Underneath their skin is no single machine. Within their husk are several hundreds of millions of these very small individual robots. Though not quite microscopic in size, they are no larger than a flea. Near as we've been able to tell, they function individually *and* as a whole."

General Spradlin addressed Becky.

"That's why I knew the creature you shot was disabled but not dead," he said. "You likely destroyed many thousands, perhaps even hundreds of thousands of the smaller units within the creature's body with each shot, but many, many times more than that survived. Give them a little time and the surviving robots will repair and rebuild their destroyed members. Humpty Dumpty will put itself back together again."

"And the black knives—?"

"Once inserted into the body of a chameleon, the blade triggers an electrical overload that fries every last one of those tiny robots. Now, the blades aren't the only way to kill a chameleon. You could blow them to bits with high explosives and spread those individual robots so far they cannot come back together. You could temporarily stop them by freezing them.

You could permanently stop them by melting them down. The knife, however, is the only way a single person in a combat situation can effectively kill them."

"What about the black chameleon, the one that I killed? Why did it look like that?"

"It didn't have its organic skin membrane," Spradlin said.

"Why not?"

"I'm not sure. Perhaps in time it grows a layer of skin. Then again, maybe it wasn't programmed for that."

"Who created them?" Becky asked. "The Russians? The Japanese? The Chinese?"

"None of the above."

There was a long, uncomfortable pause.

"You're not saying *we* created them?" Jennie Light asked.

Spradlin shook his head.

"You saw what they could do," Spradlin said. "The way this country's going, we're lucky to make a stove that lasts beyond its two year warranty. What country on this planet has the capacity –the *ability*– to create a being with that level of sophistication?"

The group was very silent for several seconds.

"You're not saying they're aliens, are you?" Becky said.

"That's *exactly* what I'm telling you," General Spradlin replied. "These creatures, ladies and gentlemen, are the first wave of an alien invasion."

The group held their tongues. There was disbelief in their faces, but they could not deny the incredible things they witnessed.

"I don't understand," Becky Waters said. "If we're being invaded, why haven't we heard about this before?"

"The chameleons were never intended to exterminate, or even hurt, a large number of us. Not unless it can't be helped. As I said before, they're infiltrators. They're here to—" General Spradlin stopped and let out a soft laugh. "—they're here to sniff around our back yard, to figure out what exactly we're capable of, and then send that information back."

"To whom?" Samantha asked.

"To the invasion fleet, of course."

The mess hall once again became very quiet.

"You're joking," Jennie Light said.

"During the Second World War, we had agents throughout Europe feeding us information on everything from Nazi troop strength and movements to each country's general mood. We had information on where tanks and aircraft were hidden. But we also knew the price of milk on the black market. This went on for years and helped us plan and implement the Normandy invasion. Our success in the European theater was as much due to brute force as it was to volumes and volumes of good intelligence." General Spradlin looked the group over. "Are you still with me?"

"Go on," Samantha said.

"Our first hands-on encounter with the ACUs can be traced back to late October, 1925. A half-crazed prospector leads his mule through the Blue Mountains, some fifty miles south of Pyramid Lake, in the state of Arizona. He was one of the last of his kind, an old-time prospector still stubbornly searching for a fortune in gold in a land picked clean of such ore years before. I won't bore you with the details, but on that day in October he made a startling find. Half buried in the sand in a ravine, he spotted what at first others thought was a 'wooden Indian.' A closer examination revealed that the object was not made of wood. It was metal."

"The prospector leads the Sherriff of a nearby town to this strange object. Together they eventually get word to Virginia City of their find. Government officials, under a cloak of heavy security, examine the object. Afterwards, the object is boxed up and shipped off to Washington D.C. The Sheriff and the Prospector join government forces and scour the Blue Mountains for many more years, looking for any other metal men. Between 1929 and 1945 they find two more of them in this area. The metal men are in various stages of decomposition and are also crated up and shipped east. The government kept every one of these discoveries a secret."

"Fast forward a few years," General Spradlin continued. "I'm sure all of you have heard of Roswell. You've heard how a UFO supposedly crash landed there and how the government covered it up. That story was a creation of very fertile civilian minds. However, almost no one knows what happened in 1952, five years later. At that time, the Cold War was red hot and Congress had little trouble offering generous funds to support a number of top secret bases. One such secret military base was Blow Glass, located outside Sandy Hills, Arizona. The U.S. Air Force was testing what was, at that time, our most sophisticated fighter aircraft there. On the sixteenth of April, their radar picks up a blip of unknown origin. The blip was following a path that would take it straight over the base. The General in charge feared a Soviet spy aircraft and issued a red alert. A squad of fighters was scrambled. Their orders were to confront and bring the blip down. However, before a single aircraft took off, the blip sped up. The General feared an imminent attack and launched fifteen missiles at the unidentified flying object. As we were to discover much later, by sheer, complete, and total luck, one of the missiles brought that blip down."

"The UFO fell to earth in three big, and thousands of smaller, pieces over five miles of desert. There was enough of it left for us to get an idea of what we were dealing with. The craft was automated, run by machines that looked very similar to those that popped up in the Arizona desert years before. So much so that our scientists confirmed they were created by the same...beings. We also found a few odd storage devices. After some five years of very hard work, we were able to uncover some of the data on those devices. The craft had indeed been collecting information about us. It criss-crossed the world many thousands of times in the three years before it was shot down. The fact that it was able to do this without us being aware of its presence was scary enough. Then came the information that made the higher ups really break out into a cold sweat. The machine had detailed information about our defensive and offensive nuclear and non-nuclear systems up to the date it was brought down. They had a complete list of our submarines and their general routes and a very complete inventory of our air and land resources. As bad as all that was, it was even worse. They had the same information about the Russians."

"So here we were, in the early years of the Cold War, with an intelligence gold mine. Yeah, the information was five years old by that point, but it was far from useless. At any other point in time, you would have heard cheers coming from every U.S. officer stationed from the Pentagon to Alaska. But given extent of the data we found, both pertaining to the U.S. and to the Soviet Union, no one was in the mood to party."

"There was only one reason to collect information on both sides," Doctor Evans said. "The things behind the craft were creating an inventory of our strengths and weaknesses. Not as individual nations, but as a *planet*."

"Our scientists figured out one other thing," General Spradlin continued. "The automated flight instructions within the ship's computer indicated it was scheduled to return to orbit and rendezvous at a point well outside of Earth orbit. Using extrapolation, we determined the rendezvous point was well beyond the orbit of Pluto and outside the confines of the solar system."

"We pointed our most powerful telescopes in that direction," General Spradlin said. "At first, we saw nothing. The days, then months and years, passed without another incident. Then, in 1972, we finally spotted them. They were so damn far away and resembled nothing more than a tiny blob of light. But we knew they were big. The size of their ship, or fleet, was roughly that of the moon. They gave off heat as well as light. Their engines were blazing. Their rockets were aimed toward us. They were slowing down. They were –they are– braking."

"From that far away?" Becky said.

"The distances between systems are almost unimaginable," Doctor Evans said. "To travel from one solar system to another in any reasonable time –and by reasonable I'm talking hundreds of years– requires incredible speed. Acceleration, like deceleration, must be gradual, or else the beings aboard the vessels will be crushed. Thus, it takes a great deal of time to slow your craft down in order to reach your destination intact."

"Then what about the chameleons?" Samantha asked. "If the gravity of a hard stop is so bad to these aliens, shouldn't the advance probes face the same forces of gravity?"

"They do, but the chameleons were designed to survive greater extremes of acceleration and deceleration, something their alien masters cannot. Perhaps that's why they're made up of the nano-robots. The pull of gravity may not affect them as much. Regardless, we tracked one of their ships as it broke orbit from Earth and followed it half-way to the armada. Based on the projected speed, we estimate they make the round trip there and back in six years, if needed. We have to assume they communicate via some kind of radio frequency as well."

"So the chameleon makers have recent information on us?"

"Yes, and their alien masters are still on their ships, gradually slowing down and sorting through their scouts' information. No doubt they're preparing for their eventual arrival here."

"How long before they're here?" Samantha asked.

"They arrive in approximately two hundred and fifty years," Doctor Evans said.

The words were followed by an uncomfortable silence. The members of the group looked at each other. Jennie Light rubbed her jaw and shook her head. Finally, no longer able to contain herself, she let out a laugh.

"Two hundred and fifty *years*?" she repeated. "We'll be dead and buried long before they're any real threat to us."

"You'll never see them," General Spradlin agreed. "But your great-great grandchildren will. All of them will. Can you sit back and ignore the coming Armageddon because you won't have to face it?"

Jennie Light looked away from General Spradlin's angry stare.

"I also want you to consider this," General Spradlin continued. "Even though the threat is well over two hundred years away, our invaders are thousands, if not *hundreds* of thousands of years ahead of us, technologically. If we have any hope, any hope at all of a continuation of our species, we have to do everything we can to at the very least catch up to them. Otherwise, the human race is done."

General Spradlin paused to let that information sink in.

"I'm not sure I get it," Samantha said after a few seconds. "Why send the scouts planet side? Why not buzz the Earth from above, from the safety of outer space, and take whatever information they can and avoid the risk of discovery?"

"For the same reason we sent probes to the Martian surface instead of getting our data from the planet's orbit," General Spradlin said. "If you want to know what's going on at the surface of a world, you have to be there."

"They've also been known to perform sabotage missions," Doctor Evans said.

"Just as our spies did during every major war," General Spradlin said. "Make no mistake: The chameleons are doing their best to ensure we never develop into a genuine threat to their masters."

"We've got much better technology than we had in the fifties," Jennie Light said. "We must have found out more on the aliens or their fleet, right?"

"We've made strides," General Spradlin said. "When the Hubble Space Telescope became operational in 1990, the very first thing we did was aim its cameras at the armada. Unfortunately, our efforts were six years too late. In the spring of 1984 the armada went, for lack of a better term, "dark". At first we thought –hoped– they experienced some kind of internal catastrophe. Maybe they lost their power source or their systems had somehow crashed. We subsequently spotted more scout ships departing from the area the armada was last seen. These new scout ships were quicker and harder —but not impossible— to detect. The optimists in our government speculated that maybe the robots in the armada remained active, replicating themselves and continuing their mission on some sort of autopilot, despite the fact their masters were dead. The realists noted advances in the robot scout ships design argued the alien masters were not dead. The armada crew was adapting and evolving. They were improving their equipment."

"Then how, and why, did they go 'dark'?"

"The answer was obvious," Spradlin said. "They infiltrated our government and knew we were on to them. When plans for the Hubble were finalized years before her actual launch, they knew they had to hide themselves. To that end, they made sure that once the Hubble was operational, it would be completely worthless as our eye in the sky. When we got our first pictures from it, we saw nothing but a star field where the armada should be. Subsequent photographs revealed a square black mass. It's just a guess, but we think the aliens created a black object, perhaps nothing more sophisticated than a thin metallic rectangle with a thickness no greater than that of an oversized kite, and positioned it a few thousand miles in front of them. At that distance, it directly blocks our view."

"Like putting your hand in front of your face to hide the sun," Samantha said.

"Sometimes the simplest solution is the best," Spradlin said.

"How long have they been here, on Earth?" Becky asked.

"That's hard to say. The robot bodies discovered before and during World War II were very, *very* old. For all we know, those chameleon units might well have roamed America for hundreds of years before their internal energy supply gave out."

"How long has this armada been coming?"

"For at least eight thousand years," Spradlin said.

"Eight thousand years?" Becky repeated. "If we assuming these aliens are humanoid like us and live to eighty or so years, then the original group that took off on this trip would be long dead."

"It is equally possible they developed some kind of cryogenic system that allows them to wake for brief periods whenever their scout crafts depart or return," Doctor Evans said. "Maybe they spend a year awake, analyzing their data and making adjustments to their flight path while preparing their next scout missions."

"Even if we were to assume the original crew of the armada is dead, the next generation of conquerors, and the next ones after them, *has* to proceed with their mission," General Spradlin said. "What alternative is there? Earth is where the fleet is going. Our planet lies a mere two hundred and fifty years away. If, at this moment, they needed to seek another world, it would take them several thousand more years to reach it. Two hundred and fifty years, at this point, is like taking a short walk around the block."

"Then we're screwed," Samantha said. "Two hundred and fifty years isn't nearly enough time to get ready. By then, we'll still be ants going up against a nuclear bomb."

"Well," General Spradlin said. "We have made some progress."

"Since figuring out when they're arriving, we've devoted considerable resources to intercepting the scout ships," Doctor Evans said. "Six years ago, we did just that. A ship was intercepted over the Beauford Sea, some one hundred miles from Prudeau Bay, Alaska. The ship crashed down just inside the Canadian border, near the Porcupine River. We recovered the craft and its three inhabitants, all ACUs. They were in some kind of stasis and encased in glass-like pods. Obviously, we didn't dare risk letting them out, so we stabilized their pods and brought the whole thing here, to Bad Penny. We had already modified an abandoned underground laboratory and it was ready to house our captured specimens. The next six years were devoted to intense research on the ACUs. We have learned a great deal about the chameleons in that time, both their strengths and weaknesses."

"Enough to get them before they get us?" Jennie Light asked.

"Let's just say we have plenty of new information," General Spradlin said. He looked at his watch. "Unfortunately, none of that information is particularly helpful at this moment and we've got more important things to worry about."

Jennie Light let out a laugh.

"What?" she said.

"By now, three nuclear submarines have converged around Bad Penny. Regardless of whatever we accomplish here, in exactly one hour the entire island will be incinerated. My job, to see what's become of the base, is done. This place is obviously lost. Our next step is to get to a radio and signal for a transport to come pick us up. We need to get the fuck out of here before the missiles fly."

With that, a fragile feeling of hope and the dim possibility of escaping this nightmare was finally presented to the survivors of the *Little Charlie*. Becky Waters, Jennie Light, and even the very pale Frank Masters smiled. But General Spradlin did not. He remained sitting next to the injured pilot, his face grim and determined.

Samantha, too, did not share in the optimism. Even if everything Spradlin said was true, there were still things about the flight back to Bad Penny that didn't make any sense at all.

"General Spradlin, I'm confused," she said. "If your whole purpose in coming here was to look the situation over, why take us along? Why not put together a staff more experienced in dealing with those things? And why set off that explosive to bring my chopper down? Why not just order me to land in that clearing?"

General Spradlin didn't answer right away. From the expression in the others of the group, they too were curious for an answer. After a few seconds the General nodded.

"Excellent question, Captain Aron," he said. "There were reasons to set off that explosive. Good reasons. But as my grade school teacher used to say: Talking about things isn't quite as effective as showing them."

In a lightning fast motion, General Spradlin pulled his black blade from its holster and, to the horror of those around him, rammed it deep into Captain Frank Master's chest.

28

Everyone was stunned by the General's swift and cold blooded action.

Everyone but Captain Frank Masters.

His eyes surveying the black knife embedded in his chest. Despite what should have been an incredibly painful if not *lethal* wound, his facial expression displayed nothing more than curiosity.

General Spradlin's right hand remained on the blade's handle. After a few seconds, he exhaled.

"Stand back," General Spradlin told the others.

They didn't need to be told. The fact that Frank Masters was still alive, if such a term applied, despite the blade rammed through his chest, prove he was another of the creatures. And he remained alive because General Spradlin's hand remained on the knife's handle. The moment he released it, the blade would initiate its lethal electric discharge and Frank Masters would be incinerated.

No one spoke for several seconds.

"How...how long have you known?" Samantha Aron finally whispered. "How is this even possible?"

Frank Masters' face remained neutral. He no longer looked sickly and weak. Color returned to his face and his eyes were alive and, as much as was possible for a machine, filled with what looked to the others like raw hatred.

"Stay very still," General Spradlin told the mechanical pilot. "You know what happens when I let go of the blade."

"What...what the hell is going on?" Samantha said.

"You asked why we sent your group back to Bad Penny and why we needed to disable the helicopter," General Spradlin replied. "They were really good questions, Captain Aron. Your timing, on the other hand, could have been better."

"What are you talking about?"

"The reason we disabled the helicopter was because we feared one or more of you were not what you seemed," General Spradlin said.

He let those terrible words hang in the air for several long seconds. The remaining crew of the *Little Charlie* looked at each other.

"The chameleons are different from us in one other key aspect," General Spradlin continued. "Their bodies are not terribly buoyant. They can float in water for only a few minutes before sinking. Once they've sunk, they have to walk along the bottom of whatever river or sea they're in to get wherever they're going. Unfortunately for them, if they're fully submerged for longer than forty minutes, the nano-robots that make up their body lose cohesion. Prolonged contact with water discharges the electrical field that keeps their individual parts together. In layman's terms, they dissolve. That's why a little island like Bad Penny is such a perfect place to store them. It's also why we have no boat dock and had to make sure the *Little Charlie* wouldn't fly again."

"But...but he triggered your bomb!"

"If he didn't, he would have revealed himself at that very moment," General Spradlin said. "He didn't want me to know. Not then anyway. Right Frank?"

Frank Masters did not reply. He remained perfectly still in the stretcher. His eyes were alien, cold and probing.

"But you broke your leg," Samantha continued. "The blood?"

"It's not that hard for those things to make their outer organic membranes bleed on command. As for the broken bone and ripped flesh, the nano-robots within the chameleon's body simply formed themselves into the shape and texture of shattered bone and changed their individual colors to approximate that of flesh. That's how they fake serious injuries. A good doctor can tell the difference."

These words proved a revelation to Samantha.

"That's why Frank didn't want Doctor Evans to look him over!"

"He protested quite a bit, didn't he?" Doctor Evans said. "If you remember, he was willing to let me examine him only after I insisted I was a scientist and not a medical Doctor."

"Then when Frank dropped that remote control he...he did it on purpose?"

"That's how you guys found out about the helicopter's sabotage?" Spradlin asked. "Very clever, Captain Masters. You knew Samantha would be suspicious about the emergency landing, so you purposely left behind evidence to prove sabotage was the cause." General Spradlin turned from Frank back to Samantha. "I suppose you confronted Captain Masters about the remote, and, after some polite protestation, he was only too happy to attribute that sabotage to me. Let me guess what happened next: You tell the others in the group and very soon everyone is suspicious of me and my men. *We're* the bad guys. Divide and conquer."

"When did you first suspect?" Frank Masters asked.

"Well before boarding the chopper and well before Bad Penny went dark. I knew the ACUs planet-side were looking real hard for their three missing comrades. We've found high security computers hacked and information stolen. I figured you guys might make a move on the base."

"And you let this happen? You let all those people die?" Jennie Light said.

"We had a strategy in place," General Spradlin said. His voice was low. "A strategy that would have avoided all this bloodshed. But we were too late to implement it. Our hand was tipped."

"The British agent," Becky Waters said.

"The one element we couldn't –didn't– anticipate," General Spradlin said. "When Bad Penny went dark, we scrambled. The *Little Charlie* was the last flight out, and we had to isolate it. We feared one or more of our three captured ACUs were on board, or any of their friends. We quickly examined each of your personnel files. I needed to know if there was a chance anyone on this flight showed any sign of being an ACU. As it happened, I found three suspects: Private Thompson, Private Bartlett, and you, Frank. Each one of you moved within military circles for a while seeking, and receiving, entry into departments that brought you closer and closer to my organization and, more specifically, Bad Penny. The three of you made sure you'd eventually get a job here. And when Doctor Evans examined your injury, I knew for sure."

The machine that was Frank Masters considered the information.

"I would have roasted you then and there, but I still wasn't certain about Thompson and Bartlett," General Spradlin continued. "I did my own version of divide and conquer when I sent Private Waters and Colonel Robinson, two people who could handle themselves very well with their weapons, with Private Thompson. Private Bartlett, meanwhile, took it upon himself to go out with Private Light. I followed them, to make sure nothing happened. Your fellow chameleons went ahead and killed both Bartlett and Thompson. It left only you."

"Couldn't be helped," Frank Masters said. "We'll adapt."

The neutral look on Frank's face sent a chill down Becky and Samantha's spines. The tone of his voice was one of triumph, not defeat.

"What are you hiding?" Becky said.

There was a gasp, and the members of the group turned away from General Spradlin and Frank Masters. With a trembling hand, Jennie Light pointed to the Mess Hall's south side windows.

Everyone looked in that direction. Just outside the Mess Hall building there were at least two dozen black forms surrounding the building and slowly making their way its entrance.

"General?" Jennie Light said.

"He can't stop them," Frank Masters said.

"Don't let them in," Spradlin said.

"How exactly do you intend to do that?" Frank Masters said.

Sweat ran down Spradlin's forehead and cheek.

"It was easy convincing you to come to the Mess Hall," Frank Masters said. "Once inside, it was even easier to surround you. I'm surprised, General. I thought you'd be a better adversary. There's no way out, now."

General Spradlin used his free hand to wipe the sweat from his forehead.

"How long have you been a scout?" Spradlin asked.

"Does it matter?" Frank replied.

"It doesn't, I suppose," Spradlin said. He eyed the handle of the black blade and loosened his grip on it. "Perhaps I'll just let this go..."

Frank Master's smile faded. His facial expression became an unemotional cipher.

"I am an automated unit," Frank said. "Though my speech patterns and outward display of emotions might appear genuine, I am not susceptible to intimidation or torture. Your threats are meaningless."

"Then indulge me," General Spradlin said. "I've known Captain Frank Masters for a long time. Was it really him, or was I dealing with one of you all along?"

"I replaced the real Frank Masters over twenty years ago," the chameleon said. "This was shortly after his parents were killed in an auto accident."

"You arranged it?"

"Of course."

The chameleon's smile returned.

"At the time, Frank Masters was in the process of joining the special forces," the thing continued. "He completed his physicals. Taking over for him proved an easy substitution."

"But you fought so valiantly," Spradlin said. "You saved so many lives."

"Part of the act. Had I known back then you worked for Oscuro—"

"Who told you about Oscuro?"

"We have our agents, General. You know that."

"Why did you let us live? Why didn't you kill us back in the forest?"

"We needed to learn everything you knew about us," Frank Masters said. "In that respect, you've been very accommodating."

General Spradlin's face turned pale.

"Your history lesson was most interesting," the chameleon continued. "Our hosts will value this information for years to come. Especially the knowledge that there are only twelve people outside of your organization aware of us. Finding them won't be easy, but we'll manage."

"Bastard," Spradlin spat. "At least you won't be giving them that information."

The fingers on General Spradlin's right hand, the one that held the blade, moved. In a fraction of a second the blade's electrical pulse would be released. However, Frank Masters proved quicker. He grabbed General Spradlin's hand and pressed down, locking it back in place around the blade's handle.

"No you don't," Frank Masters said.

General Spradlin tried to free himself. Frank applied more force and the sound of brittle bones breaking was heard through the Mess Hall. Blood dripped from between Frank's closed hand.

"What the hell are you going to do?" Spradlin muttered between clenched teeth. "Take me with you?

Frank Masters gave the General an ice cold smile.

"I don't need you," he said. "All I need is your hand."

There came a sickening snap. General Spradlin fell onto the ground. Blood splattered onto the floor. The General's right hand was gone.

In a smooth, mechanical motion, Frank Masters stood up. The injury to his leg, still grotesque in appearance, did not hinder his movements at all. Frank's hands remained over his chest, holding on to General Spradlin's detached right hand which, in turn, remained gripped to the black blade.

The rest of the group took a step back, their guns drawn. No one dared fire at such close range. Frank Masters ignored them and looked down at the General. The General's wound was bleeding profusely.

"It will be over for you soon, General," Frank Masters said. He looked up at the group. "And your little group."

"Let them go," General Spradlin said.

"You know that can't be," Frank Masters replied. "I must congratulate you. You've made it quite far. Your only failure was in underestimating how many of us infiltrated this base."

Behind him, some fifty feet away, the Mess Hall door was forced opened. Debris intended to barricade the entry was pushed aside as if it were nothing more than cardboard and tissue. Several mechanical beings, their bodies covered in blood and gore, stepped into the Hall. Behind them came another wave, then another, until there were well over forty ACUs in the Mess Hall.

The survivors of the *Little Charlie* huddled together around General Spradlin. They heard a noise and turned the other way. The double doors leading into the kitchen opened and several more waves of chameleons emerged. They too were covered in blood and gore. They had pretended to be corpses only moments before.

To Samantha's horror, one of them was Warren Bligh.

That creature, now part of a group of well over sixty chameleons, surrounded the survivors of the *Little Charlie*. Warren flashed Samantha a cold smile.

"No hard feelings, honey," the thing that looked like Warren said.

29

Samantha, Becky, Jennie, and Doctor Evans huddled around General Spradlin. Doctor Evans was the only one not paying attention to the overwhelming number of chameleons surrounding the group. He tightened a tourniquet around Spradlin's wound that considerably slowed the bleeding. From one of the chopper's first aid kits he pulled out and applied a thick layer of antibiotic crème around the stump before wrapping it with gauze and bandages. Finally, he reached for a bottle of pills.

"Swallow these," Evans told the General. "They'll ease your pain."

General Spradlin forced his mouth open and Doctor Evans threw several pills in.

All the while, Frank Masters stood before the group. He pulled the blade from his chest and dropped it and General Spradlin's severed hand on the ground. The other chameleons and robots kept a few steps back but had the survivors of the *Little Charlie* completely surrounded.

"That's some work," Frank Masters said when Doctor Evans was done fixing General Spradlin's injury. "You do know more about medicine than you let on. The care you gave me was clearly inferior." Frank Masters shook his head. "Either way, you're wasting what little time you have left. It won't matter whether General Spradlin bleeds to death or is ripped apart. He —and every one of you— will be just as dead."

Doctor Evans didn't reply.

Frank shook his head. The other chameleons made an impressive platoon. They carried no weapons but had obviously seen intense battle. Each and every one of them was baptized in the blood of the military base's personnel.

Doctor Evans lifted General Spradlin into a sitting position.

"You...you played us all along," Spradlin gasped. His body shook. "How did you know about Oscuro?"

A cold smile appeared on Frank's face. He let out a very human laugh.

"We have people in high places, General," Frank replied.

"Who?"

Frank motioned to his companions. They moved closer to the group.

"No more threats?" Frank said. "It worked so well the last time."

"Tell me, you bastard!" General Spradlin yelled. He winced and cold sweat ran down his forehead.

Frank stopped. As he did, so too did the rest of the chameleons.

"For you, the war ends here, General," Frank said. "Your suffering will not last much longer. In many ways, you and your group are among the privileged."

"Maybe they are," Spradlin hissed. "I fought you...your scouts, well."

"That you did."

General Spradlin clenched his teeth and gasped for air.

"Tell me," he muttered. "Even if it's the last thing I'll ever know. Who told you about Oscuro?"

The creature that was Frank Masters paused a moment. Whatever internal programming it possessed, designed so clearly to emulate human actions, reactions, and emotions, considered Spradlin's final request. General Spradlin knew there was nothing to stop the creature for finishing the group off.

"Please," Spradlin implored.

The creature tilted its head. Its mouth opened, and it whispered:

"The vice-president."

General Spradlin's pale face turned even paler.

"Son of a bitch," he muttered. "It can't be...he's frail, he's got a pace-maker. He's under the care of a special White House Doctor—"

Spradlin's eyes opened wide.

"Oh no," he muttered.

The cold smile returned to Frank Masters' face.

"Of course," Frank said. "He too is one of us. We adapt, General Spradlin. Human beings aren't so different from us. They're also machines, only they're built entirely of organic parts. In recent years we have cultivated organs, cloned and grown them, not unlike vegetables in a garden. Once grown, we've clothed our nano-robots in suits of flesh and incorporated these very real organs. One day we hope this clothing is complete enough to fool even the most thorough of medical examinations."

The look of shock remained on General Spradlin's face. He had nothing to say.

"How about that?" Frank Masters continued. "The man one heartbeat away from the presidency is one of ours. It must make you feel like hell that you've failed so miserably in your one, and only, job. We knew all your moves from the very beginning."

"You can't get off the island."

The skin on Frank's face began to bubble. Its shape changed, becoming leaner and longer. Brown hair became grayer. Brown eyes turned blue. Wrinkles disappeared

"We'll get out of here," the creature said. The voice was no longer that of Frank Masters. It was General Spradlin's. His features, too, were changing to that of General Spradlin. "Once I tell them we're ready to go."

"Of course," General Spradlin said.

Frank's face remained in flux, though it wouldn't be long before it was an exact duplicate of the General's own.

"Some group you've got," General Spradlin continued. "I expected more."

"More?" Frank inquired. "When we discovered this is where you held our three scouts, we made a concerted effort to infiltrate this island on all levels. We brought every scout we could spare to this place, to make sure when the moment came, we would free our companions."

"Every scout?" General Spradlin said. "All except for the vice-president and his physician?"

The smile on Frank's altered face disappeared. His eyes locked in on General Spradlin's. Somewhere deep within the creature's programming, a realization was made. Moments before, the creature that was Frank Masters offered General Spradlin the identity of their most well-placed mole. Now, it had offered a second bit of information of equal and perhaps greater importance.

"What are you hiding from me?" the creature said.

"This group you have here," General Spradlin said. "They represent the bulk of your scouts on Earth, don't they?"

As he spoke, Doctor Evans got up and took a step forward. He stood between the General and his group and the dark figures surrounding them. Frank Masters took a step back.

"What do you have—"

Spradlin abruptly turned and yelled:

"Hit the floor!"

Becky, Jennie, and Samantha followed Spradlin's orders without hesitancy. Spradlin fell over them, covering them with his body. The creature that was Frank Masters watched in silence, his mechanical brain attempting to analyze and interpret this illogical movement. His group of chameleons, likewise, stood still.

Every member of the *Little Charlie* huddled together.

All but Doctor Evans.

He faced Frank Masters and locked eyes with the homicidal creature. Then, the Doctor raised his arms until he looked like a preacher about to deliver a sermon. His head arched back. Then it arched back even more. Farther and farther. No human being could bend his head that far back without breaking his spine.

Finally, but too late, the programming within Frank Masters realized what was happening. The creature closed its eyes. An almost human look of fear momentarily crossed the thing's face.

"Very clever—" it whispered.

And then everything went white.

30

The survivors of the *Little Charlie* felt the heat and crackle of an enormous electrical discharge. For a moment, it was like they were in the center of a furious thunderstorm. The hairs on their bodies stood up, the heat around them was scorching. Despite the booming crackle of electricity, they heard the creatures around them howl. It was as if their internal programming allowed them to experience the agony of a violent death.

Neither Becky Waters nor Samantha Aron could understand what was going on. Becky had a single hope.

If this is their death, then let the journey to hell be a very painful one.

Samantha also wondered about the screams. But her mind was on Frank Masters and Warren Bligh. One was her best friend, the other her lover. She had never really known the human beings they originally were. Her stomach twisted and turned. Even as the chameleons died around her, she wanted to confront the bastards and take them on. Even if she were fried in the electrical current like the rest of them, she'd die swinging. For their deception. For their lies.

After only a couple of seconds, the electrical surge was finished. The screams of the chameleons faded, replaced by an eerie silence.

Very, very slowly, the survivors of the *Little Charlie* moved. Becky Waters opened her eyes and at once jumped back. Standing directly before her and reaching out with his deadly hands were the remains of Frank Masters. In the creature's very last action, it reached out and attempted grabbing the members of the human group. Huddled together as they were, if Frank Masters succeeded, they too would have been electrocuted.

Becky pushed away the ashen corpse. It collapsed on its side and shattered into thousands of dark little pieces.

"Asshole," she muttered before realizing Samantha was right beside her. "Sorry. I knew he was your—"

"You get no argument from me," Samantha said.

General Spradlin and Jennie Light were the last to sit up. The group surveyed the Mess Hall. With the exception of Frank Masters, most of the chameleons remained in place, erect but blackened to a crisp. A couple toward the back tried to flee. Another pair were on their knees while a third lay on the floor. The agony of the chameleons' last moments was etched on each and every one of their frozen faces. The blade Frank removed from his chest and threw to the floor, likewise, had roasted in the electric blast. It was nothing more than ash.

"This place looks like some kind of God damned museum," Jennie said.

Samantha stood up. She stepped past the remains of Frank Masters and walked to that of Warren. Despite the dark features, she recognized her lover's face. The memory of cuddling up in his arms flashed through her mind and she shivered. A deep, angry frown filled her sweaty face. She spat at him.

"Fuck you all," she raged. But her anger didn't last. A single tear streamed down her face. Samantha wiped the tear away and again stared at Warren. She caressed his black cheek, tracing her fingertips over his lips and nose. Her hand settled on its cheek. The smooth surface turned to dust under his hand, spilling down and drifting to the floor.

"Fuck you all," she whispered.

Jennie Light helped General Spradlin to his feet. They ignored the other figures and examined the remains of Doctor Evans. As with the other creatures, his body was blackened. It too roasted in the electrical storm that emanated from his body.

General Spradlin pulled his injured arm across his chest.

"Thank you," he said to Evans's remains.

The figure of Doctor Evans moved slightly.

Jennie gasped.

"Easy," General Spradlin said. Almost all at once, the Doctor's figure crumbled. Pieces both large and small fell In chunks on the Mess Hall floor, leaving behind a pile of dark ash.

"What...what exactly happened?" Samantha asked.

"Don't look at me," Becky said. "I'm just a grunt who came along for the ride."

"Help me with the General," Jennie Light said.

Becky, Samantha, and Jennie stepped past the ashes of the creatures. Samantha grabbed a chair and slid it to General Spradlin's side. He sat down.

"They're all gone?" General Spradlin asked. His face was very pale.

"As far as I can tell, yes," Becky said.

General Spradlin nodded. Despite the intense pain he felt, a look of genuine relief flicked over his face.

"We...we better get to the control tower," Spradlin muttered. "Quick."

"Why?"

"We need to call off...the bombing..."

"You told us we had an hour," Samantha said.

General Spradlin managed a very weak smile.

"I lied," he said.

31

The four survivors of the *Little Charlie* found a gore filled Humvee with its key still in the ignition abandoned on the main road some two hundred feet south of the Mess Hall. Unlike the Humvee they found earlier, this one's engine was intact.

"They didn't expect us to make it any farther than the Mess Hall," General Spradlin said.

Samantha and Jennie helped General Spradlin into the passenger side seat of the vehicle while Becky Waters covered their movements. They didn't expect resistance or another attack, but weren't about to assume all their troubles were over. The three women mounted the vehicle, Becky last, with Samantha in the driver's seat. She headed directly south, hurrying past the administrative buildings that made up the remainder of the base. All that was left, beyond the forest, was the landing pad.

On the way, Samantha stopped at the base's only four way stop. Her action, she realized belatedly, was automatic and pointless. There would be no vehicle coming from the other side. There would be no pedestrians who had the right of way. Her gaze drifted off to the side, toward the rusted tool shed. The occupants of the vehicle stared in that direction as well, for there was much to see.

The structure looked like it had exploded. Its sheet metal walls were peeled back like torn flesh. A faint black smoke rose from the shed's center.

After a few seconds, General Spradlin gently tapped Samantha's shoulder.

"Let's go," he said.

It took them a couple more minutes to reach their destination. When they did, they were shocked by what they found. Little remained of the security station Samantha Aron drove through the previous evening. The metal and wood structure was in pieces. They drove past it and to the pad's parking lot. There they found Samantha's Humvee, the one she used to get to the landing pad the evening before, lying on its side.

Beyond the parking lot, the tower looked like it was the victim of a brutal raid. Every one of the building's windows was shattered, leaving crumpled vertical blinds fluttering in the morning breeze. Within the tower was utter darkness.

The group wearily eyed that darkness, wondering what lay inside. Samantha shut the Humvee off and slid out of the vehicle. Becky and Jennie exited as well. They opened the passenger door and helped General Spradlin out. By now, his features were deathly pale, his breathing shallow. He was covered in sweat.

"Is it possible...could there be more of them?" Samantha asked.

General Spradlin shook his head.

"They're gone."

General Spradlin examined his fellow survivors. Becky and Samantha were hesitant to enter the control tower. Sweat shimmered on their foreheads. Jennie Light, on the other hand, carried herself well in the morning heat. She stood the closest to the structure, her lean figure tense.

"What if Frank lied?" Samantha said. "What if there are more of them?"

"He could have lied, but why?" General Spradlin said. "He was certain we were finished. There would be no reason to spread any disinformation. Not at that point."

"Yeah but—"

"He knows those things better than all of us," Jennie intruded. "I'm guessing he's right."

She walked to the door leading into the control tower. It was smashed open and its metal frame was twisted. Jennie Light stepped into the building and disappeared into the darkness.

Outside, the remaining three survivors watched. A few seconds passed. Finally, Jennie Light stepped out and waved.

"Come on in," she said. "The water's fine."

Becky and Samantha helped General Spradlin into the building. The entire floor was very dark. Jennie pulled at several vertical blinds, snapping them from their places. Light streamed inside the control tower, revealing a floor littered with shattered electronic equipment and documents.

"They've destroyed everything," Jennie Light said. She walked to the opposite end of the room and removed more vertical blinds from a window. Before her were the remains of the base's radio.

Jennie Light turned and let out a laugh. Sitting in the corner a few feet away was a coffee machine. It too was shattered to pieces.

"Absolutely everything," she said.

"What about the communication jammer?" Becky Waters asked. "Did you see anything—?"

In the corner of the room, just a few feet from the shattered coffee maker and on a wood table lay a black metal box. The table and the box were the only things within the room in one piece.

"Do you think?" Samantha said.

"What else could it be?" Becky said.

Samantha helped General Spradlin to the box. He took a few precious minutes to look it over. He could feel the stares from the women behind him.

We're about to be bombed! Hurry up!

General Spradlin nonetheless took his time to examine the featureless box. There were no buttons or any indentations. There was no indication of any way to open it. As General Spradlin got closer, he could feel heat emanating from within it.

"The good news, if you could we could call it that, is I think this is the jammer," General Spradlin said.

"The bad news?" Jennie Light asked.

"I haven't a clue what to do with it."

"You've never encountered a device like this?"

"Yeah, I've seen devices like it. All of them, each and every one, had a trap. Our alien friends don't much care for us getting hold of any of their technology. For all I know, if we so much as touch it, it'll blow."

General Spradlin motioned for Samantha to help him step back.

"It's too risky to do anything with it," General Spradlin said.

"But if we don't disable it..."

"It doesn't really matter, does it?" General Spradlin said. "Even if we were to somehow, miraculously, figure out how to turn the device off, we still have to signal the subs. Have you taken a good look at the radio equipment?"

"There must be some way to fix it," Samantha said. She gave the equipment a quick examination. "Maybe we can—"

Her voice faded as she looked at the mangled radio equipment. General Spradlin was right. The radio was beyond any help.

"How long do we have?" Becky asked.

"Thirty six minutes, give or take," General Spradlin said.

The women around him were silent. Jennie Light approached the metal box. She took a deep breath and, like General Spradlin, looked it over.

"One thing's for sure," she said. "We need to get rid of this before we can communicate with anyone out there."

"Don't touch it!" General Spradlin said.

It was too late. Jennie Light closed her eyes, reached down, and picked the device up.

Nothing happened.

"That's a relief," she said.

The others approached Jennie Light. On the bottom of the box were several indentations.

"What could they mean?" Becky asked.

"They have to be controls," General Spradlin said. "But there's no way to know what they do."

Jennie Light shook her head.

"Then we'll have to use trial and error."

"You played the odds and survived one incredibly foolish risk," General Spradlin said. "Don't push it."

"Even if I don't, we're dead anyway."

General Spradlin had no reply to that.

"Be careful," Samantha said.

Jennie Light laughed.

"I'll try my best."

She pressed a button. When she did, an inner green light came on. She pressed another. This time, the light was red.

"A code?"

"Could be," General Spradlin said.

She pressed another button. Green again.

"This thing is getting warmer," Jennie Light said.

"It's also starting to...squeal," Samantha said.

Jennie Light pressed a third button. Green again.

"It's getting *really* hot."

General Spradlin bit his upper lip but said nothing. Jennie Light pressed another button. Green yet again.

"The noise..." Samantha said.

The whine had turned into a wail.

"Throw it out the window!" General Spradlin yelled.

Jennie Light did as told. She heaved the box with all her might through one of the shattered windows in the front of the control tower. The box landed next to the Humvee they drove into the landing pad.

"Get down!"

The four survivors of the *Little Charlie* fell to the floor and covered themselves. The electronic whine from the box became an earth shattering scream. The box lit up from the inside until it looked like it was melting. The scream reached a fever pitch.

And then the box exploded.

32

The explosion shook the control tower and sent debris flying in all directions. The structure held, but barely. Whatever was left of the windows erupted and embedded itself in the wall above the four soldiers. For their part, they were thrown back by the shockwave and also slammed against the building's inner wall.

A fireball filled the parking area. It rose into the sky before leaving behind a heavy black cloud.

Afterwards, the soldiers painfully got to their knees. They looked in the direction of the explosion.

There was little left of the Humvee they used to get to the control tower.

"Looks...looks like the jammer's done," Jennie Light said. She brushed dust from her clothing.

General Spradlin coughed. Samantha and Becky helped him to his feet.

"That was a...a very stupid thing you did," General Spradlin said.

"Stupid or not, the jammer's gone," Jennie said. "We can send out signals now."

"With what?" General Spradlin said. "We've got no other radio."

"There has to be something," Jennie Light said. She thought about it for a few seconds. "Those creatures took good care to destroy every personal communication device on the base. But what about cell phones?"

"You know they aren't permitted on the base," Becky Waters said.

"You mean us grunts aren't permitted to have them on the base," Jennie Light countered. "I'll bet some of the officers in this place didn't follow that particular order."

"You might be right," General Spradlin said.

"Then what are we waiting for?" Jennie said. "Let's find a cell phone!"

Jennie Light headed to the back of the control tower. She hastily pushed aside destroyed equipment and file cabinets and searched through the debris. Samantha and Becky did the same at opposite sides of the room. General Spradlin could do little but watch their progress.

For several long minutes, the trio of soldiers sorted through the wreckage. Jennie Light noted General Spradlin sitting limp on his chair. His eyes were half-closed.

"Don't leave us just yet," Jennie said.

General Spradlin's eyes opened wider. He shook his head and straightened in his chair.

"Feeling week," he mumbled.

"Talk to us," Samantha said.

"About what?"

"Tell us about Doctor Evans," Jennie said. "What the hell was he? Another one of them?"

"In a manner of speaking," Spradlin replied. He rubbed his face and wiped sweat from his forehead.

"Don't tell me you're going to get cryptic on us now?" Jennie said. "Not after all we've been through?"

Samantha and Becky's attention, like that of Jennie, had shifted to the General. From the looks on their faces, it was obvious they feared he was fading away.

"Keep searching," Spradlin said.

"We will," Jennie said. "While you tell us about Doctor Evans."

General Spradlin considered her request. Presently, he spoke.

"Everything I said about the Armada was true. But there's more...much more we know about them."

"Like?"

"Their most recent home world revolves around a yellow star our scientists designated A-43169," General Spradlin said. "We say it is their most 'recent' home world because they are a race of travelers with no permanent home. They jump from planet to planet in search of resources. When they reach their new planet, they become a hoard of locusts. They ravage the planet's resources, a process that may take a hundred years to fully accomplish. When they're done, they leave behind the withered husk of the planet. Then they lift of and head for greener pastures."

"How did they find us?" Becky asked.

"Given the distances they travel between worlds, they spend plenty of time and energy analyzing their course and potential ripe targets," General Spradlin said. "We had the bad luck of being the closest system with the most abundant resources from where they were. Their deep space probes first discovered us some twenty thousand years ago. Perhaps longer. Data on our planet suggested it was perfect for their needs. They sent more sophisticated probes our way, anticipating the eventual path they'd take. These probes touched down in what would eventually become known as North America some ten thousand years ago. The aliens were...delighted...by what the probes found. Earth had a hospitable atmosphere, temperature, and, most importantly, ecology. Earth was designated their next target after they were done on A-43169. Their arrival was scheduled for many thousands of years into the future. In the meantime, they conducted further examinations to make sure all remained as it should be and prepared our planet for their arrival."

General Spradlin stared out a shattered window.

"We plan our lives around tomorrow or next week," Spradlin continued. "Some of us, when we're young, plan for careers and some far thinkers even plan for their retirement. These creatures think along the lines of millennia. They have to. Their trip from A-43169 to Earth, in the end, will take over nine thousand years and exhaust almost all their fuel and supplies. When they arrive, they have little option but to land and immediately begin ravaging our world. This is when they are at their most vulnerable. Their greatest danger is arriving here after all these years only to find that some disaster has rendered their new world unusable."

"Disaster?"

"Such a thing happened some sixty-five million years ago on Earth. Back then, our planet had a thriving environment, ecosystem, and population of reptiles. Dinosaurs were Earth's predominant life form. Then, just like that, they were wiped out. Scientists call it the Cretaceous-Tertiary extinction. The cause of this event is still somewhat in dispute. One thing we do know is that an asteroid hit this planet around that time and what was once a very habitable place became very inhospitable for many, many years. If our visitors arrived here at that point, they might not have found the resources they needed. That being the case, they could well have faced extinction."

"So they continued their observations on our planet. They realized this world was in a most fortunate place. In orbit behind us lie the largest planets of this solar system: Neptune, Uranus, and, especially, Jupiter and Saturn. Those planets are like our big brothers in that they defend us from cosmic bullies. Countless asteroids which may have threatened our existence have either been deflected or eaten up by these giants. This was certainly the case back in 1994 when the Shoemaker-Levy 9 comets hit Jupiter. Had they struck Earth, mankind would have been wiped out."

"But the aliens weren't about to stake their continued existence on our planetary neighbors alone. They had to make sure absolutely nothing threatened us until they arrived. To that end, they send other crafts our way, armed satellites which, even now, orbit the outer fringes of our solar system. We've identified at least five of them just outside the orbit of Neptune and suspect there are many, *many* more. Their purpose is to analyze incoming comets and asteroids and predict their paths. If they're coming our way, the satellites take them out."

General Spradlin grimaced from the effort of talking. He pressed his injured arm against his chest and let out a breath.

"So everything was in place and ready," he continued after a few seconds. "But they wanted more."

"More?"

"They searched long and hard through our flora and fauna for just the right elements. They discovered the possibility, at the dawn of mankind, that Earth possessed sentient life forms."

"Our ancestors," Samantha said.

"With so many years before their arrival, they had to anticipate our development and progress. Estimates were made as to how much more advanced our fledgling civilization would be by the time they arrived. The aliens' greatest minds examined their data and found it insufficient. They needed eyes on the ground, spies among us, to see for themselves just how fast we were developing. But they couldn't come here themselves. The laws of physics made such a trip impossible for them. Therefore, they created a series of robots capable of withstanding the sudden, crushing acceleration and deceleration required to enter Earth's atmosphere in a relatively short amount of time and modeled these creatures on our unique physique. Their mission was to infiltrate us and get the information their masters needed. Unfortunately for them, they didn't have much time to implement their plan. Their current home world was used up and they had to leave. They chose, despite reservations, to make the journey to Earth even though they still didn't know enough about us. Yes, we were primitive at that time and there was a very real possibility we would still be very primitive –if we survived– when they arrived. The armada lifted off and began their journey here. The creatures within set their instruments on automatic and entered their cryogenic units. They drifted off into an eight thousand year sleep."

"When they awoke some seven hundred years ago, on the outer fringes of our solar system, their ships had begun the long process of slowing down. The scientists aboard the armada immediately sent more probes our way to make sure their destination remained habitable. It was, but the scientists were shocked to find their projections regarding our progress were inadequate. We were much farther along than they expected. We had rudimentary nations and were on the verge of our Renaissance. At the rate we were advancing, the aliens feared we'd have nuclear weapons well before they arrived."

General Spradlin paused before saying:

"That scared the shit out of them."

"Why?" Becky asked. "They're still far more advanced than us."

"They may have no love for humans, but what scares them is the possibility we might put up a fight."

"How can we possibly be any match for them?" Samantha asked.

"We wouldn't —indeed we couldn't— win a war against them," Spradlin agreed. "But if we know we're going to lose a war to a race that takes no prisoners, there's a chance we might turn our weapons from them and toward the planet itself. If we're going to die, we'll take those sons of bitches down with us."

"Scorched earth," Becky said.

"Humanity dies in the blasts," Spradlin said. "And the aliens starve."

"So why didn't they take steps back then to get rid of us?" Becky asked.

"That's a very good question. The fact that they have left us alive suggests they have uses for us. Given their ravager mentality, I'm not terribly optimistic about what those uses are."

"How the hell do you know all this?" Jennie Light asked.

"Isn't it obvious?" General Spradlin said. "We're in contact with them."

33

Five simple words. In any other context and about any other subject matter, they might have elicited a polite nod or, perhaps, indifference. At this moment and regarding this subject, the words set off the equivalent of a nuclear firestorm.

Samantha, Becky, and Jennie were glued in place, their full attention on General Spradlin. For several more seconds, no one spoke. For several more seconds the three women survivors of the *Little Charlie* digested this incredible revelation. Finally...

"How...how is that possible?" Jennie Light asked.

"It turns out the inhabitants of the armada are not all that different from us," General Spradlin said. "They don't all share the same opinions and often argue about their course of action. Some have openly questioned their nomadic, parasitic way of being. They wonder whether it's time to lay down genuine roots and no longer conquer and subjugate planets in their path. They may not feel any sympathy for the cultures and peoples they've destroyed in the past, but pragmatism tells them they may eventually reach a point where there is no other nearby planet they can use for their nutrients and fuel. For years they've worried faulty scouting data could send them to a world with any number of dangers that might threaten their existence and strand them without the means to move on. This group represents a small minority in the armada, yet they have changed some minds."

"Enough to halt their attack?" Samantha said.

"I'm not sure," General Spradlin admitted. "But everything evolves, and their culture is no exception. This group has followed our progress. Some of them even have a grudging respect for us. They want to negotiate. They're willing to share our resources."

"Share?" Jennie asked. "In exchange for what?"

"Information," Spradlin replied.

"How can we trust them?" Becky said. "What if this is a stalling tactic, a way to make us give in?"

"It's possible, of course, but they sent us something very important as a sign of good will."

"Doctor Evans," Jennie Light said.

Silence again descended on the control tower. A breeze kicked up and the verticals danced against the shattered windows.

"Doctor Evans was a chameleon," Spradlin said. "When he...arrived...we were weary. We feared we were sent a Trojan horse. But Doctor Evans did everything we asked and provided considerable information about the Armada and its history."

"How do you know any of the information was accurate?" Becky said.

"We couldn't verify everything, but we were able to verify quite a bit," General Spradlin said. "The fact is that until Dr. Evans came along, the aliens went to great lengths to keep us from having even a piece of one of their robotic scouts. Giving us Evans was a big –a *very* big– good will gesture. For three years we examined this being. For three years it allowed us to poke and prod its inner workings. That's how we gained such an in depth knowledge of its strengths...and weaknesses."

"The black blades?" Becky asked.

"Doctor Evans gave us the schematics for them. He told us how to make them. Even more importantly, he told us every individual chameleon scout from the armada has its own suicide switch designed to be used in case it, or its group, was in danger of capture. Doctor Evans used the suicide switch back in the mess hall to destroy those other creatures."

General Spradlin leaned back in his chair and again winced as pain roared through his body.

"He saved our lives," General Spradlin concluded. "Let's make sure his sacrifice wasn't in vain."

Becky, Samantha, and Jennie returned to their search of the control tower. Long minutes passed and the deadline to make the needed call approached too fast. Becky and Samantha looked increasingly frustrated with the search, while Jennie kept her cool. She turned over boxes and chairs, tables and shattered equipment.

And then she let out a yell.

"I found something!"

The group converged quickly around General Spradlin. In Jennie's hands was a cell-phone.

General Spradlin let out a relieved laugh.

"You've come to our rescue, Private."

Jennie Light beamed.

The cell phone was very compact. It had a blue casing and a small screen. She switched it on and muttered a quick prayer. The cell phone's screen lit up.

"I'll be damned. It's got juice! Now let's see if it gets a signal."

They waited for the telltale bars to appear on the phone's screen. It was only a matter of seconds before they did. Two bars. One more than they needed.

"We're going to make it after all," she said.

"Most of us," General Spradlin muttered.

"Most of us," Becky repeated. She laid a comforting hand on Samantha's shoulder.

Jennie handed the phone to Spradlin.

"Excellent," he said. "And with a whole eight minutes to spare."

Becky and Samantha embraced each other. Jennie laughed, and was joined in the laughter by the others.

General Spradlin rose unsteadily to his feet.

"Let me get by the window," he said as he stepped away. "Get a clearer signal."

The women followed behind as Spradlin approached the window. Half-way there, he let out a loud groan. His hands wrapped around his midsection and he tumbled forward to the ground.

"General!" Becky yelled.

Spradlin eyes shut tight. They slowly opened, to see the trio of women standing over him.

"Look...looks like I'm in worse shape than I thought," Spradlin said. "Officer Light, could you get me my chair, please?"

Jennie Light hurriedly brought a chair to the General's side. Samantha and Becky placed him on it.

"Thank you," General Spradlin said. He held up the phone. "Still in one piece, thankfully."

He shook his head.

"You know," he said. "This phone represents more than our personal salvation. As I said, the aliens do not want any of their technology to fall into our hands, which makes this phone very special indeed."

General Spradlin turned the phone over, examining its body.

"The aliens we are in contact with told us Evans' suicide switch would work on all chameleon scouts within its immediate area. But they were wrong. Isn't that so, Private Light?"

Jennie Light stiffened. She looked at Becky and Samantha and then back at the General.

"What are you talking about?"

"Very convenient you finding this phone, isn't it?" General Spradlin said.

"Someone left it behind," Jennie insisted.

"But the chameleons were so damn thorough going over this base," General Spradlin said. "They got hold of every weapon and communication device on the island yet they just happened to miss this one cell phone? A cell phone left behind in the very nexus of the base's communication?"

"I don't—" Jennie began.

"And let's not forget how incredibly lucky it was for you to somehow activate the self-destruct code on that communication jammer," General Spradlin continued. "There were ten indentations on the bottom of that device. I'd say the odds of finding the self-destruct code –hell, *any* code– on it has to be several million to one. Yet you got it on the very first try."

Samantha and Becky took a step away from Jennie Light. The Private's eyes remained on General Spradlin.

"Of course, that's the more subtle stuff," General Spradlin said. "We've been moving for hours and have barely stopped. In all that time, I haven't seen you sweat. Not even once."

"General," Jennie Light began. A smile appeared on her face. "You couldn't be more wrong."

"I wish it were the case."

Jennie shook her head and opened her mouth to say something. Instead, she jumped Spradlin. Her left hand locked around his throat, her other snatched the cell phone from his hand.

General Spradlin gasped. His now freed hand reached for the knife sheath tied to his belt.

"You idiot," Jennie Light said. "All three of your blades are gone. The last two roasted along with Doctor—"

Her final thought was left unspoken. A curious expression appeared on Jennie Light's face. She released General Spradlin and turned around. Becky Waters stood just behind her. With Jennie's back to him, the General noted a black blade protruding from her back. It was the blade Spradlin found in the Mess Hall kitchen. The one he told Becky to hide. She did so, until now.

"She's not frying," Becky said.

"She's different," General Spradlin replied. "Give her a minute."

Jennie Light took a step forward. Her movements were jerky, uncoordinated. The flesh on her pretty face darkened. The nano-robots within her were burning up, though at a slower pace than the creature Becky killed in the forest.

"You'll die, too," Jennie Light said. Her voice was no longer human. She held up the cell phone. Becky and Samantha reached for it. They tried to remove it from the stricken chameleon's hand, but Jennie Light had more than enough strength left in her to crush it.

"Shit!" Becky yelled as the pieces of the phone fell to the ground.

Jennie Light eyed Becky. Her blackened lips parted, revealing a horrid smile.

"We'll die together," she said.

"No, we won't."

The thing that was Jennie Light slowly, ever so slowly turned. Her eyes, already almost completely black, opened wide. General Spradlin stood behind her, several feet away. In his hands was a cell phone, the one Jennie Light had found.

"W-what?" Jennie Light asked.

"When I was much, much younger, I was a big fan of Harry Houdini," General Spradlin said. "He was the greatest escape artist and magician there ever was. Like all the great magicians, he was a master at the art of misdirection."

General Spradlin sat back on his chair.

"When I fell to the ground a moment ago, you were all focused on me. None of you noticed that I used the fall to switch your nice little alien artifact with my very own personal cell phone. It was here in my jacket pocket. You see Jennie, I had a cell phone on me this entire time. When you presented this cell phone, I knew it was yours. But how special was it? I had to see how far you'd go to keep it out of my hands."

The creature that had been Jennie Light stumbled toward him. But her movements were slow, uncoordinated. She stopped.

"In your haste to do just that, you didn't look closely at the phone you snatched back from me," Spradlin continued. "The cell phone you smashed, *my* cell phone, didn't even look like yours. Not at all."

Jennie's mouth locked up. She could no longer speak.

"I suppose this is how you and Frank communicated with the other ACUs and coordinated the Mess Hall ambush," General Spradlin continued. He addressed Becky and Samantha. "I suppose this is also how you back up any information you find on us. If anything should happen to you, your fellow chameleons make it a priority to retrieve the data in a unit like this one and get it back to the armada."

Jennie Light's jet black eyes stared at General Spradlin. Despite the trauma to his body, the General could hardly contain himself. He let out a laugh.

"Touching a nerve am I?" he said. "We always wondered how you talked to each other. In the few chameleon bodies we studied, we found no internal communication devices. Even in Doctor Evans. He had no explanation for it, so I knew my contacts in the fleet didn't tell me everything. It was to be expected, to some extent. The fact that you had no internal communication devices seemed counter intuitive. You're machines. How hard could it be to insert a radio device of some kind within your bodies? Ah, but your masters were clever. Maybe at one time the chameleon units had them. But with the advances we've made in communication, perhaps your masters feared we would find a way to monitor your transmissions, both to track you down as well as listen in on what you were telling each other. So your clever, clever masters found a much safer, more rational course of action, especially for this day and age. Nowadays everyone has a cell phone. Why not you guys? We can't monitor every cell phone transmission on the planet."

Jennie Light turned her withered face away. Her black eyes focused on the door leading out of the control room.

"I'll bet we'll find some interesting things inside this device, won't we?" General Spradlin said. "I wonder..."

Jennie Light could no longer hear General Spradlin's words. The world grew dark to that machine. She took two steps toward the door before falling heavily to the ground. Thin wisps of smoke rose from within her body.

"Ashes to ashes," Spradlin said.

Becky folded her arms.

"Never was for playing Charlie's Angels," she said.

"Charlie's...?" Spradlin said.

"TV show," Becky said.

"Movie," Samantha added.

General Spradlin shook his head.

"Never heard of it."

"You need to get out more, General."

"I think I've had all the fresh air I can take for several lifetimes," General Spradlin said.

Becky let out a laugh. Samantha shook her head.

"Why did you string her along out like that?" Samantha said. "She could have killed us all!"

"That's what she would have done the second after I made the call," Spradlin said. He leaned back in the chair. "Once the code was given, we were worthless to her. The creature masquerading as Private Julie Light kills us and changes her appearance. Like Frank Masters, she would most likely have duplicated me. When the helicopters arrive, they find the phony General Spradlin lying on this floor, severely injured, surrounded by your bodies. The creature would make it look like the two of you died heroically while saving my life. She could dial down her vitals until they're very faint and hope no one checks up on her too closely. If they don't, the fake General Spradlin is boarded up and flown off to get medical care. The chopper never reaches its destination and our chameleon disappears into a crowd."

"Clever," Becky said.

"Not really," General Spradlin countered. "You see, our group has devised ways of proving we are who we say we are just in case an attempt is made to...duplicate us. Members of our group have microchips implanted just beneath our skin. The aliens may not want their chameleon bodies to emit any radio waves, but we don't have that problem. The signal is very, very high frequency and immune to most communication jamming equipment. I wasn't sure if it could break the jammer the creatures set up on Bad Penny. Luckily for us it did."

"How do you know that?"

"Because when activated, the microchip sends out a signal every five minutes for as long as my heart beats," General Spradlin said. "Alan Robinson had an identical chip. Doctor Evans a somewhat similar one. There was no special code I personally needed to send to stop the bombs from falling and there never was any time limit. The moment the boys out at sea stop receiving all three of our signals, they were to assume we were dead and Bad Penny was lost. At that point, they were to wipe this island off the face of the Earth."

"You lied."

"It was part of the game," General Spradlin said.

"It kept *you* alive."

"It kept all of us alive," General Spradlin said. "It was in their best interests, at least based on what they thought they knew, In the end, the real reason they kept me alive was because they wanted information from me. And I, of course, wanted information from them."

"You survive another round in your game of poker," Becky said.

"The cost was so high," Samantha said. "An entire base worth."

"Three hundred people died in exchange for Jennie Light's cell phone," Becky said. "Was it worth it?"

General Spradlin was silent for a few seconds.

"This cell phone and the information stored within it could be the key to saving humanity," General Spradlin said. "As a bonus, we've also destroyed almost every chameleon on the face of this planet and discovered the Vice President of the United States is one of them. Yes, we lost three hundred brave soldiers. Considering what we got back, it might be a bargain."

It was Samantha and Becky's turn to be silent.

"We found out one other thing, too," General Spradlin said.

"What?"

"Someone in the armada knew we had one of their chameleons."

"How do you figure that?"

"Isn't it obvious?" General Spradlin said. "Jennie Light was *insulated* from Doctor Evans' suicide switch. Up until now, I've never heard of any ACU possessing such an ability, so I have to assume this is something the aliens have only recently devised. Which begs the question: Why insulate one of their chameleons from the suicide switch unless they knew we had a chameleon capable of using it?"

"Your contacts within the armada were discovered," Becky said.

"That's a safe assumption to make," General Spradlin said. "They used Jennie Light as a back-up infiltrator on this mission. If by some miracle we survived, Jennie Light would slip under our radar and infiltrate my organization. Had she succeeded, she could have destroyed the entire operation."

General Spradlin held up Jennie Light's cell phone.

"This time around, we were a little smarter than them," Spradlin said. He walked to Becky's side and laid the cell phone in her hand.

"The cost of getting this device was high," he said. "Given the...sacrifices...you understand how important it is to guard this device. I'm putting the both of you in charge of doing so. Don't let anything happen to it."

"General, we can't take this."

"You can and you will," Spradlin said.

"Why don't you keep it?" Samantha asked.

"Because I have an appointment." General Spradlin looked at his wristwatch. "I have to leave the island."

"Leave? How?"

"Don't worry about that," General Spradlin said. "We'll get back together in no more than two days. The boys listening in to my microchip transmission will see I'm on the move. That'll be their cue to come in here in full force. When they do, they'll be understandably suspicious and *very* trigger happy. You will do everything they say. Get on your knees in plain sight and keep your hands raised high in the air. Don't do anything –*anything*– to provoke them. They'll assume the worst, so be patient while they verify you are who you say you are. Expect to be handcuffed and treated very rough at first. Expect to be searched. And expect them not to be all that nice about it. Once you're off the island, you'll be placed in separate cells and debriefed. Tell whoever is interrogating you everything that happened in as much detail as you can recall. Do not embellish and do not exaggerate."

"Like that's possible."

"Please, *please* don't forget to tell them that the Vice-President and his personal physician are ACUs. You understand?"

"Yes, sir," Samantha and Becky muttered.

"Finally, tell them this phone was a chameleon's," Spradlin continued. "You tell them I don't want anyone to touch it. They are to put it under quarantine until I personally get a chance to look it over."

"Where exactly are you going?" Samantha asked.

"There are a couple of loose ends that need to be tied," Spradlin said. He faced Becky. "Please give me the backpack you found."

Becky blinked. She had forgotten all about the backpack that belonged to the chameleon that killed Alan Robinson. She removed it from her shoulder and handed it to General Spradlin. Spradlin opened it and examined its contents. Satisfied all was in order, he closed it back up.

"We'll see each other very soon."

"Then what?" Samantha said.

"Then you get to join my group," Spradlin said.

"Join you?" Samantha said. "What if—"

"I'm afraid you have no choice in the matter," General Spradlin said. "We're fighting for the survival of the human race. Can you possibly refuse to join that cause?"

Neither Becky Waters nor Samantha Aron replied.

"That's what I thought," General Spradlin said. He walked to the door leading out of the control tower.

"Wait!" Samantha said.

General Spradlin stopped.

"Your injuries," she said. "You need treatment. If you start bleeding again—"

"It's not as bad as it looks," Spradlin said.

Becky and Samantha blinked. The General did indeed look far healthier than he had since Frank Master took his right hand. His features were no longer as pale and his walk was rock steady. A chill passed through Becky's spine.

"You're not—?" she whispered and swallowed.

"Another Doctor Evans?" General Spradlin said. He shook his head. "No. I'll need a good while to convalesce."

"Convalesce? This isn't some cold. You lost your fucking hand!"

"Doctor Evans did a good job fixing me up," General Spradlin said. "I'll be OK. We'll talk again in a day or two."

34

By the time he reached the beach, General Spradlin heard the distant sounds of helicopters in flight. The men and women in the choppers would take their time approaching the island, circling from a distance while coming in closer and closer and keeping a wary eye out for any potential threat. Even now at least three spy satellites were pointed at Bad Penny, and someone surely must be watching the General walk along the island's south shore.

Just in case, he looked up into the sky and waved.

His men would still hang back. They knew enough about the way he operated to give him his space.

General Spradlin strolled further south. He would soon reach the island's southern tip. Should he choose to do so he could continue walking along the shore as the coast turned toward the north and east, but there was no point in doing this. General Spradlin was certain what he was looking for was close by.

He searched through the weeds and overgrowth and, after a few minutes, found it hidden under a pile of palms. Once he pushed them aside, a deflated and neatly folded black rubber Zodiac was revealed. Under it was a small plastic case and within the case were three metal cartridges of compressed air and a single black plastic oar.

General Spradlin spread the rubber boat out before screwing one of the metal cartridges to a nozzle on the inside of the craft. It took some effort given his injury, but when the cartridge was locked in place, the hiss of air rushing from it and into the boat was heard over the breaking waves. The boat inflated in a matter of seconds. It was a small boat, meant to be used by no more than two people at a time.

General Spradlin pushed the craft into the water and climbed aboard. He awkwardly paddled out to sea, allowing the current to take him further and further away from shore.

General Spradlin was satisfied with the direction he was taking and leaned back and relaxed. He knew this boat would be hidden at the southern tip of Bad Penny because during the evening and at the most likely time for the British agent to infiltrate the island, the tides pushed from the south and east and toward the north and west. This meant he was dropped off somewhere to the south and east. His drop off point, the General estimated, was no more than two or three miles away.

By midday, the currents shifted and flowed from the west and pushed out toward the east. After recovering his gear, the British spy wouldn't need to row too hard when he left the island. The tide would take him farther and farther east, to eventually rendezvous with his ride home.

General Spradlin closed his eyes. He pulled the wrapping from his injured arm and examined the wound. The injury was already closed up and covered in a layer of bright new red skin. General Spradlin felt the stub, noting the protrusion that already, a little less than an hour later, was forming.

It would take a year, at least, to grow a new hand. Even then, it would be stiff and awkward, like a limb on a newborn infant.

Spradlin scowled.

He couldn't help but recall some of the other serious injuries he received since starting this job. The worst of them, like the stiletto a would be assassin jammed into his lower spine at the battle of Gona and, much later, when a grenade took out his legs in a dark alley in Prague, took a very long time to heal.

General Spradlin shook his head and sighed. It was pointless to dwell on the past when there was so much to worry about in the here and now.

He looked back at Bad Penny. The tide was indeed strong and his raft was at least a couple of miles from shore. He saw a single helicopter buzz the island. The others had no doubt already landed. Their occupants, even now, were checking out Private Waters and Captain Aron.

He grinned.

Treat my boys gently, he thought.

The women were in for some serious shit the next few days and things weren't going to be easier when General Spradlin took them under his wing.

The General's face hardened.

They'll survive, he thought. *Hopefully, a little longer than Robinson. Or Parker. Or Hendricks. Or...*

Dark thoughts swirled within the General's mind. There were so many names. There were so many people he'd worked with over the years.

So many.

35

It was very cold in the capitol.

Snow flurries swirled through the busy streets and a stiff breeze blew across the Jefferson Monument, sailing past its cavity and eventually making its way to the White House. Even when the weather was at its most brutal a few brave souls – tourists most often– wandered just outside the White House fence. Many stopped to take pictures of themselves here, while others paused to examine the t-shirts and hats sold from vans parked along the side streets.

Motorcades guarded the heavily fortified black SUVs that often passed through those streets. Sirens blared and those same tourists, for they were the only ones who found this event so unique, craned their heads in a futile attempt to figure out which VIP was passing them by. There was little chance they would find out. The vehicles' bullet proof windows were tinted a heavy black. It kept their cargo well hidden.

A black limousine left its armada of security behind as it passed through the rear entrance to the White House. Photographers snapped pictures from their reserved spaces a good distance away, aware that any visitors to this place were always noteworthy.

The limousine parked off to the side, beneath the skeletal shade of an elm, and several armed officers took their places. Their focus was on their surroundings; their job to make sure the vehicle's passenger made it safely across the short distance between the limousine and the White House entrance. Another group of journalists, these with seniority and high level connections, stood a short distance to the side.

They watched as the Vice-President, an elderly, balding, and slightly overweight man, exited from the vehicle. He waved at the journalists and they, recognizing it was their moment to act, shouted questions. Instead of answers, the Vice-President offered his standard sarcastic smile.

"I'm pressed for time," he said. "Depending on my schedule, I may be available later."

His tone was amicable, even playful. He would not be available later, of course, he never was.

One of the Vice-President's aides stood beside the door leading into the White House. He was a very young man, the visual opposite of the Vice-President but a true believer of the cause.

"Welcome, Mr. Vice-President," he said. His voice was all but drowned by the reporters' last shouted questions.

The two shook hands. The awe the young man held for his boss was all too evident in his expression. The two entered the building. When the reporters' voices died down, the aide frowned.

"Rude vultures," he muttered.

The Vice-President patted his aide on the back.

"Aren't they all?" he said.

Other White House staffers saluted the Vice-President as he walked down the entry hallway. Those that were on friendly terms with him shook his hand. Others smiled and offered a slight bow before hurrying off to their current tasks.

All the while, the Vice-President moved deeper and deeper into the White House, passing priceless portraits, marble busts, and other stately décor. The hallways were ample and painted a warm antique white. Armed security lingered every few feet. They watched silently as the Vice President and his personnel passed. Most offered hushed greetings while others scanned the floor, their vision not unlike a sniper hunting for an as yet unseen target.

The Vice-President greeted still more staff before finally making his way to an ornately designed double door. Sitting behind a desk beside the door were a trio of armed guards. The Vice-President greeted these guards and stopped before them.

"How's it going, Glen?" he said while extending his hand. One of the three security guards, a muscular man wearing a dull blue suit, rose from behind his desk and grasped the Vice-President's hand.

"Well, Mr. Vice-President," Glen said. His voice sounded like it was coming from a very deep cave. He offered a small, polite smile and motioned the Vice-President toward the door. The room the group guarded looked like an ordinary conference room but was, in fact, one of the White House's central intelligence areas. Computers hidden behind wood panels had access to a wealth of data and virtually every contact throughout the world.

Glen produced his entry card and, as if seeing him for the first time, addressed the Vice-President's aide.

"You're needed in 22a," Glen said.

"For what?"

"Barbara Sotherby asked to see you," Glen said. "Something about Sudan."

"I already sent her an email," the young man said. He was irritated at the thought of leaving his boss' side.

"Perhaps she has some other question?"

"Go on," the Vice President said. "I'll be here."

The Vice-President's aide nodded.

"I'll see you in a few minutes."

The young man walked briskly down the hallway, disappearing around a corner.

The Vice-President's attention was back to the Security Agent. He again nodded. Glen ran his security card over the scanner. As he did, a low, audible buzz was heard. Glen opened the door and motioned the Vice-President through.

The Vice-President entered the conference room and found it was empty. He faced the Security Agent.

"Where is the President?"

"He should be here shortly," Glen said. "He asked that you wait for him."

The Vice-President sighed. He worked in the halls of power for decades. He was not accustomed to waiting for anyone. Even the President of the United States.

"He offers his apologies," Glen continued.

The Vice-President pulled up a chair and sat down.

"Don't worry about it," he said. He could barely contain his annoyance. "I've got nothing at all better to do. Nothing at all."

"Yes sir," Glen said. He closed the doors to the conference room and stood a few feet behind the Vice-President.

The Vice-President reached into his jacket and pulled out his cell phone. As he did, Glen's eyes casually settled on the device. The phone was identical to the one found on Bad Penny a little over an hour before. The image of that device had already circulated among several well-placed White House staffers, including Glen.

The Security Agent bit his lower lip.

For a moment, he felt a series of conflicting emotions. Anger, betrayal, and, yes, even disappointment. There were few both inside and outside the White House who liked the Vice President. The man was notoriously arrogant, ill-tempered, and mean. But he was still the Vice President of the United States, and Glen's love of country made him respect the man's office, even if he didn't necessarily care for the man himself.

The emotions faded quickly as Glen reached into his jacket. Seeing the cell phone was confirmation of the Vice President's status.

It was time.

When Glen's hand emerged from his jacket, it held a long black blade.

36

General Spradlin shielded his eyes from the sun. Two hours passed since he floated away from Bad Penny. He could no longer see the island to the west. Indeed, he could see absolutely no land at all protruding from the monotonous sea. He was completely alone.

It's time.

General Spradlin reached into the British agent's backpack. He ignored the binoculars and camera and grabbed the ordinary looking rectangular box. He briefly examined it.

"All right," he muttered.

He pressed on the sides of the box until a side panel sprung open. Revealed below the thin panel was a single black button. General Spradlin pressed it.

"Show yourselves," he muttered.

General Spradlin waited patiently. The tide took him further and further to sea. There was no way he'd get back to the island under his own power, and no chance at all to make it to the U.S. Coast.

That thought, however, didn't disturb him. He sat back, relaxed, and waited.

A half hour later, General Spradlin noticed a disturbance below the surface of the sea. A huge, shadowy form, like an enormous whale, shot past. The sea boiled with bubbles. Suddenly, an enormous conning tower ripped through the water and rose into the air.

General Spradlin recognized the tower's shape and dimensions and almost at once recognized the submarine as a British Astute class model. She looked brand new.

Clever, General Spradlin thought.

A handful of crewmembers dressed in dark jumpsuits appeared on the conning tower and exposed deck. Those nearest to General Spradlin carried handguns and rifles. When they realized the man in the rubber boat wasn't who they thought it would be, one of them let out a shout and the others aimed their weapons at him.

General Spradlin decided it would be best for everyone concerned if he raised his good hand over his head.

"Who the hell are you?" someone yelled from the conning tower. Not surprisingly, he spoke with a British accent.

General Spradlin squinted in the direction of the tower. He spotted three figures dressed in light colored clothing standing there. They too held weapons and pointed them in the direction of General Spradlin. The one who yelled at him had graying hair. The insignias on his suit indicated he was the Captain of this vessel.

"Ahoy, *Avenger*," General Spradlin said. "I see you launched a few months early."

The Captain didn't immediately reply. He had no idea of what to make of the American dressed in U.S. military fatigues on board the British SIS's boat.

"Who the hell are you?" the Captain repeated.

"I know that voice," Spradlin said. He closed his eyes and made a show of concentrating. "Captain Jonathan Elliot, right?"

The man Spradlin accurately identified was stunned into momentary silence.

"I asked you a question," Captain Elliot said.

General Spradlin grinned. He motioned to his injured arm and bloody shirt.

"I could say I'm Captain Hook, minus his hook," Spradlin replied. "But the fact is I'm the guy with your spy's radio transmitter."

Spradlin slowly reached out with his good hand. He showed the Captain the rectangular box he used to signal the submarine.

"Your man didn't make it."

The features on Captain Elliot's face hardened.

"What happened to him?"

"He got into something he shouldn't have," General Spradlin replied. His features also hardened. "What he found killed him."

"You...?"

"No," General Spradlin said. "And neither did any of my people. Your boy released something that should have stayed locked up. That's what killed him. It also killed every single soldier stationed at Bad Penny."

Captain Elliot took a few seconds to digest this information.

"Ex...explain yourself," he finally said.

"I'd rather do that with the individual who authorized this mission."

Captain Elliot thought about the request but said nothing.

"Pardon the pun, but I'm a single unarmed man," Spradlin said. "If you wanted to, you could shoot a few holes into this raft and watch as I sink to the bottom of the sea. After you're sure I'm gone, you could spin your vessel around and return to England with your tail between your legs, hoping no one learns of your role in the death of over three hundred American soldiers."

"We are not killers."

"Of course you aren't," Spradlin said. "And I'm not here to start a war between our...friendly...governments. I'm here to have a chat with the man who sent your boy into Bad Penny."

"He's not here."

"Captain Elliot, the time to play games is long past," General Spradlin said. "I know more about the man who authorized this mission than even you do. He's not the type to start something like this without being real close to see the results. So how about it, Elias? You're going to show your face?"

Captain Elliot took a step back. He considered his reply and was about to say something when...

"That will be all, Captain," came a voice from somewhere within the interior of the conning tower. A shadowy figure appeared beside Captain Elliot. He laid a sympathetic hand on Captain Elliot's shoulder.

"You may lower your weapons," the shadowy figure told the crew. "Please throw a rope to our guest."

One of the crewmembers did just that. General Spradlin grabbed the rope and was hauled to the submarine's side. Other members of the crew helped General Spradlin onto the deck of the *Avenger*. Once on, they all stepped back and gave their unexpected guest his space.

The shadowy figure from the conning tower climbed down the ladder to the submarine's deck. The man was elderly and almost skeletally thin. He dressed elegantly and his hair was white with age. His skin was very tan and his teeth were remarkably white and perfectly straight.

"Leave the deck," the elderly man ordered the crewmembers.

As the crew withdrew into the submarine, General Spradlin couldn't help but stare at the man before him. The first time they met, Elias Vulcan's features were, to put it politely, complete shit. His hair was matted and filthy. His skin was burned red by the sun. His clothing, if you could call it that, consisted of rotting animal skins.

Much had changed since then, since Paul Spradlin was a Veteran of the First World War and relocated to Arizona, where he was elected Sheriff of a now forgotten small town. Back then, he looked forward to living the rest of his life in that town. Today, he couldn't even remember its name.

"I wish I could say it was nice to see you again, Elias," General Spradlin said.

Elias Vulcan's eyes were hard.

"Is it true what you said about Bad Penny?"

"Yes."

Vulcan was silent.

"Don't tell me you actually care," General Spradlin said.

"I was gathering information," Vulcan said. "No one was supposed to die."

"If you hadn't sent your agent to check in on me, they'd all be alive," General Spradlin said.

"And if you didn't keep everything from me," Vulcan began. He shook his head. "You're dealing with things far beyond your capacity. I gave you the gift, Spradlin. I did so because I thought we could work together for the common good. We're two of a kind now. Like you, I want to *save* this world."

"This planet is gone and you know it."

"Have you given up, Paul?"

General Spradlin did not reply.

"No, you haven't given up," Vulcan said. "It's not in you to do so. What *are* you up to? You fight their scouts, you devise weapons to kill them...but all you're doing is getting rid of strays while and an army the size of the moon closes in. What is your goal?"

"That's my concern."

"Let me in," Vulcan said. "Please."

"I can't do that, Elias," General Spradlin said. "You're one of them."

"They haven't contacted me in millennia," Elias said. "I've been abandoned. I'm free."

"The only difference between those ACUs and you is that you've been forgotten," General Spradlin said. "With those three others, you were their beacon at the dawn of mankind. You watched us grow while keeping this planet lit up, should the armada somehow lose track of their next target in all that time."

"I'm not in contact—"

"Not now," General Spradlin said. "Your programming somehow adapted. It let you live while your companions died. I know this adaptation made you self-aware, and I know it allowed you to act more...human. But as much as you think yourself one of us, you aren't. You outlived every person you ever came in contact with and the constant losses and loneliness made you yearn for company. You searched for your companions' bodies, finding one of them in Arizona. You did your best to revive this...machine. You couldn't. Whatever life it had left inside was nothing more than a dim spark. And then you had the brilliant idea to revive your companion by fusing it with a human body. Mine."

General Spradlin gritted his teeth.

"Yes, you made me like you," General Spradlin said. "But whatever changes were done, I remain human while you're...you're still a machine. All your adaptation doesn't change the fact that you still belong to them. The moment they realize you exist, they'll take back control. And when they do, you'll be no better than the creatures that killed every soldier in Bad Penny."

Elias Vulcan turned away from General Spradlin and stared at the sea. A breeze blew in from the west and the elderly man caught sight of a pair of seagulls circling overhead. They stared down at the strange sight below them before flying off in the direction of Bad Penny. As they flew by, they called out. Their squawks interrupted the gentle sounds of waves lapping against the submarine's hull.

"You really think they'll take me back?"

"Yes."

"And then?"

"I don't know. You're an antique, Elias. You may well be obsolete. They might scrap you. If they don't, they might send you to their next world, or the one after that. It won't be long before you find out."

The birds disappeared in the distance.

"This is a beautiful world," Vulcan said after a while.

"It is."

"I hope it stays that way for as long...as long as possible," Vulcan said.

The elderly man reached into his pocket and pulled out an envelope. He handed it to General Spradlin. General Spradlin opened the envelope and found a letter. It was directed to the letter writer's mother.

"What's this?" Spradlin asked.

"A parting gift," Vulcan said. "Examine it closely. *All* of it."

General Spradlin folded the letter and pocked it.

"You're right," Vulcan said after a while. "We shouldn't see each other again. Not if there's a chance..." Vulcan paused. "I hope...I hope you're wrong. I hope you can save this world. I've grown very fond of it."

With that, Elias Vulcan walked back to the conning tower and climbed to its top. He descended into the submarine.

General Spradlin returned to his rubber boat. After a few minutes, the submarine slowly began moving back toward Bad Penny.

When they were within a couple of hundred feet from the island, General Spradlin released the rope holding his boat to the sub.

He rowed the rest of the way back to shore.

37

On a busy street in downtown London a plainly dressed middle aged woman stepped past the shops lining the street. Her goal was to move past these crowds and reach her home, but she stopped when she noted the headlines from papers displayed in the corner newsstand. Those newspapers were filled with front page headlines regarding arrangements for the funeral of the U.S. Vice-President. His sudden death the past week was hardly a surprise given his reported declining health.

Eulogies poured in from all corners of the world. A few were genuinely heartfelt, but most read like polite courtesy. Around the world, the Vice-President was even less popular than the current U.S. President. He was viewed at home and abroad as the power behind the power and his off the cuff, unscripted remarks regarding any number of topics caused the administration considerable embarrassment.

They wouldn't have to worry about that anymore.

The lady's eyes, hard and shiny like porcelain, scanned the headlines. In their rush to out-report each other, the papers for the most part missed the fact that the Vice-President's personal physician had also passed away. The physician's death, listed only in a couple of obituaries the middle-aged woman found on the internet, noted his was due to a skiing accident.

Another lie.

The lady read some more. The other big news was the downing of a U.S. Military Transport craft off the east coast of the United States. Mechanical error was blamed for that tragedy which resulted in the deaths of over three hundred U.S. soldiers. To date, few remains were found.

She left the newsstand and crossed the street, walking south for a few blocks before reaching the downstairs entrance to her loft. She held her right hand tight over her purse and rapidly climbed the stairs to the second floor. Once there, she removed her apartment keys from her bag and used them to gain entry to the apartment. It was sparse and comfortable, consisting of a living room, a kitchen, and a single bedroom and bathroom.

The lady stepped into the living room and drew the curtains. The apartment became as dark as it was quiet. She sat down before the table and laid her purse on it. From within, she pulled out the letter. It was addressed to her post office box and contained no return address. Despite this, she knew it was from her son.

The lady made no effort to open the envelope. Instead, she laid it down in front of her. Ever so gently, she rubbed her fingers over its right corner, directly over the postage stamp.

To the casual eye, the image on the stamp, a stoic portrait of Queen Elizabeth, seemed to come alive. The delicate lines that made up her face rolled away, becoming nothing more than an ugly smudge of aquamarine blue. The lady's finger froze in place. The colored smudge moved closer and closer to her finger until it seeped into the pores of her skin. In seconds, the smudge was gone. The postage stamp now had a bright white oval in its center and no image of the Queen.

The lady moved her hand away. The nano-robots embedded in the stamp had done their job and the information stored within their memory was downloaded directly into her. She replayed those images, seeing herself put these special stamps in her son's apartment. She placed nano-robots in several other locations but the stamp was the fail-safe. If he didn't make it back, neither would the nano-robots embedded in his clothing and gear.

Her son was a curious sort. He had a love/hate relationship with his mother, something that the elderly woman's programming found difficult to adapt to and emulate. At times, the programming opined that he would discover the substitution, in which case the old lady would take over her "son's" identity, eliminating him as it had done to the agent's real mother. In two years, though, this action proved unnecessary. When she discovered her son's next mission would be Bad Penny, it became imperative that whatever he learn there be revealed to her. Despite their latest arguments, she insisted he write, to tell her all was well. Guilt was a good incentive and investment. It paid off.

Through the images and audio in the nano-robots on the envelope's stamp, the elderly lady relived her son's final days, starting with his packing. She watched as she grabbed the stamps and stuff them into her son's backpack. The following day passed in darkness. She heard voices, usually hushed tones, nothing she could identify. She fast forwarded those images, until her son confronted the *Avenger's* Captain.

Darkness became light as her son removed the letter from his backpack and affixed one of the stamps on it. She saw the Captain and her son. She heard him plead for the Captain to send the letter should he not make it. The man was hesitant, but she knew he would relent. The fact that she had her son's letter proved this.

A small portion of her programming noted her current identity was no longer needed.

The submarine's Captain eventually put her son's letter in his shirt pocket and everything went dark again. Luckily, the letter shifted and the nano-robots made out hazy images past the shirt's cloth. She followed the Captain's dull routine after her son disembarked. The man drank an awful lot of coffee while he waited for her son's return.

Then they received the radio signal. The Captain and his crew were, at first, very excited. Their mission was accomplished and they could finally return home. The submarine surfaced amid good cheer. But instead of finding her son on his boat, they found...someone else.

The mood within the sub turned very grim. The Captain hurried to the conning tower and gazed out at sea, toward the boat that should have carried her son. It was a stranger, a man who spoke with an American accent. She used her best image enhancement programs to make out his features, but other than the fact that he was missing his right hand and his shirt was bloody from that injury, she could not make out details of the American's face.

She allowed the information to play out in real time as the Captain questioned the one handed man. They talked for a little bit.

Query: Who is Captain Hook?

The images and sounds moved onward. Clearly, the one handed man knew more about the submarine and her secret mission than the Captain thought possible. There was great tension, and the Captain's heart beat rapidly.

And then the stranger appeared. He climbed up the conning tower and took control of the situation.

A secret passenger aboard the submarine?

Even more surprising: The one handed man and the stranger on the submarine seemed to know each other.

Curious.

She was eager to see more but, abruptly, the images and sounds abruptly ended right there.

Not possible.

A low buzz intruded into her cognitive process. Someone had ordered her nano-robots to stop recording information. It was the only way they would quit performing their assigned task.

If they can command the nano-robots to stop recording, they can program them for any—

The lady's hands came to her head and her eyes shut tight. She grimaced as pain swept through her system. A new image appeared in her mind. It was the one handed man. He was talking directly to her.

"You are the very last of the chameleon scouts on our planet," the man said. "You are now under my control."

The elderly lady tried to move. She couldn't.

"Reprogramming the nano-robots on the stamp was easy enough," the man continued. "As was inserting the computer virus that just locked you down."

The door to the elderly lady's flat opened. The one handed American entered the apartment and sat down in a chair before the elderly lady. In his hand was a black remote control unit. A red light blinked on it.

"Can you hear me?" he said.

The elderly lady moved her eyes. It was the only part of her body she had control of.

"Good," the one handed man said. "I want you to understand: I am in complete control of your entire body. If I wanted to, I could have sent a far more destructive virus into your system or ordered you to walk into the Thames. But you're more useful to me...alive. In a few minutes, I'm going to give you a command and you'll be free to move. But you will no longer be able to hurt another human being, myself included. You will be directed to return to your spacecraft and ordered to leave our planet. You will do so, returning to your armada and your masters. You will tell them they will no longer benefit from you – or any other chameleon's–services. We've cracked your code."

Having said what needed to be said, the one handed American pressed a button on the black remote control unit. The red light stopped blinking and he put the device in his jacket pocket.

Movement returned to the elderly woman. The machine's first thought was to attack. The fingers on her hands turned to razor sharp claws and she approached the one handed man. She raised her hand to strike, but couldn't complete the action. Something kept her a few feet away from the American. It was as if he was coated in an invisible shield. She stepped back and her hands returned to their normal state.

"You fight us, but you have no hope," the elderly woman said.

"We'll see about that," the one handed man replied. "When you get back to your masters tell them it's in their best interests to turn their armada around. Find some other world to ravage."

"Their course is set. They will not turn."

"Too bad," the one handed man said. "When they get here, all they'll find is dust."

"You would destroy this world to finish us?"

The one handed man said nothing.

"I don't believe you."

"You should," the one handed man said.

The creature thought about that for a few seconds.

"What are you thinking?" she said. "Do you expect me to lead you to my ship?"

"There was a time I would have given almost everything to get my hands on you or your ship," the one armed man said. "Now? I could care less. Give them our message."

He rose from the chair and walked to the door leading out of the apartment.

The elderly lady followed. They walked down the apartment building's stairs and to the street. When the elderly lady exited the building she found the one handed man standing beside the building's entrance. He was flanked by two young women.

The one handed man and his companions watched as the elderly lady disappeared into the crowds. When she was gone, the one handed man and his companions walked off in the other direction.

EPILOGUE

She walked off to the west with little control over her movements.

She was forced to make this journey entirely by foot, for the altered programming within her forbade use of any other transportation. Her interactions with people were limited. When she walked alongside the highways, including the M40 and M54, many trucks and cars slowed or stopped. The people within the vehicles offered her a ride but she could do nothing more than politely refuse.

On she walked, her journey taking her over three hundred kilometers to the Snowdonia National Park. There, in the Gwydir Forest, was her spacecraft. Even as she drew nearer to her destination, she knew the journey was wasted. The one handed man's message would have no impact on her master's plans. The fact that she was infected with his programming meant she would be terminated after delivering her worthless message.

But she was a machine, and such things did not matter to her.

Her clothing was ragged from the long trip, ripped in spots and damp from a recent rain storm. She removed the branches and rocks that hid her spacecraft and examined the vehicle to make sure it was operational. The spacecraft was small, not much larger than a medium sized car. Its outer shell was a shiny silver metal. The creature opened the ship's hatch, revealing space for two occupants. The creature placed her hand on a panel beside one of the seats and the ship's controls flickered to life. She checked the vehicle's status before beginning the pre-flight preparation.

When she was almost ready to leave, she heard a rustling sound coming from the woods. She faced the source of the noise, and presently found an elderly man walk out of the brush. He was skeletally thin, with white hair and perfect teeth. He walked directly toward her.

"Thank you, I do not need any assistance," the creature said, for this was all she could say.

Still the skeletally thin man approached. His right hand reached down to his waist, and the creature saw a knife holster at his side. He drew a black blade from the holster.

"I do not need any assistance," the creature repeated. She wanted to attack, she wanted to defend herself, but her programming wouldn't allow it.

She could do nothing but watch as the skeletally thin old man walked directly up to her. He looked over her shoulder, at the spacecraft, and nodded.

"It'll do," he said.

"I do not need—" the creature began.

The elderly man placed his free hand over the creature's mouth.

"It's funny how alike we are," the elderly man said. He smiled at the creature. Her hair was matted and she looked like a lost soul. He fixed her hair and withdrew his hand.

"We've both had changes to our original programming," he continued. "Your first instinct is to defend yourself, but you can't. As for me, there was a time I couldn't do this."

The elderly man thrust the black blade into the creature's stomach. When he released its handle, the electrical discharge roared through her body. As the creature fell to the ground, her outer flesh turned to black ash.

The skeletally thin man stepped past the remains of the creature and walked to the spacecraft. He examined the controls.

"They've made some modifications," he muttered. "Nothing I can't handle."

He sat inside the craft and looked at the forest around him. For several seconds he took in the beauty of his surroundings. He had spent many years here. Many, *many* years. He knew this would be the last time he'd see the forests of Earth.

"Goodbye," he said.

Though he was a machine, there was sadness in his voice.

THE END

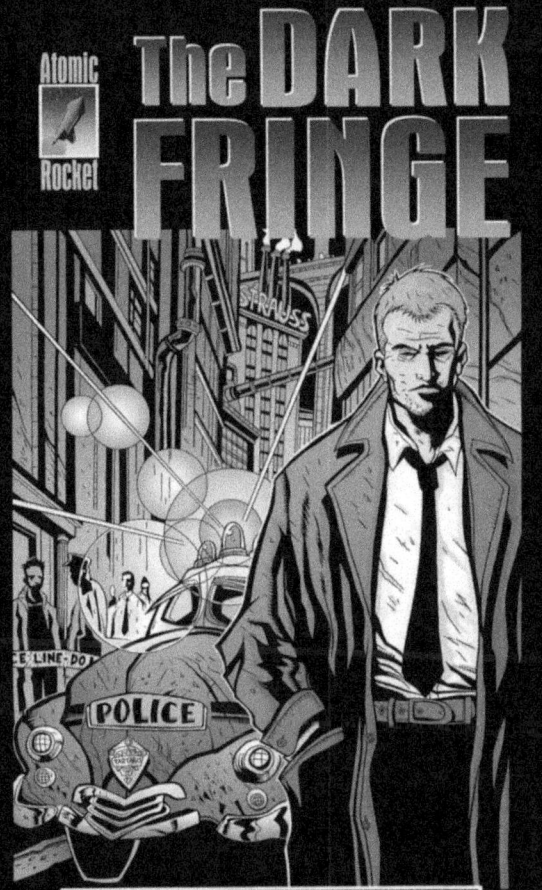

From the grittiest corners of a dark metropolis...
...to the coldest reaches of outer space...
...and all those uneasy places in between...

SHADOWS at DAWN

E. R. Torre

Fourteen tales of Mystery, Suspense, and the Fantastic.

Visions of a dead actor haunt a lonely young man...
Fate leads him on a journey to the man's home town...

E. R. TORRE

HAZE

It started with Blood...

...see how it ends.

Return once more to the world of
The Dark Fringe.

COLD HEMISPHERES

E. R. Torre

An elderly Hitman's most dangerous job
Is the one he can't complete.

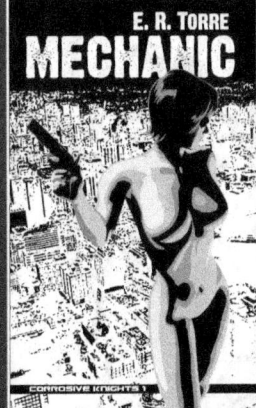

HER NAME IS NOX. HIRE HER, AND SHE WILL GET
THE JOB DONE...

E. R. TORRE
MECHANIC

CORROSIVE KNIGHTS 1

...CROSS HER AT YOUR OWN RISK.

For over two hundred years a deadly secret has been kept.
A secret that could shatter the delicate peace between two
galactic empires and result in the death of billions...

CORROSIVE KNIGHTS 2

THE LAST FLIGHT OF THE ARGUS

E. R. TORRE

That secret is about to be revealed.

Arizona, 1925: A Sheriff makes a discovery in the fiery desert that changes everything.
Bad Penny, the Present: On an idyllic island army base, a hidden menace is about to be unleashed...

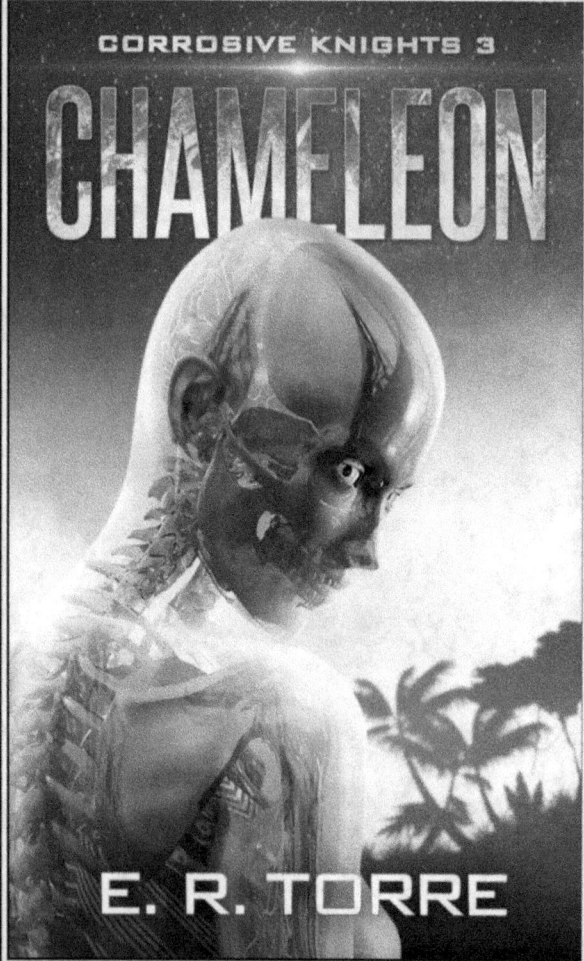

CORROSIVE KNIGHTS 3

CHAMELEON

E. R. TORRE

For the seven passengers of a military transport helicopter, the next twelve hours could signal the end of mankind.

Centuries ago, an unstoppable enemy
forced humanity to flee to the stars.

CORROSIVE KNIGHTS 5

GHOST OF
THE ARGUS

E. R. TORRE

Today, humanity will take the fight to *them*.

A scavenger on a lost planet
carries a terrifying secret...
CORROSIVE KNIGHTS 6
FOUNDRY OF THE GODS
E. R. TORRE
Copyright © 2017 E. R. Torre
What lies beneath the desert sands
within the Foundry of the Gods?

The Corrosive Knights series comes to its explosive end...

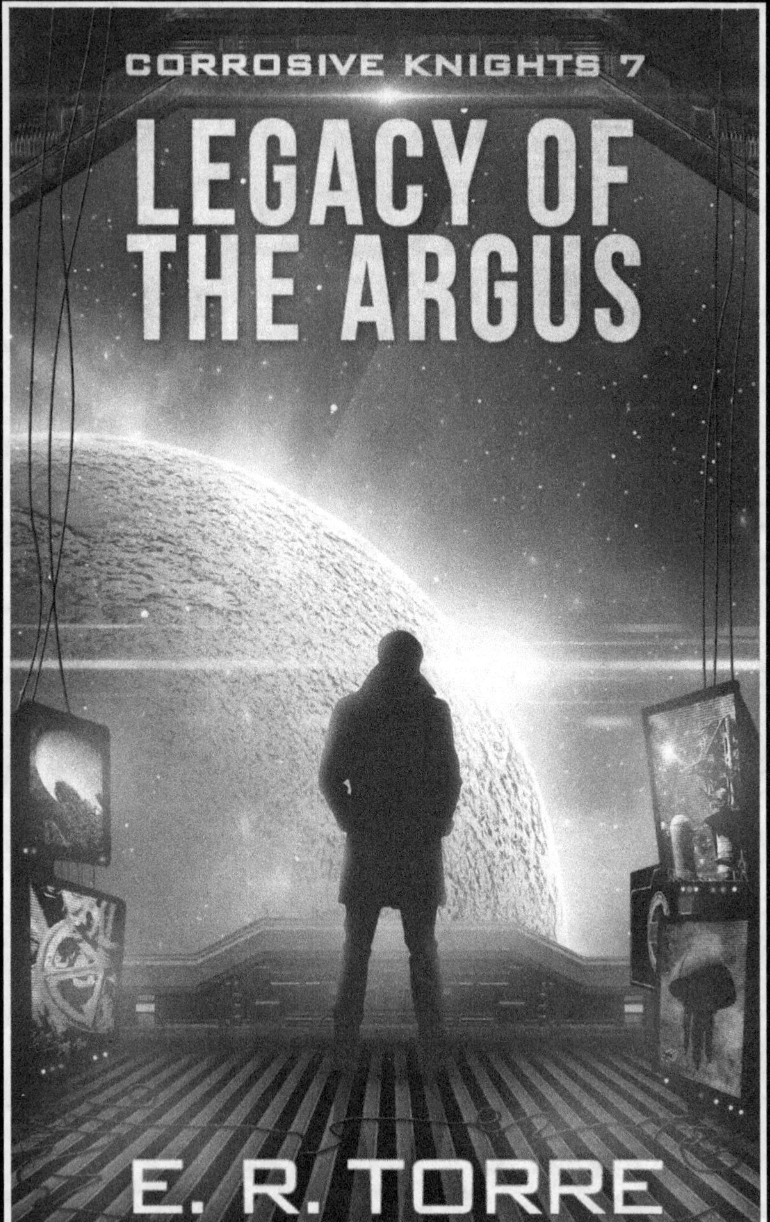